CAMP

BOYFRIEND

Friends Forever!

Joane Rock

J.K. Rock

Karen Rock

SHC

Spencer Hill Contemporary, an imprint of Spencer Hill Press

This book is a work of fiction. Names, characters, places, and incidents are products of the author's imagination or are used fictitiously. Any resemblance to actual events, locales, or persons, living or dead, is entirely coincidental.

Please visit our website at www.spencerhillcontemporary.com

First Edition: July 2013.
J.K Rock
Camp Boyfriend : a novel / by J.K. Rock – 1st ed.
p. cm.
Summary:
Teen girl gets caught between her old self and her reinvented self, and two boys, one in each world.

The authors acknowledge the copyrighted or trademarked status and trademark owners of the following wordmarks mentioned in this fiction: Advanced Placement, Bambi, Batman, BMW, Breathalyzer, Bugles, Calvin Klein Obsession, Cheetos, Comic-Con, Diet Coke, Dungeons and Dragons, Elmo, Energizer Bunny, Eveready, ex-lax, Facebook, Field of Dreams, Frisbee, Gatorade, Geological Society of America, Gollum, *GQ* magazine, Gucci, Harry Potter, Hayden Planetarium, Hershey, IMAX, iPhone, Jell-O, Juicy Couture, Keds, Lamborghini, Light Saber, *Lord of the Rings*, Magic Marker, Mario Kart, Mercedes-Benz, Motel 6, National Geographic Channel, Olympics, Ouija board, Pepé le Pew, Pepto-Bismol, Peter Pan, Poison Ivy, Polo, *Popstar!* Magazine, Pringles, PSATs, *Seventeen* magazine, Silly String, Skunk-Off, *Survivor*, Swatch, Tabasco, Thriller, TiVo, Twitter, U-Haul, Wizard of Oz.

Cover design by Jennifer Rush
Interior layout and chapter artwork by Marie Romero

ISBN 978-1-939392-50-3 (paperback)
ISBN 978-1-939392-51-0 (e-book)

Printed in the United States of America

To the wonderful students that we've worked with past and present, thank you for inspiring us with your lives and stories. We hope we've done them justice!

Munchies' Manor:

Emily (Counselor):

Lauren:

Alex:

Trinity:

Piper:

Siobhan:

Jackie:

Voted most likely to…

(be cast in a remake of any '80s film)

(pilot a mission to Mars— take that Kirk!)

(break the world record for biggest bubblegum bubble)

(predict the apocalypse)

(live in a Sequoia tree to save it from lumberjacks)

(win a Nobel Peace Prize by using chess strategies to bring peace to the Middle East)

(turn down a modeling career to compete in the Olympics)

Divas' Den:

Victoria (Counselor):

Hannah:

Brittany:

Rachel:

Madison:

Kayla:

Voted most likely to…

(fall asleep on a train and wake up in another country)

(marry wealthy, divorce rich, repeat…)

(marry a vampire—if she can find one that's not afraid of her)

(make the US Volleyball Team, then OD on too much RedBull)

(appear on the side of a milk carton)

(kiss the boys and make them cry… on Wall Street)

The Wander Inn:	Voted most likely to...
Bruce "Bam-Bam" (Counselor):	(win an award for best pyrotechnics in a James Bond movie)
Seth:	(discover a plant that solves our energy crisis)
Julian:	(write sequels to the Lord of the Rings trilogy)
Vijay:	(own the most exclusive Manhattan club, close it in a week, open another, repeat...)
Danny:	(live at home until he's forty, and then marry his babysitter)
Garrett:	(write an 'I Survived Camp' blog followed by millions)

Warriors' Warden:	Voted most likely to...
Rob "The Hottie" (Counselor):	(be a stunt double for Zac Efron)
Matt:	(win a Heisman Trophy)
Eli:	(host a ripoff show– Punk U)
Devon:	(be the next "Bachelor" and get turned down on the Final Rose show)
Jake:	(own a chain of fitness centers)
Buster:	(become a WWA star, wrestling name: BUST-A-MOVE)

HONORABLE MENTION: Lake Juniper Point Director: Mr. Woodrow ("Gollum"): Most likely to have his whistle surgically removed from his stomach.

Chapter One

Ten, nine, eight...

At Jefferson Davis High School, we drummed our fingers on our desks and half-rose from our seats, counting down the last seconds to summer vacation. I held my breath and eyed the wall clock. Would I go through with tonight's plans to sabotage my so-called perfect life?

Seven, six, five...

Today, everyone was actually psyched to be here. From slacker to brainiac, we listened to the ticking and waited for our break to officially begin. If only my life was on TiVo—then I could fast-forward to the fun.

Four, three, two...

Even the teachers were excited. Music had vibrated through their lounge door all day, their laughter so loud our red-faced principal looked ready to give *them* detention. You'd think they'd survived the zombie apocalypse when we'd barely survived their burial mounds of homework. But we forgave each other—all sins forgotten—when the school year ended...all except the one I was about to commit.

One!

You couldn't hear the bell ring for the collective cheer. Fists pumped the air. Notebooks sailed into the trash. Sneakers beat a path to the door out of Mrs. Kazinski's health class. Goodbye to a semester's torturous viewing of human sexuality films—most of which weren't half as enlightening as the girls I sat with at lunch.

Kids screamed, shouted, and high-fived without penalties from the absent hall monitors. If only I could celebrate with them. The end of school began my indentured servitude to my older sister while she planned her Texas-sized wedding. And that was just the start of my summer problems.

"Hey, Lauren." My boyfriend, three-sport standout Matt Butler, grabbed my hand as soon as I hit the corridor of sophomore lockers. "Ready to ditch this place for a couple months?"

He gave me a lazy stare that could turn most of the female student body into babbling idiots. Even our principal, sixty-something-year-old Ms. Collins, must have had heart palpitations around Matt, considering the way she smiled at him and let him get away with anything. She was too old to be a cougar, so we'd dubbed her a saber-tooth tiger.

But Matt's green eyes, dark hair, and retro sideburns were undeniably hot. And the fact that he was all abs and square shoulders didn't hurt either.

"In a minute," I stalled, trying hard to smile despite the dread balling up in my stomach. "I've got to clean out my locker." My solar system magnets came off easily, but I had to abandon my 'Save Pluto' sticker. Hopefully whoever had my locker next year would appreciate it.

"Look out! Coming through!" One of Matt's football friends—a huge lineman they called Crash—barreled down the hall on a skateboard. He knocked over freshmen like bowling pins, propelled on two sides by a couple of running backs who lived in the weight room.

Matt pounded knuckles with the oversized musclehead while I grabbed a NASA sweatshirt and stuffed it in my bag.

"Matt and Lauren," Crash shouted, winking at me while he held out his arms like a surfer to ride the waves of discarded folders and test papers. "You'll be at the beach tonight, right?"

My gut knotted even more, and for once I wished it was only PMS. Actually, maybe it was the flu. That would make an awesome excuse to miss the party at Turtle Creek later, but it would only delay what had to be done.

"We'll be there," Matt called, loud enough for his friend to hear even though Crash was halfway to the other end of the hall by now.

Matt, meanwhile, had never taken his eyes off me.

"Won't we, babe?" He ran the back of his knuckles along my cheek, a sweet gesture that made me second-guess my plan for tonight.

Oh God.

My stomach cramps increased in velocity, knocking into one another like molecules in collision theory. I distracted myself by watching Crash and his buddies. They made no effort to avoid a couple of students carrying the hovercraft that had taken top honors at the school's science fair.

"Whoa!" Crash shouted as he plowed into it, making me wince. All of that hard work and ingenuity—gone in seconds.

Matt turned at my expression and surveyed the damage. Grinning, he shot his football buddies a thumbs-up sign, oblivious to the feelings of the kids who'd poured their hearts into this piece. They must have been crushed. Witnessing Matt's reaction while our valedictorian fought back tears erased any doubts I had about tonight. Call me crazy, but I was breaking up with the hottest guy in our school.

"I'll be at the beach," I told him, backing away. I didn't care who saw me rush toward the destroyed hovercraft to help. I had a soft spot for the school nerds.

After all, I used to be one.

"See you at seven-thirty?" Matt called through the hysterically laughing crowd.

"Sounds great." My gritted teeth flashed in a bright smile. It was an expression I'd perfected during my transformation from geek to popular girl this year after moving half-way across the country to a new school. Amazing what losing my glasses and braces and joining the cheerleading squad had accomplished. Sometimes I felt like a science experiment gone wrong, like a broken hovercraft lying in pieces on the school floor.

"I need to talk to you." He smiled in a way that had heads turning toward me from every direction.

Matt attracted attention. At one time, that kind of flirty look would have sent me running to fill ten pages in my diary. But I'd seen through Matt's gorgeous exterior. Laughing with his friends when they mocked or pranked other kids made him as guilty as if he'd done it himself. I'd been too dazzled by his attention to notice at first. Now it bugged me and I couldn't wait to get some space. Hopefully our "talk" wouldn't be about something serious. How awful if, after months without the "L" word, he said it tonight. I definitely needed to tell him my news first.

Summer camp started next week and I couldn't return to the Smoky Mountains while I remained Matt's girlfriend. I had other plans for my eight weeks at Camp Juniper Point. I missed my old friends and our goofy fun, like staying up to watch predawn meteor showers or casting Harry Potter spells with wands we made out of twigs.

"Same here," I muttered as I helped pick up the pieces of a project I wished I'd done myself.

I was over being popular, and I was done with being Matt's girlfriend. I'd decided as much last night when I'd gotten an email from Seth Reines.

My camp boyfriend.

*   *   *

I slipped inside my house and eased the mammoth door shut, the central air conditioning raising goose bumps on my arms. One of many things I resented about my new Texas hometown was that you could sweat one minute and freeze the next. Speaking of icy things, my mom and sister were quarreling in the living room to my right. Again.

"But Momma, this bride's wearing semi-gloss lipstick. Look," Kellianne drawled—the only one of us who'd acquired a southern accent besides our Texan mother. As for Dad, he'd barely said a word since being laid off from his geology professorship at Cornell University and taking a job at Mom's family's oil company. Meanwhile, I stubbornly refused to call anyone "darlin'" and held on to my upstate New York accent. It was the only relic of the old me to survive the move. Well, that and my telescope.

"Semi-gloss is inappropriate for church. Do you want to look like a lady or a roadhouse tramp?" Appearances mattered to Mom, especially in front of her Dallas socialite friends. It was part of the reason she'd made me over when we'd moved. If Dad hadn't been so preoccupied, he would have put a stop to the eyebrow waxing and hair highlights, insisting, as he used to, that I was fine just the way I was. And I'd believed him until he disappeared into his work the way stars vanished under Houston's bright glare.

"Maybe I won't walk down the aisle at all." Kellianne's voice sounded teary.

"Oh hush now. Every bride gets the jitters. And at two hundred and fifty dollars a plate we can't afford them. Why do you think your father's working so hard? Here's a tissue."

I set down my school bag, stepped out of my Keds, and slid across the foyer's marble floor toward our curved oak staircase.

Hershey, our chocolate lab, lounged at the top of the landing, her square head resting between her paws. Her ears pricked up as I tiptoed upward. I put my finger to my lips and shook my head, hoping she'd understand my plea for silence. No way was I getting dragged into another round of endless debates about seating charts, floral arrangements, music choices, picture locations, cake flavors, entree options...the list grew longer by the day. It didn't matter that Kellianne had a wedding planner. Mom said the day should have the Carlson family "stamp" on it, and that meant we all played a part.

But I had my own problems to deal with, ones a little more important than deciding if Kellianne looked better in ecru or eggshell. Like there was a difference. Besides, everything looked good on my blonde bombshell sister, something she'd loved flaunting in my plain Jane face until I'd started wearing makeup and upgraded to a C cup bra.

Hershey's tail thumped as I avoided the squeaky left side of the tenth stair. *Please, please Hershey*, I begged silently, knowing she'd demand a belly rub before letting me pass. She rolled over, round stomach and tongue protruding. She really was cute. Annoying. But cute. I smoothed her short fur and tickled her under the chin. Three more steps and I'd be in my room and home free.

"Woof!"

I whirled and frowned at her wriggling body. Her backside lifted while her front legs pressed to the floor. Great. She was ready to play while I needed to escape Wedding Alcatraz.

"Hush." I grabbed her favorite play toy, Turtle, and threw it down the stairs. She barked and bounded after it, skidding like Bambi when she hit the polished floor.

"Lauren, honey, is that you?"

I shut my eyes. So close to a clean getaway.

"Lauren!" Kellianne shouted. "Come look at this lipstick and tell me what you think."

Frantic for an excuse, I blurted, "I've got to finish my NASA Aerospace Scholars application."

"It's not due until September. Besides you can't send it in until your father gets Congressman Owens' letter of recommendation," Mom yelled. My hand gripped the banister. Would Dad remember that promise? It seemed about as low on his list of priorities as I was.

"Hurry, this is more important," Mom added.

Lip color was more important than studying with some of the world's top scientists? Hershey mimicked my snort. Maybe in Mom and Kellianne's world. But not in mine. Of course, what I wanted didn't seem to matter. My life was in orbit around everyone else's. I could be in a coma and they'd be at my hospital bed with color swatches.

I'd hoped to curl up in bed with a good book, distract myself from doubts about tonight's social suicide plan. Just the thought made my heart skitter along my ribs like a trapped spider. Now I'd have to endure an afternoon discussing lace versus tulle, roses versus calla lilies, and chicken versus fish. At least beef was a given. In Texas, a wedding without steak wasn't even legal.

Resigned, I slumped back down. Next week I'd be at camp, away from Bridezilla's clutches. My chest loosened, letting me draw my first easy breath of the day. I could practically smell the Smoky Mountain evergreens and Seth's outdoorsy scent. This week would go by in a snap if I could stay focused on that.

I hurried into the kitchen to see if Dad had dropped off the reference letter—he hadn't—and grabbed a glass of sweet tea to console myself. Hopefully he'd give it to me before I left for camp. Getting the application in early meant I had a better chance of making it into the competitive online and weekend program.

In the living room, my mother and sister sat on the couch, their blonde heads bent over a magazine.

"Use a coaster, Lauren," Mom ordered without looking up from a shot of a pouting bride, her peach lips shining. "And not a good one—get the crocheted ones Aunt Flo gave us for Christmas."

"Do we really have to invite her, Momma?" Kellianne twisted her ring. "Remember how she was at the engagement party—reading auras and talking about crystal powers. What if she brings her Tarot cards and predicts my marriage won't last?"

"Is that her guess or yours?" My smile faded when Kellianne covered her face. Crap. Sometimes my sister seemed as armored as a rhino and other times as thin-skinned as the tissue she held to her nose. I leaned over and gave her a quick hug. "Hey. I'm kidding. You and

Andrew are great. I'll ask her to read my future. It'll keep her off your back, okay?"

My sister nodded as I plopped in a deep-cushioned chair and gulped my lemon-flavored tea. My nose curled at the smell of clashing perfumes wafting from the bridal magazine. Even bug spray would be better. Kellianne's glistening blue eyes flew to mine.

"She'll probably warn you that you won't keep Matt looking like that." She shook her head at the broken-in jeans and rumpled Batman tee I'd rescued months ago from a 'To Donate' bag of my old clothes. Today had seemed like the perfect day to resurrect my former look. "Don't you want to be at Matt's side when he joins his daddy's business?" Kellianne pressed her acrylic nails into her temples. "They own the biggest car dealership in town, and while that's not in the same class as *Andrew's* business, it's still decent."

Kellianne's fiancé was Andrew Jackson Buford III, heir to the state's biggest cattle ranch and as close to Texan royalty as we got. They'd met at Texas A&M University, where she'd earned her Environmental Science degree and an engagement ring. My sister was actually no slouch in the brains department, and it still surprised me that she'd agreed to give up her dream job when they'd set the wedding date.

"I'm going to be too busy discovering our cosmic roots and revealing humanity's place in the universe to worry about that, Kellianne." Ice cubes clanked as I swirled my straw.

My sister rolled her eyes. "Are you still in that astronaut phase? Do you want to be a princess when you grow up, too?"

"Girls," my mother warned. "Can we focus?"

I ground my teeth, mad I'd let Kellianne bait me. Charity events, country club dinners, and junior league socials might suit Kellianne, but they were definitely not in the cards for me, Tarot or otherwise. I wanted to explore planets glimpsed on mathematical charts, orbit the world rather than rule it, discover places I'd yet to imagine.

"Fine. What do you think, Lauren?" Kellianne pointed at the picture, puffing her full lips out like the model. "Is semi-gloss trashy or classy?"

My mother raised her plucked eyebrows and flared her nostrils.

"Ummmm," I stalled, not sure which answer would please them both. "How about a matte lipstick for church, then switch to the same color in semi-gloss for the reception?"

Smiles broke out across both their faces. Bingo. Another epic wedding crisis avoided. One down, a thousand more to go...

"Thanks, Lauren." Mom squeezed my hand. "We can always count on you."

I wondered if she'd feel the same way after tonight. Her values were traditional and she'd always stood by her man. Would she be okay with me breaking up with Matt?

Like Dad, my mother had earned a geology degree from Cornell. But when the college offered him a professorship, she stopped looking for a job, married him, and become the perfect housewife and mother. Not that I faulted her choice, but I'd caught her watching the National Geographic Channel many times, and I knew she maintained her membership in the Geological Society of America, and read its monthly magazine the day it arrived. When we'd returned to her wealthy parents' hometown and had an easy in with their oil company as a consultant, I noticed she'd seemed happy to put her skills to use. I wondered if a part of her wished she'd chosen a different path long ago.

"I'm rethinking that tiara, Kellianne. It doesn't have nearly enough crystals." Mom flipped a page and studied another bride.

Then again, maybe not.

They debated headpieces that wouldn't flatten Kellianne's hair while I self-consciously fluffed my straight, auburn-streaked brown locks. This morning, I'd skipped the hairspray that normally kept it at acceptable Texan standards—meaning fuller than a small shrub.

Seth used to tug on my ponytail whether it was wet from the lake, sticky from bug spray, or dusty after a hike. He'd called me a natural beauty, despite my glasses and braces.

What would he think of me now? Uncertain of how Seth or my bunkmates would view the new me, I hadn't posted any recent pictures to my Camp Juniper Point Facebook account. I had a separate account in the camp group that was visible only to campers, allowing me to keep my school and camp worlds apart.

As if sensing my attention had wandered, Kellianne narrowed her gaze at me over the magazine. "What am I going to do without you this summer? Momma, can't you make her stay?"

My heart stopped. What if Mom agreed? I'd missed camp, and Seth. After a year of trying to fit in—succeeding on the outside, but failing on the inside—I understood that he and I shared something special. Since he was a year older than me, it was our last summer together and my only chance to make our relationship year-round. I had to go. I would walk there if I had to.

"We've gone over this." Mom tucked a loose strand back in her updo. "The wedding planner will handle the big issues. Then, Lauren and I will assist you with things that need a more personal touch." She handed Kellianne a tissue. "No need to get upset. Remember, we made that list for Lauren."

List? What list? I was looking forward to hanging out with my old friends and Seth. Speaking of which, I still hadn't responded to his email.

Kellianne unfurled a piece of paper as long as my arm. For a moment I fantasized about it fluttering over the side of a canoe and disappearing into the depths of western North Carolina's Nantahala River. Preferably while Seth paddled me around, his muscles flexing as he worked with his oar. Would he remember the meteor shower we'd planned to watch this summer?

"Here are some things I need you to do." Kellianne waved the paper under my nose and reeled off a list about bridal party gifts, place cards, and thank-you notes. My heart sank. Even

13

ten states away, I'd still be her wedding slave. Sure. I'd have plenty of time to fit all that in around five camp activity periods a day. Maybe I could address the shower notes while rock climbing, or write out her place cards on a whitewater rafting trip.

"Fine. Got it." I snatched the list but halted my headlong rush out of the room when a thought occurred. "Is Dad going to be home for dinner?"

Mom's face fell into disappointed lines. "Something came up on one of the oil rigs, so he flew down this afternoon to supervise."

Emptiness rose at the thought of another evening without Dad. What did that make it? Eight, nine days without a family dinner? I understood that his new job was demanding, but it was like he'd forgotten he had a home too. Forgotten about me. He used to be my wall of support. Now he was a shadow that flitted in and out of my life. "He'll be back before I leave for camp, right? To say goodbye?"

Kellianne and Mom exchanged a long look, and then Mom cleared her throat. "I'm sure he'll do his best, dear."

I trudged upstairs to my room, heart heavy, and closed my door behind me. A picture of Dad and me in front of Manhattan's Hayden Planetarium caught my eye. Our grins were as bright as the IMAX show we'd watched while Kellianne and Mom shopped on Fifth Avenue. Back then, we'd all had clear priorities and alliances.

I pushed away thoughts of Dad, grabbed my laptop, and sat cross-legged in the middle of my canopied bed. While the computer whirred to life,

I glanced at my open closet, wondering what I'd pack for camp. Would Seth recognize me wearing designer labels and carrying a Gucci backpack?

His email popped up on my homepage.

7 days until the bonfire and our FKOC

Our First Kiss of Camp. Just the phrase made my heart race. We'd started the tradition two years ago when we'd snuck away during a bonfire sing-a-long. While a rousing chorus of *John Jacob Jingleheimer Schmidt* sounded behind us, we'd sat on the dock, swinging our legs over the inky waters. I remember the electric feel of his skin every time his calf touched mine, the jittery sensation in my stomach that made me babble about different types of meteors... Being that close made it impossible to focus on anything but us. And he must have felt the same way because he had cupped my cheek, bringing me closer until our lips brushed as softly as a moth's wings. After five years in the friend zone, we'd reached official boyfriend-girlfriend status, at least for that summer and the one after that.

I flopped back on my pillow and pulled a picture of Seth from my nightstand drawer. I traced his short, sandy blonde curls and looked into his amber eyes. I loved the way they lit up whenever he saw me. Would they still glow when I told him about Matt? Not that I should feel guilty. Seth and I agreed to break up at the end of every summer and get back together the next year. It was his idea, in fact. No pressure, he'd said. But for me it was. I was tired of the two months on, ten months off schedule.

I touched my finger to my lips and then to Seth's picture. After I cleared my conscience and broke up with Matt, I'd answer his email.

To have the summer of my dreams, I'd have to survive the worst night of my life.

Chapter Two

"A Batman shirt and ponytail? Seriously?" My frenemy Jessica greeted me when I arrived at the beach that night. "I thought you were kidding at school with that lame outfit. But hello? This is a party, not Comic-Con."

The small patch of sand near Turtle Creek was already full of kids ready to cool off in the 90-degree heat. I'd arrived a few minutes after seven-thirty and there were at least twenty people throwing Frisbees or riding the rope swing out over the water. A few of the boys had brought in coolers with sodas on top and beers hidden underneath, while the girls compared bikini tops.

I gave her a fake smile that masked the panic attack building about tonight. Taking a deep breath, I told myself not to let her get to me. "What's up, Jess? Didn't know you knew about Comic-Con. You must make a perfect Poison Ivy." I'd survived the cliques of Jefferson Davis High this long and wouldn't let a witch with French tips bring me down now.

"Hey ladies," Matt announced himself, arriving on the scene and sliding an arm around my waist. "Looking good tonight, as always." His warm lips tickled my ear as he whispered, "Meant to tell you at school—Batman is now my favorite superhero."

His eyes were all over me, but Jessica preened, her toes turning inward like she was six years old. "Hi Matt," Jessica's breathless voice displayed none of the venom she'd just shot my way. "You look good yourself."

I had to give Matt props, since he barely heard her. He made a vague sort of nod in her direction and steered me away. He wasn't all bad. But I couldn't help contrast his popular persona to Seth's quirky style. Matt and I hung out mostly at games or at parties, leaving us little one-on-one time. I still barely knew the boy beneath the shoulder pads and helmet. Seth and I, on the other hand, had long talks while we watched the stars and counted lightning bugs. I taught him about the cosmos while he shared the genus and species of every living thing around us. I missed him. Missed *us*.

"I need to talk to you." Matt lowered his voice, his hand palming my back, providing the sort of thrill I should not be feeling from him.

"Sure." Steeling myself, I tried not to notice his warm fingertips through the soft cotton of my T-shirt. Soon, it would be Seth touching me, and then everything would be right again. "I need to tell you something too." I took in a deep breath and opened my mouth. Breaking up with Matt meant I needed to tell him about Seth. As hard as that would be, it wouldn't be right otherwise.

"Dude!" One of Matt's friends shouted from the water. "Water football starts in five minutes. Hurry up."

Air exploded from my lungs and my shoulders drooped. The wait was killing me, but I didn't have the heart to ruin Matt's night before it began. I gave him a weak smile and glanced at the creek.

Most of the guys had already gone in. There was a bend where a wide, shallow area made a good spot for water sports. Great for Matt and his friends, maybe. But that meant I'd spend an anxious twenty minutes with Jessica and company while I waited to confess my real feelings.

"Promise you won't take off until we talk?" Matt asked, still by my side despite the collected cheers and catcalls from a handful of his friends.

"Not a chance." I gave Matt a little shove toward the water. "Go have fun. I'll be here."

With a nod, he stripped off his shirt and jogged toward the creek, muscles rippling and girls' necks twisting for a better look. Matt definitely wouldn't have a problem moving on after me. Honestly, I was shocked we'd lasted this long. I looked decent in my cheerleading uniform, fit in with his popular crowd, and brought his favorite Gatorade to games, but there were lots of girls who could do the same. As a junior next year, he'd be more sought after than ever and have his pick.

"I'm open!" he shouted to his friends, calling for a pass as he jumped in with a splash.

I trudged Jessica's way, where she held court with two of her lackeys. My steps slowed as I approached, not wanting to tangle with them tonight. Way too much to deal with already.

Instead I veered toward a log beside a rounded bush blooming with burgundy flowers—*Berberis thunbergii*, Seth would have told me. A Japanese barberry bush. I inhaled the delicate scent and remembered the wildflower bouquet Seth had given me on our final evening at camp last year.

His wide shoulders had made my heart skip a beat when he'd jogged up my cabin's steps. I'd slipped outside and returned his slow smile when he pulled a slightly wilted arrangement of yellow black-eyed Susans, purple blazing stars, and white Queen Anne's lace from behind his back.

"So you won't forget me." His hands lingered on mine as he gave me the fragrant gift. He must have used his free activity period to manage this surprise. I looked up at him, touched. Did he honestly think I'd forget him?

"This way you can bring a little of the Smoky Mountains to Texas." He stroked my upper arms, worry puckering his strong brow.

My happiness evaporated at the reminder that my parents would be arriving tomorrow and that Seth and I would be apart. Not even a couple. We'd agreed to break up again and see where things stood next summer. It'd worked last year, and I'd hated to risk losing him by disagreeing. With everything else unraveling in my life, I needed Seth to be a constant.

I led Seth to our porch swing and snuggled against his side. The soft periwinkle light enfolded us, the first glimmers of Venus appearing in the darkening sky. His arms wrapped around me and I rested my head on his shoulder, breathing in his clean, outdoorsy smell.

"Everything is changing so fast." The bouquet trembled on my lap.

Seth tipped up my chin and leveled his golden eyes at me. "Everyone is going to love you in Texas, Lauren. You're amazing."

I wrapped my arms around his neck and buried my fingers in his thick, blond curls. PDA was enough to earn us Mess Hall duty, but we were leaving tomorrow. What was the worst the counselors could do?

He cupped the back of my head and kissed me, the warmth of his body seeping into mine. After a moment, we pulled apart, both of us out of breath. "I'm going to miss this," I murmured.

"I'm going to miss you." His hands smoothed across my back. "I can't believe next summer will be our last together."

I ignored the anxious pang those words inflicted. If all went according to plan, this time next year, we'd be a year-round couple, I'd thought. No more summers-only and no more endings. "Let's not think about that now." I brushed my lips against his and gasped when he crushed me to him, banishing my worries with a long, deep kiss.

"Hi, Lauren," a voice came from beside the barberry bush, breaking me out of my reverie.

"Hey Paige." I waved to a girl on the cheer team. She was Crash's girlfriend and was a grade below me. Was it just my imagination, or was she avoiding the rest of the girls?

"I don't want to bother you–" Her eyes darted toward Jessica as one of her friends burst into giggles over some private joke. "But if you have a minute—"

She hugged her arms around her waist and bit her lip.

"What's up?" I was game for anything besides wedding planning or a round of 'stab your friend in the back' with Jessica's crew. And I definitely needed to stop thinking about Seth until Matt and I talked. I glanced at my iPhone. Five minutes down, fifteen or so to go. My gut twisted itself in a double knot.

"I'm having some trouble with the new routine, and Jessica said there's no way I'll make the squad next year if I don't get the timing down."

How charming that we had our very own tyrant to ensure quality control.

"You'll make the squad." I'd have a vote on everyone who tried out, just like the rest of my teammates. But then again, maybe *I'd* be the one getting the boot next year. Breaking up with Matt meant losing the built-in status that came with being his girlfriend.

Without him, would I freefall back into Nerdy Anonymity, never to return?

And if I did, would that be such a bad thing? Being Seth's fulltime girlfriend was all I needed.

"But if you had time over break, I thought—" Paige shrugged a shoulder, her pink glittery tank top meeting tonight's dress code better than my superhero tee. "We could get together to practice. I could—I don't know—make your banners for you next fall to pay you back."

"Wow." That was generous, since each cheerleader had to make a banner for two of the guys on the football team, and one of the guys on the basketball team when that season came around. The banners weren't just Magic Marker on poster board either. They were competitive works of art. "That's a great trade, Paige, but I'm going to summer camp for eight weeks and when I get home my sister is getting married. I'm not sure if I'll have time."

"Oh." *Crestfallen* had only been a vocab word for me until that moment. "Okay. I understand."

"I'm sorry," I rushed to explain, feeling like I'd just kicked a puppy. "If I was going to be around, I'd definitely—"

"It's okay." She twined her finger around a little braid tucked behind one ear. "Is the camp for cheerleading?"

Behind us, someone cranked up the tunes to drown out the sounds of the boys fighting over whether or not a pass was intercepted. A couple of girls gyrated their hips and looked to see if the boys were checking them out.

"No." I leaned against the tree. "It's a summer camp in western North Carolina."

"So is it a sports camp?" Paige's brow furrowed, uncomprehending. "Or an arts camp?"

"Both. It's a traditional camp. My dad went there." Paige was more interested than I would have thought and had lots of questions. Had I misjudged her? Not given her a chance? Maybe I could have had a friend this year...a real one. We must have talked for a while, because the next thing I knew, a crescent moon, my favorite, appeared in the southern sky, and the guys were out of the water.

"There you are." Matt's voice wrapped around me just as Crash arrived to retrieve Paige, teasing her that he was going to throw her in the water.

"Here I am." I swallowed hard, knowing the point of No Return had arrived.

Nearby, most everyone paired off into couples. A few of the guys weren't dating anyone, but even they had invited girls to hang out with. The six of them were the noisier group at one end of the rocky beach, while some of the other couples disappeared altogether. Thankfully, Matt had never pressured me too much to take that long walk into the woods at twilight. Yet another reason he'd been a good boyfriend. I'd never felt ready and couldn't go all the way with him when a piece of my heart still belonged to Seth.

"Come on," Matt gestured toward the quieter side of the party. "I brought a dry towel."

He laid out the towel and pulled on his T-shirt. His hair still dripped onto the collar in a few spots. My heart pounded hard; there was no turning back.

"I want to apologize," he started as he sat beside me on the blue terrycloth. "I haven't even asked you about your sister's wedding or anything lately. I've had a lot on my mind."

"That's okay." I was kind of surprised he even remembered Kellianne had gotten engaged. We didn't spend a lot of time at each other's houses, and I had only mentioned the wedding a few times, over post-game pizzas in town. "I don't expect you to share that headache with me. Unless, of course, you want to weigh in on the merits of semi-gloss lipstick versus matte for a church ceremony."

"Uh. Right. Not my area of expertise." We shared a laugh before he grew serious again. Wrapping an arm loosely around one knee, he turned forest-green eyes on me. "Lauren, my mom and dad are getting divorced."

It took a while for the words to sink in.

"Ohmigod, Matt. I'm so sorry." I'd been so wrapped up in my own family drama this year that I had missed his. While I'd just had the vague worry of divorce floating around my head, given the amount of time Dad spent away from us now, Matt had to deal with the real thing.

I reached for him, my hand on his arm before I could think twice about touching a soon-to-be ex-boyfriend. No matter how I felt, this sucked for Matt.

"My dad cheated on my mom." His voice turned harsh. Unforgiving. "I'm so pissed at him—" He shook his head. His jaw flexed.

"That's awful." A sinking feeling washed over me.

Matt was going through hell. I'd be a total jerk to break up with him when he already had a huge life crisis on his plate. Then again, how could I not when I intended to be with Seth next week? Guilt pinched at my heart.

"Thanks." Matt squeezed my hand hard. "I know I've been out of it lately, but that's why. I—I'm so glad I have you, Lauren."

His heartfelt words delivered the death blow to my break-up plan, at least for tonight.

"Me too," I murmured, feeling like a traitor to him and to Seth. But weathering the divorce news alone would really suck, and it wouldn't be right to give him another thing to worry about.

I squeezed his hand back. Maybe I could spend time with him for the next few days and cheer him up before I broke the news to him on Wednesday or Thursday.

"We can write to each other this summer," I continued, hoping to reassure him so he wouldn't feel like I was bailing. "And we're allowed to use our phones for an hour once a week."

Seth would understand if I needed to exchange a few texts with a guy who was going through this kind of family trouble. He was always there for everyone.

"I want to do more than talk on the phone." One corner of Matt's mouth kicked up, a reluctant smile starting. "There's one bit of good news in all this."

"What's that?" On the other end of the beach, someone lit a bonfire, the bright flare making me realize how dark it had gotten.

"My dad knows he messed up, so it was a good time to ask for what I *really* wanted this summer." Matt turned toward me, his fingers covering mine where they rested on the towel. "I told him I'm going to miss the first week of weight-training."

"You are?" Butler men played football, and players all hit the weights in an intensive program that started during the summer, even before practices began. It was tradition. "Why?"

Being a gridiron hero counted for something in this town. Matt's father still used footage from when he won the state championship in an ad for his car dealership.

"I need a break." Matt shook his head. "Playing three sports means I'm in training all the time. And I've done it because he's always expected me to. But this summer, I just want time to—get away from him. From everything."

My heart pounded harder. A vague unease made me shift uncomfortably beside him.

"What do you mean?"

Matt tipped his forehead to mine. "I'm going to Camp Juniper Point with you."

I opened my mouth to protest, but he was so happy and oblivious that he took it as an invitation. He leaned in to kiss me while I shook in panic. Matt was coming to camp with me, and there wasn't a damn thing I could do about it.

How would I explain this to Seth?

For that matter, how would I make Seth my boyfriend for real when I'd be showing up at camp with another guy?

Suddenly, helping with Kellianne's wedding felt like a cakewalk compared to the hell that waited for me in North Carolina next week.

Chapter Three

The smells of evergreen, spruce, and pine drifted through the bus window, surrounding me like a favorite song. I inhaled and leaned away from the sculpted arm Matt had draped around my neck. His large hand dropped to my shoulder and pulled me back against the vinyl seat, trapping me in my role as his girlfriend.

Un-freaking-real.

Between Kellianne's non-stop errands, and Matt's trips to the lawyers' offices for custody statements, and shopping expeditions to buy camp supplies, we'd barely seen each other. I hadn't had a chance to warn him about Seth and now it was nearly too late.

"I can't believe we're finally here." Matt's sparkling eyes reflected the setting sun. I couldn't believe it either. After enduring a week as Kellianne's wedding slave, a rerouted five-hour flight that took us to the airport in Charlotte instead of the one in Asheville, and an hour-long wait for the camp shuttle bus, it had seemed like we'd never make it. And I'd started thinking that might be a good thing.

How could I avoid hurting Matt and be with Seth? Or help Matt settle into camp without causing Seth pain? If Hercules had had a thirteenth task, this would have been it. Impossible.

"Welcome to Nantahala National Forest." I pointed to a large wooden sign engraved with gold-painted letters, the last of the sun reflecting on the metallic finish. As we turned onto a smaller route, the bus lurched. Or was that my stomach? The shadowed blue-green summits of the Appalachian's Smoky Mountains loomed in the distance –Tennent, Cold, and Toxaway, I recalled, having hiked them all. A familiar red barn flanked by a weeping willow and grazing chestnut horses told me Camp Juniper Point was less than fifteen minutes away.

"Beautiful," Matt murmured in my ear before nibbling it. I pushed him away, pretending to be playful but feeling serious. Arriving at camp late, with a stylish look, designer gear, and a hot new boyfriend would put me on the diva list. And prima donnas at camp were as annoying as mosquitoes, at least to my friends and Seth.

Now, playing the role of Jessica...Lauren Carlson.

The bus engine whined as the driver downshifted to slow our momentum. He could have come to a full stop and I would have cheered at the delay. Just as I opened my mouth to tell Matt about Seth, two white-tailed deer emerged into the dwindling light from a thick mass of roadside brush.

Matt nearly bounced off the seat. "I should have brought my rifle! Did you see that?"

His excitement faded at my expression.

"We don't shoot near camp." It felt right saying "we" since Seth agreed with me on this. An avid outdoorsman, he excelled at any *Survivor*-style events our counselors dreamed up, from hiking to hut-building. And if he'd ever needed to survive in the wild, he'd use a bow, not a gun.

Matt's frown made me feel guilty for counting all the things I preferred about Seth. But there wasn't any comparison between the two, and I was long overdue to be straight with him.

I wrapped my fingers around Matt's broad hand. "Matt—"

He squeezed my hand. "I can't wait to have fun. The only thing that's helped this week is knowing I'd get to be with you. This couldn't be more perfect."

My courage waved a white flag and surrendered. Matt had gone through a tough week and was finally happy. I hated to ruin it. I'd tell him once we reached camp—let him enjoy this good mood a little longer.

"You'll have fun here." I tightened my fingers around his. "There's an awesome volleyball tournament that runs all camp season." He excelled at every sport he tried. "It's more cutthroat than Crash at last year's championship game."

Matt shuddered against me, no doubt picturing Crash's perp walk like I was. Who knew selling ex-lax laced brownies to the opposition would be considered criminal mischief? At the time, it'd just seemed like payback after our rivals branded our mascot Jefferson, a two-thousand pound bull, with their ram's-head logo. My lips quirked as I tried to suppress a laugh and failed. Matt responded with a deep chuckle that intensified when I couldn't stop giggling. The bus driver's eyes flashed at us in his rearview mirror.

"Do you remember Crash's excuse?" Matt choked out.

"'But officer, I thought they looked constipated,'" we chorused, sending us into another laughing fit. The driver cranked up the radio and shifted to ascend another slope. Spruce trees lined the shoulder, their needles looking like they'd been dipped in powder-blue dye.

Matt shook his head. "Man, Crash can be such a moron."

I stopped snickering. He always acted like he thought Crash, and his goons walked on water. Where had this new attitude come from?

Matt leaned forward. "Hey—isn't that the sign for your camp?"

A forest-green sign loomed. I squinted in the dim light and made out a painted conifer-lined river and the words, "Camp Juniper Point."

My heart sped up even as my stomach dropped. My hands clenched, Matt's fingers getting caught in the involuntary motion.

"Ouch!" Matt joked, untangling his hand from mine and shaking it.

He couldn't have said it better. Arriving at camp *would* cause lots of pain. Hopefully, Seth wouldn't see Matt until we'd spoken. Knowing we weren't a couple was one thing—but seeing me with another guy would hurt him even more.

After the night at the creek, and Matt's surprise news, I'd finally answered Seth's message.

Looking forward to seeing you at the bonfire too.

My finger hovered as I'd stared at my response, rereading the coded break-up message Seth wouldn't fail to miss. We'd known each other so long. By not mentioning our First Kiss of Camp, he'd understand that things were different. But just in case, my hands had returned to the keyboard as I contemplated how to explain that I was bringing another boy to camp, one I was dating but didn't love. Not the way I cared about Seth.

But Kellianne had burst in the room, impatient for us to make her fitting, and hit the send button for me, sending our relationship to its electronic death. With one push of a button, we'd returned to the friend zone and Seth was still in the dark about Matt. It didn't surprise me that he hadn't emailed back. Seth took time to process things. And I knew better than to force him. Hopefully, by giving him space this week, he'd hear me out in person.

"You ready?" Matt rubbed my knee as we bumped down the dirt road that led to camp.

"As ready as I'll ever be."

Which is to say—not at all.

*   *   *

"That's the last of 'em." The bus driver tossed a heavy duffle bag at Matt, lumbered up to his seat, and drove off in a cloud of choking dust.

"Where is everyone?" Matt squinted in the twilight as he shouldered his bag and picked up my suitcases. "Are we the first ones here?"

"Hardly." I led him up the path toward the office, the stone pavers painted with handprints the camp had created during my first year. Along the left side of the path, the chubby yellow fingers of seven-year-old me were on a stone decorated with a lopsided yellow star and blobby blue planets that resembled squashed berries. I skimmed my foot along it as we passed by, and smiled at my early astronomy aspirations.

"The rest of the camp probably arrived at dawn. It's always a race to get the best bunk."

Matt pointed to a large, pine-sided building bathed in soft amethyst light. "Is that one of the cabins?"

I laughed. "That's the field house. It's where we play all kinds of sports, even fencing. Our cabins are a lot smaller. Do you know which one you're in?" I nearly tripped over an exposed root, worried that it might be "The Wander Inn," Seth's cabin.

"I think it's called War or Warrior something."

My breath whooshed out. Of course Matt would be assigned to the jock cabin. "Warriors' Warden?"

"That's it." Matt stopped beside our baseball field. "Whoa, you guys have everything."

He dropped our bags and laced his fingers in the chain-link backstop.

"It's called the Field of Dreams." I leaned against the cold, crisscrossing metal, amazed at how four bases and a dirt mound gave guys heart palpitations.

Seth had hit one out on this field last year, and I'd been there to cheer him on. God, I needed to tell Matt about him...

"Matt. I'm really glad you're here but there's something I've got to tell you—"

A shrill sound blasted behind us, making us jump and turn. Camp Director Frank Woodrow, otherwise known as Gollum for his sneaky ways and a whistle obsession so insane we'd dubbed it His Precious, glowered at us. He blew it once more before polishing it on his shirt and tucking it away.

"What are you doing here, sneaking around?" he snapped, wielding his flashlight like a lightsaber.

I could have asked him the same question. Then again, professional "fun sucker" was part of his job description, "gotcha" his middle name. Sometimes I wondered if Gollum hibernated all winter, then emerged from his cave for summer camp, grumpy as a newly woken bear.

"We just arrived, Mr. Woodrow." I moved closer. "This is my—ah—boyfriend, Matt Butler. He's new this year."

Matt flashed his company grin and extended a hand. Gollum's long nostrils pinched as he ignored Matt and narrowed his close-set eyes at me.

"And who exactly are you, missy? Trespassers face serious consequences." His hand twitched toward his whistle pocket. Who was he going to summon? A goblin army? His mother?

I spoke fast, hoping to avoid another eardrum-shattering blast. "I'm Lauren Carlson. I've been coming here for eight years now. Don't you recognize me?" My eyes stung as his flashlight blazed in my face once more.

Gollum shook his bald head, eyes widening behind thick black frames. "Impossible. Where are your glasses? Braces?"

Matt chucked me under the chin. "Hey, I want pictures of that girl." He grinned. "For blackmail purposes, of course."

I elbowed him, annoyed rather than charmed. Seth never teased me about my looks. Even if it was a joke, it still stung.

"I got rid of them when I left camp last year, Mr. Woodrow. But it's still me." At least, I hoped so.

Gollum pursed his mouth, his overgrown moustache looking like it had eaten his upper lip. "All right then. Matt, follow me and I'll get you set up. Lauren, I trust you know the way and won't fall off a cliff." He chuckled at his reference to the time I'd tumbled off an overlook with a little help from our camp's queen of mean, Hannah Trudeau.

Matt looked over his shoulder as the camp director steered him northward, to the corner of camp farthest from the girls' section. Did they really think the distance kept the campers from hooking up? It was like separating a pair of oversized magnets. We couldn't resist the pull, no matter how hard they tried keeping us apart.

I picked up my luggage and watched Matt disappear into the deepening gloom, hating myself for not warning him about Seth. I couldn't let him hear the news before I got the chance to tell him myself.

At least I still had time to sneak in a quick visit with Seth—if he was still talking to me after that short email. He deserved a warning as much as Matt did.

I broke into a trot, anxious to get to my cabin, "Munchies' Manor," and drop off my stuff. If I could explain to Seth in person, maybe he'd understand and agree to wait for me until I had a chance to talk to Matt. I needed to be honest with both of them.

A part of me hoped he'd insist that I break up with Matt right away. Or maybe I kind of hoped he'd confront Matt himself and set the record straight—that Seth and I belonged together. Since I hated conflict even more after a year of Mom and Kellianne's pre-wedding battles and Dad's full-on retreat, I needed help from my camp friends to figure out how to handle my Matt situation.

My foot had barely grazed the first porch step of my cabin before a willowy blonde in her mid-twenties sprang from the door. An overhead lamp backlit her long messy curls, held back with an enormous, glittering clip that could have doubled as a disco ball.

"What's up, home girl!" I caught a flash of rainbow-striped leg warmers as she sped down the stairs. Before I could move, a tight hug lifted me off the ground.

I was speechless in the face of such enthusiasm.

"I'm Emily, your new counselor." The blonde pulled back slightly, her nose nearly touching mine. "And you must be Lauren. I mean, you have to be since you're like the last person here and everything."

Suddenly I remembered my previous counselor's trip to Ireland this summer for a step-dancing competition. Emily must have taken her place. I didn't know what to make of our new counselor. Between the leg warmers, hair clip and an oversized neon Swatch watch, she looked like she'd crawled out of an Eighties time capsule. And she was touchy-feely times ten. She grabbed one of my bags and started back up the stairs.

"It sucks being the last one. You get the worst bunk and everyone takes up your space and talks about you behind your back, right?" Her huge smile flashed, showing a little too much gum.

I smiled back weakly and followed her, trying not to notice the Smurfette-patterned thong peeking over her lime-green biker shorts.

"Not that anyone trashed you—I eavesdropped all afternoon, so you've got nothing to worry about. Trust me."

I stepped over clothes spilling from suitcases, wet towels, and open bottles of bug repellent and sunscreen. The place was a wreck and way beyond regulation. Had Emily stayed behind to clean it up? As a first-year counselor, Gollum would be watching her every move.

But instead of picking up the mess, she flung herself on a lower bunk and thumbed through a purple journal with an astrological sign on the cover—Trinity's, by the look of it. I wondered if my new-age roommate's Tarot cards had predicted that a lunatic would expose her deepest secrets.

I grabbed for the journal, but Emily snapped it shut and held it behind her back. "Hello—this is private. Looks like I need to teach you guys about a little word I like to call respect."

My throat tightened around a surprised gasp. Was she for real?

She sat up and untangled her hair clip from the top bunk's wire springs. "Your friends were worried about what took you so long, and why some guy named Seth hadn't stopped by." She freed the clip, which now perched sideways in her frizzy updo. "So who is this guy—a stalker? Crazed ex? Your true love? You can tell me anything." She held up crossed fingers.

"Um. I'd kind of like to get to the bonfire." I looked away and noticed a jumbo bag of caramel-flavored Bugles—definitely contraband material now that the camp had made a health-food push. I nudged it behind a blue recycle bin, my social activist friend Piper's version of luggage, as I headed toward the door

"They're just starting. We have time," Emily insisted even as I retreated. "Another counselor's covering for me so I could be here when you arrived." She picked up some wet towels and hooked them on bunk corners to dry. "Give me a sec and we'll head down together." She babbled on even as I waved through the screen door.

"Sorry. But I have to see someone!" I ignored her call to come back, knowing I was breaking regulations but not caring. Jogging through the camp, I hoped the evening air would clear my head. In the distance, I could hear singing, so the bonfire must have started. Was it too late to get a moment with Seth alone?

At the bonfire, junior, intermediate, and senior campers squirmed for more room on the circled logs. Many wore their green camp shirts, the white lettering and logo reflecting the fire's red and yellow glow.

"B-I-N-G-O" they sang as I peered from the shadows. My eyes lit on Siobhan, Alex, and a few of my other cabin mates. They swayed to the music, laughing when Alex added an impromptu howl at the end of every chorus. I wanted to join the goofy fun I'd missed for months, but knew this would be my only window of time to seek out Seth.

Most of the guys lounged on the logs nearest the blaze. One of Matt's new bunkmates was holding Matt's hand to the fire—a macho rite of passage they performed when the counselors weren't looking. They cheered as Matt gritted his teeth and darted his fingers in and out of flames. He blew on them like birthday candles, then fist-bumped his new buds as Hannah and her vapid followers from the "Divas' Den" cabin applauded. Yep. Fifteen minutes after arriving, Matt was already on the popularity fast track. Thankfully, he hadn't seen me.

But where was Seth? His friends sat quietly on another log, unusual for the boisterous nerd herd. I caught the eye of one of the guys from his cabin, but he pulled up the hood of his sweatshirt and looked away. My heart sank. Seth must have told them about our split, receiving all he needed to know from my email. If this was their reaction, what could I expect from Seth?

He must be so hurt. If only I could tell him that I was, too.

A loon trilled in the sudden quiet when the camp song ended. Suddenly I knew where to find Seth. I swerved down the beach path and broke into a dead run until I skidded onto the narrow strip of gritty sand. Seth sat at the end of the dock, the site of our first kiss, his head bent over the dark waters below. The rising moon shimmered on the wake left by a pair of swimming loons. The rare birds stopped me in my tracks. I'd only seen their black-spotted backs once before, the year Seth finally became my boyfriend. Was it a sign? My eyes drank in the faint twinkling of the North Star and hoped so.

Seth was the one who'd taught me about loons and everything else that I knew about nature aside from the stars. I still couldn't believe I was here but not with him. Last year, it seemed as much a given as Venus's bright light in the western sky.

I padded quietly along the wooden planks and stopped behind him. Across the lake, juniper trees swayed in a light summer wind that ruffled Seth's curls. My nails dug half-moons in my palms as I forced myself not to smooth the wayward strands that made him look more California surfer than science geek.

"So who's the guy?" Seth spoke without turning, his voice deeper and shoulders broader than I remembered.

So much for breaking the news to Seth first. Secrets at camp had the lifespan of fruit flies. Damn it, damn it. I should have sent him a longer email.

I rubbed my palms on my shorts, wishing he'd look up at me, give me a sign we'd get through this. "His name's Matt. We dated in Texas and—"

"You wanted to be together for the summer," he finished for me, his voice breaking. "I get it. But how could you bring him to camp? We grew up here together. Had our first kiss here."

I sat beside him and matched my swinging sandals to the rhythm his swim shoes beat in the humid air. A chorus of "You Are My Sunshine" drifted on the breeze behind us. My heart squeezed. I'd been waiting for this moment for so long—to be back with Seth, sitting on the dock, just like this. Except everything felt wrong.

"I didn't plan to bring him. Matt and I aren't close that way. I was going to break up with him, but—"

Seth's wounded gaze lifted to mine, his expression puzzled. "So why didn't you?"

The loons took flight at his abrupt question. I followed their path, wishing I could flee these treacherous waters too.

"Because he needed me. I can't explain because it's private, but..." I buried my head in my hands. "God, this is a mess."

Seth's warm arm wrapped around me. Instantly my body longed to snuggle against him, loving the familiar feel of his hard body against mine.

"I've been thinking about you—and this summer—all year. Catching tadpoles, rafting, watching meteor showers together. I never imagined you bringing someone else."

I dropped my head to his shoulder. Doing anything else would have been like reversing the flow of gravity.

"We can't be together until I settle things with Matt."

Seth withdrew his arm, picked a small rock off a pile, and side-armed it across the water. We were silent for a moment, watching the stone skim the surface.

He exhaled when it disappeared beneath the dark water. "It's the way it has to be. I wish things were different, but I don't blame you."

I ground my teeth. How could he be so understanding? He had to be hurting. Was it wrong to wish he'd show it a little?

"I messed everything up." My eyes burned with frustration at all the ways my life was falling apart. And Seth was a big part of that.

"Lauren." Seth brushed a knuckle under my chin and tipped my face up to his. "Don't cry."

My heartbeat went wild, the moment echoing so many times he'd kissed me. I took in the slight growth of facial hair that gave his angular face a new, sexy look. And yes, in spite of everything, I wanted him to kiss me.

"I didn't know what to do." I hoped he heard my unspoken question. That I needed help figuring my way out of this mess.

That I still cared for him as much as ever.

"You did what you thought was right." He dropped his hand and squinted at the opposite shore. "You always do."

We had so much in common...especially that. But right now I wished he'd be more selfish. Not so damn accepting of it. I mean, I was glad he was Mr. Compassion and all, but it felt like he was letting go without a fight. And part of me wanted him to care enough to stand up for us. Our relationship.

"It's not what I want," I argued, waving away a gnat flying around my forehead. "You are. Matt needs me right now to work through...something. But once he's okay..."

Seth was silent for a long moment and it took all my willpower not to wrap my arms around him, nuzzle his neck and kiss the thin white scar on his chin that I knew had come from a wrestling match two years ago. But we were only friends now. Emptiness rose inside me as I sat beside Seth. We couldn't have been closer, or further away.

"Don't count on the future, Lauren. It never turns out the way you hope." He turned shrouded eyes on me again. I flinched, knowing he spoke from experience. When he was four, his mother dropped him at daycare and never returned. He'd waited for hours until his dad picked him up and told him that she'd left them for good.

"And that's it?" The words were torn from the deepest part of me, my voice ragged. No arguments to make me change my mind?

Seth put his hand lightly on my wrist and drew in a ragged breath. "What else can there be? Except–" his voice grew husky, "this."

I only had a second to wonder what he meant before he closed his eyes and kissed me.

My thoughts went haywire. But the pressure of his lips against mine sent my worries packing. He kissed differently than Matt. Slower. My lips parted under his, welcoming the contact that I'd been missing.

Our First Kiss of Camp. If he still cared about that tradition, he must still care about me. I lifted my hands to his shoulders to pull him closer, but he eased back instead.

"God. I shouldn't have done that. I'm sorry, Lauren. If we are meant to be together, we will be." He got to his feet while I stared at him, dazed.

The sound of his retreating steps on the dock pulled me out of my romantic fantasies.

"Seth!" I jumped up.

He stopped short of the beach and turned.

"What are you doing?" It was a dumb question. What I meant to ask was, *why are you leaving before we've settled anything?*

"I need time to...figure things out." He stuffed a hand in his pocket, eyes sliding away from mine. "I can't go back to the bonfire tonight and see you. With him. In fact, it might take me a little while before I can handle seeing you together."

The ache in my chest twisted. God, I didn't want to hurt him. The night air felt colder all of a sudden. I wanted him to come back.

"I'm sorry." I felt so helpless.

He backed up another step. "Don't worry about me, Lauren." The corners of his lips lifted slightly. "I've just got to wrap my head around this." His eyes searched mine. "Will *you* be okay?"

His concern for me was a knife in my heart. I didn't deserve such a good guy. Tears burned the backs of my eyes.

I must have nodded, though, because with a last, long look he turned on his heel and sprinted away.

I raced after him, but the forest had swallowed him by the time I reached the beach. My heart pounded harder than the June bugs against the dock light, a cheery campfire song reminding me how tough it would be to pretend everything was fine. Were Seth and I over?

I gazed skyward and spotted Jupiter, comforted by its appearance in a world changing at the speed of light. How could I have hurt the one person who understood me best, who knew who I was underneath the new clothes and new look? I watched the loons land gracefully in the water and resume their circular trek around the lake. Their calls floated back to me, the lonely sound mirroring the void Seth's absence left behind.

My eyes closed. What had I done?

Chapter Four

Early the next morning, I sat on my bottom porch step, swirling my bare toes through the ground fog. A night of tossing and turning hadn't made me feel any better about how I'd left things with Seth or Matt, so I'd come outside to watch the stars give way to the sunrise. I hadn't gone back to the bonfire last night, unable to sit beside Matt when I'd upset Seth so much.

At least my friends had been happy to see me. They all still slept after our late night of talking and laughing. When they'd come back from the bonfire, they'd swarmed me like long-lost sisters, smothering me with hugs. For a moment, I'd almost been able to pretend this was going to be a regular year. My closest camp friend, Alex, honed in on my longer, straightened hair, tugging the length and declaring it pretty while the others moved right ahead to asking about Seth.

They'd all been surprised and confused to learn we weren't getting back together this summer. Right. Me too.

The air was the pre-dawn color of a faded black and white photo, the silence so complete it felt like a dream. As if I'd conjured him, Seth appeared out of the mist in front of my cabin.

"Hey." He sounded a little out of breath as he joined me. Water dripped from his sodden curls and made his grey tee and black swim trunks cling to him. "Do you have a sec?"

I choked back a laugh. Did I have time for the guy responsible for my lack of sleep two weeks running?

"Sure." I slipped into my flip-flops, and debated taking his hand when he held it to me. For about two seconds. Easing into that familiar touch, I walked with him through the grey-black forest.

The feel of his large hand enfolding mine made my nerves short-circuit, and I shivered in my thin sleepshirt and shorts. The morning birds rousted themselves and began calling as we glided like shadows through the pine-scented air. On the beach, azure rimmed the dark horizon, the hue deepening to indigo as my eyes shot upward to the lingering stars.

"Oh!" I pointed to the faint white streaks overhead. "Meteors."

Seth smiled down at me, his even features barely visible in the gloom. Not that I needed to see them. If I were an artist like my cabin mate Trinity, I could draw his face by heart.

"Yeah." Seth stared up at the sky. "I spotted them when I swam to shore and thought of you."

Our eyes met and clung together. "I'm glad."

When he tucked a tendril of hair behind my ear, I realized I'd hadn't brushed it yet. But the tender way Seth looked at me reminded me it didn't matter.

"Let's sit on our rock."

My feet squished through the damp sand as I followed him to a larger boulder. But I couldn't take up my usual position in front of him. This was real and we needed to talk. Last night had been too raw to say what really needed to be said. Maybe now we could figure things out. I settled across from him.

He drew a deep breath. "I'm leaving."

"What?" I must have misheard him.

"I can't stay here until I figure out how to deal with...us not being together."

I blinked my way through the words that didn't make any sense. "So you're *leaving*? How long? Why?" I jabbed my finger into his chest. What. The. Hell. I was going through a major crisis and what...he was running away? This wasn't like him. But then a niggling memory came back. When he was ten, he'd rehabilitated a wounded bird until Gollum made him return it to the wild. He'd taken off back then too—heading to his grandparents' house. Since they owned Camp Juniper Point, they lived just a few miles down the river.

Was our relationship the wounded bird? The one he'd tried and failed to fix?

He caught my hand and pressed it to his lips, his topaz eyes reflecting the fingers of sunlight feeling their way across the lake.

"You wouldn't have brought Matt here if you didn't have feelings for him."

I opened my mouth to deny it, but nothing came out. He had me there. I did care about Matt. Just not the way I felt about Seth.

Seth cupped my chin. "You need time and so do I."

"What if I asked you to stay?" I jerked my chin away and clenched my teeth.

"Don't ask me to do that." He looked down, his face tense. "I'm giving you space so that when you choose me, if you choose me, there won't be any doubts."

I jumped off the stone and put my hands on my hips. With the wind tossing my uncombed hair, I must have looked crazy. But I was beyond caring.

"I don't need you to give me my freedom. And you don't need to disappear to help me figure out what's right for me."

"Like that Matt guy?"

"I didn't ask Matt to come with me, okay? Don't you think I'd rather be with you?"

"I heard he plays quarterback for a 4A state champion, right?" Seth ran a hand through his short curls. "He's everything my father wished I'd be."

Seth's father was the head of the wrestling program at Indiana University and had always pressured his distance runner, hiker, and kayaker son to wrestle, or to take up a sport that would land him a high-profile athletic career. But Seth's dad wasn't here now. I was.

"Don't you get it?" I blew my long bangs out of my eyes. "It doesn't matter how rich, or successful, or famous you are. When it comes to you, I'm—

I'm always going to be the girl who memorized the genus and species of every wildflower in these mountains to impress you. You were the first boy who made me feel beautiful and loved, even when I was covered in poison oak, with a full mouth of metal and thick glasses. You are my first love, and I want—more than anything—for you to be my last. But that can't happen if you leave."

Seth shut his eyes and shook his head, a crease appearing between his brows. "You're my first love too. The only girl I've ever wanted." He cleared his throat and lifted his lids. His golden eyes blazed at me like the morning sun spilling over the horizon. "But I can't ignore the fact that you have a boyfriend at camp any more than you can. You've got to figure out your feelings for him before we can be together again. And that won't be easy with me around." He swept me up in a tight embrace and whispered in my ear, "Tell me you understand."

My anger deflated like a popped balloon. It was selfish to ask him to help me get through the mess I'd made, especially when I hadn't given him the warning he'd deserved. I needed to handle this on my own. "How long will you be gone?"

His warm breath rushed across my temple. "A few days, maybe. First I'm going to hike something—big. Then I'm going to my grandparents. On Friday, at the dance, we'll see how things stand then. Okay?"

I gulped over the daggers lining my throat. Speaking my thoughts would slice me to ribbons.

After a wordless nod, he pressed a kiss to my forehead, gave me a final hug, then hoisted his backpack and tramped into the woods. I watched his shadow move among the trees until he disappeared from view. It felt like he'd vanished from my life as well.

"Lauren!" I looked up and caught my friends Alex and Siobhan jogging down the beach. Alex doubled over when they reached the rock while our yoga expert, Siobhan, looked completely unfazed.

"We've been searching all over for you," Alex gasped. Her dark hair had grown so long it swept the sand before she straightened.

"I told you she'd be watching the sky," the ever-logical Siobhan put in. The strengthening sun glinted off of her obsidian bob. The new length accentuated the high cheekbones she'd inherited from her Cherokee father and the large hazel eyes from her Irish mother. Her face, awash in fresh light, was splattered with freckles.

"Are you okay?" Alex asked. Both girls crowded beside me on the rock, their thin arms wrapping around me. "Were you thinking about Seth?"

The breakfast bell sounded in the distance, and we all groaned.

"Let's get back to the cabin before Emily notices." Siobhan stood and pulled me to my feet. "No matter what, Lauren. We've got your back, okay?"

"Okay." My heart swelled. I might be here with the wrong guy, and might have lost the right one, but at least I had my friends.

*   *   *

Dewy grass tickled my sandaled feet as my cabin mates and I trudged toward breakfast thirty minutes later. Shards of light stabbed through the towering pines, making us squint and draw our hoodie strings tighter. Only Alex had thought to wear sunglasses, perched crookedly on the bridge of her nose. Our collective misery was palpable after our late night. Even the singing birds quieted as we passed beneath them.

"So where's your medal, Miss National Scholastic Decathlon Winner?" Alex nudged Siobhan.

Siobhan kicked an apple core at Alex's foot. "If I'd brought it, you'd probably take it to Arts and Crafts and make it a head piece."

"Or a belt buckle." Jackie dragged a twig behind her in the dirt, her tall, willowy grace obvious even in warm-up shorts and an oversized tee. "Remember when she went through that cowboy phase after watching *True Country*?"

"Who could forget the summer of a thousand ten-gallon hats?" groaned Siobhan. "She wouldn't even take them off during swim."

A couple of us snickered, and Alex swatted Siobhan. "Hello. I had serious hathead and Rob was the lifeguard that day."

We all sighed, imagining one very crush-worthy counselor.

Piper picked up the discarded fruit. "I got my school to recycle leftovers in a compost pile. I should talk to Gollum. See if we can start a camp community project."

"Gross. Put that thing down." Alex wrinkled her nose, making her glasses rise.

Piper dropped it in the paper sack she always carried for litter and shrugged. "One man's trash is—"

"Piper's treasure," we chorused with gusto, making Piper laugh and a couple of blue jays fly squawking from a nearby tree.

Jackie leapt in front of us with cat-like grace. "Want me to take care of the litterer?"

"Oh, so now that you won your volleyball division, you can take on anyone?" Alex shoved Jackie in the shoulder. "Besides, you're too smart to start dumb fights. We all know you took four AP classes and aced your PSATs, so don't even start."

Wow. My friends really had accomplished a lot in a year. I studied the leftover polish that colored my toenails a delicate pink as I shuffled along in flip-flops. For the first time, compared to the rest of the group, I felt like a failure. What would dating the most popular guy in school and making the cheer squad mean to them?

"I started an art club and we painted a mural on the auditorium wall." Trinity twirled a dandelion before blowing its white seed pods. She turned my way. "Lauren, you'd love it. We did a night scene complete with the constellations and an aurora borealis. When the lights are out, the stars twinkle."

"That's so cool." I put an arm around her and gave her a squeeze. Finally. Friends who knew what the aurora borealis was.

"So have you applied to that NASA thing yet? It was all you talked about last summer!" Siobhan stopped and waited for Trinity and me to catch up. "I'm sure you'll get in."

"You mean the *'once-in-a-lifetime opportunity'* she wouldn't shut up about?" Alex laughed, her smile taking the sting out of her words. They were proud of my accomplishments.

I shrugged, feeling uneasy. "I finished the application, but I still need my letters of reference. My dad's getting one from our congressman." At least I hoped so, I silently added.

"Cool." Jackie grabbed a branch and swung from it before landing ahead of us.

The mess hall's roof appeared through a gap in the trees and unease squeezed my stomach. I imagined what would happen when Seth didn't show for breakfast. I had to get to Matt before the rumors got to him.

Immune to the chilly air and ungodly hour, Emily pranced ahead.

"Come on, girls! Last one in is a rotten egg." Her high-pitched laugh ended in a snort that sent a descending squirrel scurrying back up a white oak tree, or as Seth had taught me, *Quercus alba*.

An exuberant cartwheel revealed Emily's hot pink bike shorts beneath her oversized Camp Juniper Point sweatshirt. "Mornings rule!" she shouted, thrusting pine needle-coated hands upward. Her side ponytail bobbed in agreement. At least that made one of us. I already wished I could skip the day, crawl back into bed, and pull my sleeping bag over my head. If my life had an eject button, I'd hit it now.

"Is she for real?" mumbled Siobhan as she trailed beside me in flip-flops and frog-printed pajama bottoms.

"Someone needs to take the batteries out of the Energizer Bunny." I swiped at a mosquito trying to land on my nose.

Trinity turned around, her round face pale. "Her aura's like a kaleidoscope on speed. My eyes are aching."

Alex passed Trinity her sunglasses as boys jogged across our path. Like bird dogs, we froze, Alex's mouth dropping at the sight of the boys' counselor, Rob. We'd all drooled over him since we'd hit puberty; right now, he was showing off exceptional six-pack abs, his camp shirt tucked into the back of his running shorts.

I looked for Matt, worried that his bunkmates had filled him in on my Seth history. Matt smiled at me as he came around the bend, white T-shirt plastered to his steaming body. His friendly expression relieved some of my anxiety, but it was just a matter of time before everything exploded in my face.

Emily completed a round-off, knocking out Rob. They landed in a pile of last autumn's brown leaves, Emily on top. The boys stopped short while we gaped at the spectacle and tried not to laugh.

"Oh my God. I am, like, so sorry. Seriously. Are you hurt? Because I know someone who knows first aid," Emily babbled, her hands running up and down his hardcore body. Was she checking for injuries or feeling him up? Either way, she was scoring some major points in my book.

"Go Emily," Alex whispered next to me, obviously thinking along the same lines. "I should try that move on Vijay."

I shot her a look as I envisioned the boy from Seth's cabin. "Didn't your parents forbid you to date until you were married? And since when do you like Vijay?"

"Since he got ten times hotter than last year. A lot of the boys are way cuter this summer—didn't you notice?"

It was a running joke that should have made me laugh. We said the same thing every year. But I thought of Seth's newly cut body and averted my eyes.

"Not really."

"And you know I don't do my parents' 'Wholesome Home' thing here. That's their blog, not my life. At least not at camp, where I can have *fun* for two months of the year." She pointed to the tangle of limbs still on the ground, oblivious to my dark mood. "How gorgeous is Rob?"

Piper leaned over and sighed. "Do you have to ask?"

My gaze went back to Rob whose blue eyes twinkled up at Emily, the left-sided dimple we adored appearing in his cheek.

"I'm fine, Emily. Are you okay? Maybe I should check you out?" But before his hands made contact, Emily sprang back, practically knocking over Matt, who hadn't taken his green eyes off me.

Alex shot me a wide-eyed look. Had Emily actually dismissed resident hottie Rob? Any girl would give her weekly fudge pop to be with him.

Even ten-year-old campers twirled their hair and pushed out their training bras when the twenty-something camp god came around.

Rob's muscular thighs flexed as he got to his feet, eliciting a sigh from Piper.

He flashed Emily a white smile and rejoined his group.

"Let's go, ladies! Ten minutes to clean up, then breakfast," Rob shouted to the boys and sprinted away. All but Matt scrambled after him. He jogged in place for a second, gave me a quick wave, and dashed off after the rest of his cabin.

"Ladies?!" Emily stomped ahead of us. "Is that supposed to be a putdown? Male chauvinist."

We lingered behind.

"Was that 'the other man?'" Jackie turned to me, an undercurrent of tension in her tone. "He's not as tall as Seth."

"That's definitely him—you should have seen his pink aura when he spotted Lauren." Trinity grinned.

Because she was happy for me? Or because of the crush I knew she'd had on Seth all these years? She'd never shared it, but one time Alex told me she caught her writing about it in her journal. Luckily, Girl Code meant she'd never act on it. Thank God. No way could I handle that on top of everything else.

"How did he end up in Warriors' Warden? Sucks for him." Piper picked up an empty water bottle and tucked it in her bag.

"He's hot." Alex surveyed me. "But not what I pictured. He looks like a jock head."

Okay, there was no disguising it. That sounded judgmental. Why did they assume all athletes were bad? Jackie was a jock, after all. But, of course, she was a girl. My friends had all had issues with popular male jocks at one time or another.

Taking a deep breath, I blurted, "He's a varsity quarterback."

For his sake, I hoped that missing a week of strength training this summer wouldn't jeopardize his spot on the squad. If I'd broken up with him in Texas, he wouldn't be at risk. And maybe that would have been the right thing to do. But I'd acted on instinct, not wanting to hurt him more than he already had been. No matter how noble I thought I was, however, I'd committed a major no-no in the dating world—leading a guy on. I needed to fix this before more damage was done.

"A quarterback? Shut up!" Alex lightly punched me in the shoulder.

"Seriously." I wished their surprised looks weren't fading into...dismay?

Maybe they were just concerned. For me. I hoped that was all.

"Trippy." Trinity resumed walking. We followed after her, our silence awkward.

I trailed behind the group, my anxiety over the Matt-Seth situation turning my feet into lead. If my friends reacted this way—their comments quickly fading into tense silence—what could I expect from Matt?

We caught up to Emily on the wooden steps of the dining hall. She whirled, light sparkling off her gold-spangled scrunchie. "Everyone take seconds. I don't want anything left for that chauvinist pig. 'Ladies' my a—" she broke off and marched us inside.

Wow. Our counselor was the only female at camp immune to Rob the rock star's charms. And from the interested look on his face, she was the first he'd flirted with in a while. I couldn't wait to see how this played out, especially since someone else's love life drama would distract me from my own.

The sound of scraping forks, pouring juice, and the dull roar of one hundred or so chattering campers filled the room, seeming all the louder now that an uncomfortable silence stretched between me and my friends. Long wooden tables lined up in three rows that ran the length of the high-ceilinged, exposed beam room. Fly strips dangled from the rafters, already full of black insects. An appetizing decorative touch.

We lined up and grabbed plates. On each one rested a wheat pancake with a raisin-patterned smiley face surrounded by sliced strawberry petals. A sunflower. It was a cute way to trick the little kids into eating healthy. I looked at Piper to share a grin over the breakfast, but she seemed suddenly deep in thought over which flavor syrup to pour on her pancake, ignoring me.

We sat shoulder to shoulder on worn wooden benches at a table topped with a "Munchies' Manor" sign. Thankfully, having to sit with our cabins spared me from sitting with Seth or Matt's cabin. My trembling hand grabbed a pitcher of

OJ and poured for the uncharacteristically mute group. Juice splashed on my grey sweats.

I set down the last cup. "Okay. Is it just me, or did things get awkward after we saw Matt?" Eyes flitted around the table, the tension so thick you could cut it with a spork.

"It's nothing." Siobhan peered around the table as the rest of my friends lowered their heads and started cutting their pancakes.

"Seriously. Why is everyone acting weird?" I stabbed my pancake in its beady raisin eye and took a bite.

"It's just that you're different. The new look, the new boyfriend. Give us a little time to get used to everything, okay?" Piper picked up a strawberry slice and nibbled.

The rest of the group nodded, making my chest tighten. Alex and Siobhan had said they had my back. Did the rest of my friends? Since they'd been friends with Seth as long as me, I understood why they'd be protective. Prefer him even. But still.

"Look. My mother hijacked me into this make-over, and the Matt thing is too complicated to explain right now, but trust me, nothing's changed that counts. I'm still me." *And I still want to be with Seth*, I added silently.

Siobhan nodded and gave me a genuine smile. If anyone understood mother pressure, it was Siobhan. Her mom had force-fed her piano, dance, and art lessons since she could walk, and demanded perfection in all things. Siobhan's implied acceptance of the situation unleashed a firing squad of questions from the others.

"So Matt is really a jock?"

"When did you meet?"

"How long have you been going out?"

"Is he good in bed?" Emily gulped Piper's juice as she joined us, twirling a chair around and straddling it.

I nearly choked on a raisin. "Excuse me?"

Emily shrugged, her left clavicle bared through her sweatshirt's one-shoulder cutout. "It's on the D.L., girls. Fo' shizzle. So what's the sitch?"

Was she speaking Greek?

"There is none. I mean, we haven't—that is—it's private." I sputtered. How had our counselor gotten this job? Clearly she'd left "wildly inappropriate" off her resume.

At that moment, a hush fell as the top of the camp food chain entered the hall and shoved their way to the front of the line. The Warriors. They must have finished their morning jog. I was glad when Matt hung back and waved a young girl ahead of him.

He might be a jock, but he wasn't full of himself the way some star athletes could be. I looked to my friends to see if they'd noticed, but they were still staring at Emily with wide eyes.

"Yo, Butler. Over here!" hollered one of the guys from his cabin's table.

Of course, that made my friends notice.

Matt gave the little girl in line an apologetic look and joined his new friends. So much for decency. I shot him a dirty look, which he missed when Eli Rogers, their cabin's undersized comedian, squirted him with syrup. Matt blasted powdered sugar at Eli but hit another bunkmate instead. Eli straightened and laughed, pointing at the white coating on the other kid's beefy shoulders. I held my breath, wondering if Matt was about to get hammered by the biggest guy at camp. Instead, the overgrown Warrior hooked an arm around Matt's head and knuckle-rubbed his hair. His booming laugh shook the rafters.

Finally, Matt spotted me and waved. I waved back as he pointed me out to his bunkmates who, for the first time in the eight years I'd known them, smiled at me.

The screen door banged open. I held my breath, heart hammering as Seth's cabin mates entered—without Seth. Nauseous, I stopped chewing and met my friends' worried eyes. If I told on him, he might get in trouble, especially with Emily being all ears about everything.

"Where's Seth?" Siobhan whispered.

"Garrett!" Alex called, always impatient for information. Garrett's perfect features, wide-set hazel eyes and mussed brown hair attracted lots of attention as he wound his way over. He'd liked our cabin ever since he and his dad argued on Parent's Weekend a couple years ago. Some of the Munchies had helped him back to camp after his father ditched him on the banks of the Nantahala River. The jerk. Age did not guarantee that adults acted like grown-ups.

"Hey." He waved to a few other campers sitting nearby. "Looking good, Lauren. I like the new hair." He fingered the highlighted ends, making me blush.

Which was weird, since this was Garrett. A bud since forever. But it was nice to be noticed, and Garrett was one of those guys who paid attention to what we wore and how we looked. I hoped his father had stopped being such a jerk to him.

"My mother gave me a make-over when we moved to Texas." I smiled, glad he wasn't acting distant toward me like the rest of Seth's group.

"Well, she did a good job," he laughed. "So what else have you been up to besides...cutting Seth loose?" His gaze turned assessing and I wondered how much he knew.

I flinched. "Seth and I broke up last summer." My fingers crossed under the table. Officially it wasn't a lie, since it had always been his idea to break up at the end of the summer each year. But it wasn't the whole truth either.

Seth's leaving to give me space was noble. But somehow that'd made things harder. If he'd been rude, I could have been mad at him. If he'd been willing to wait, I could have had hope. But the way we'd left it, that lakeside kiss intruding in my memories, everything felt in limbo. A purgatory of emotions. How would I resolve things with Matt *and* win Seth back? Garrett raised an eyebrow. "If you two are so casual, why did he leave this morning?"

"For good?" Jackie shot me an accusing look, and Trinity did her best to keep the disappointment off her face.

Garrett shrugged. "His stuff is still at the cabin, but he took off before we woke up and hasn't come back."

Emily's chair scraped back. "Mr. Woodrow!" she shouted. "We've got a runaway named Seth."

An eerie silence descended on the room, hundreds of eyes fixed on me. I squirmed at Matt's puzzled expression.

"Did he leave a note?" Emily asked Garrett.

"Yeah—just that he needed to clear his head and would be back in a couple of days." Garrett shifted in his Keds, looking uncomfortable in the spotlight.

Alex raised an eyebrow, then slid a defensive arm around Garrett's waist.

While Mr. Woodrow strode over, heads came together at nearby tables. Garrett's news jumped from one group to the next, creeping closer and closer to Matt's crew. I watched in horror as my camp nemesis, Hannah, sashayed toward him and whispered in his ear. Her manicured hands stroked his bunching shoulders as two pairs of eyes lifted to meet mine–Hannah's gloating, and Matt's hurt and confused.

My vision swam. I couldn't reassure Matt that Seth and I were over when I still held out a hope I'd salvage things with Seth. Besides, with all the attention on us, I'd humiliate Matt more by going over to him now and increasing the drama.

"Who's that guy you're staring at?" Emily pointed the chewed end of a straw at Matt. "Are you cheating on Seth?"

"No. Matt's my boyfriend. Seth is, is..."

"The other man," Emily marveled, nodding.

Gollum's whistle blew until the cafeteria fell silent. "Anyone with information about Seth Reines's whereabouts, meet me outside immediately. And that includes you," he pointed to Garrett, glowering, before he pointed at me.

"You too, missy. On your feet. Let's go." He blew his whistle once more, marching us outside.

My bunkmates followed.

"Wow," Emily chattered. "Guess who won the cabin drama jackpot?" She squeezed my upper arm. "I hope Seth wasn't totally crushed. Do you think he's okay?"

"Hope so." I remembered all the times he'd won our camp's *Survivor*-style challenges. Then again, a lot of wrong could happen when you hiked mountains alone. If anything happened to him, it would be my fault.

Bam-Bam, Seth's counselor, appeared. He was kind of surly and intimidating, but Seth had always insisted he was a good guy. Right now, his jaw flexed as he glared at all of us. "Can I have a word, Mr. Woodrow?"

Since I'd started camp, I'd never seen the Iraq veteran smile. He'd been an explosives expert—the source of his nickname—and his background was something Gollum liked to flaunt to parents who were nervous about leaving their kids all summer. Despite the slouchy clothes and an inside-out fishing hat, Bam-Bam looked like he could fend off the Taliban if they came calling in the Carolina backwoods. He'd reported for duty at the first sound of a crisis.

Emily batted her eyelashes at Bruce. "Seth's missing."

"Would you know anything about that, Bam-Bam?" Gollum demanded. "Keeping track of your charges is part of your job."

"He called his grandfather last night. Said he'd need a ride in the morning." Bam-Bam spoke quietly, clearly trying to keep the conversation private even though, with a lot of interested bystanders, that was totally impossible. "He seemed upset and said he wanted time away. I'd hoped, after he slept on it, he'd change his mind, but he was gone before we got up."

"Since when do kids have phone privileges on the first day of camp?" Gollum puffed himself up as he turned a dull shade of red.

"I thought we cut the kid some slack since his grandparents own the camp." Bam-Bam met Gollum's angry gaze with a calm, level one.

No doubt it was tough for Gollum to cut anyone slack. He looked deflated. For my part, I was glad Seth was with his grandfather. Safe. And maybe he was right...this time apart would help. He was wrong to think I'd care about anyone more than him. But I did need time to break things off gently with Matt. Apologize for not having the guts to do it sooner.

"Well, great! Problem solved." Emily beamed at Bam-Bam, and then turned to us to stage-whisper, "So cute, right?"

A flock of glances flitted around our group. Jackie covered her mouth and Alex snapped her gum to cover her muffled giggle. Wow. Emily was immune to Rob and fell for Bam-Bam? Crazy. Gollum swung around to scowl at all of us. The whistle shrilled.

"Show's over, kids. Nothing more to see here. First activity starts at 09:00. Let's move out, people." Gollum marched towards his office, forcing us to get going too.

"Awesome! Sign-ups," Alex said, leading us back to the dining hall and Matt.

Matt. I was an idiot for not finding time to tell him about Seth. I lowered my gaze when we re-entered the building, remembering the way Matt had looked at me when Hannah had clued him in about Seth.

Even though inner-tubing and ceramics were the last things on my mind, I followed the group to a large bulletin board full of sign-up sheets beside the entrance. Since there were five activities and a free period, we each chose one on behalf of the group. We'd done everything together after Piper had barely survived an archery class alone with Hannah's posse. The Divas' Den girls hadn't liked us since Hannah and Alex had crushed on the same kid a few years ago. The cabin challenges had taken on a new fierceness that summer, and the competitive fire had only grown. Now, all the Munchies did activities together whenever possible. There was safety in numbers.

"I vote for swimming," Alex said, and I was grateful that someone had moved the topic away from Seth. "I've got the sickest bikini. It's white with these little yellow–"

"Daisies?" Jackie put in, pointing across the room to a member of Hannah's gang who'd pulled up her T-shirt to show off the same bathing suit top to Rob.

"Crap. And she's like totally a D cup." Alex looked down at her chest and sighed. "Fine. Put us down for tubing."

Jackie scrawled our names and turned to Trinity. "You want to pick an outdoor activity?"

Trinity toyed with a green bead at the end of one of her dreadlocks. "Did they add meditation this year?"

Jackie scanned the board. "Nope."

Trinity sighed. "Let's go with the low ropes course. That's always fun."

"I've got an essay on Macbeth to write." Siobhan pinned back the bangs that were angled lower than the back of her bob. "So I could definitely use some fun. How about Frisbee for our athletic activity?"

Everyone liked that idea.

"And volleyball." Jackie put her hands on her slim hips and pinned us all with a look. "Guys. We have to beat Divas' Den in the tournament this year. We need the practice."

She definitely had us there. Hannah's cabin had won our bracket every year and loved flaunting their trophy. Sometimes they brought it to meals and hummed "We Are the Champions" when they walked by. We all hated it, but I think it burned Jackie the most since she was the only dedicated athlete in our group.

I grabbed the pen and scribbled our names, resenting Hannah all the more this year after the Matt incident. The Divas' Den girls were so going down. "Piper, what do you want?"

She rearranged the order of the boy band bracelets on her wrist and lifted her large brown eyes. "Oh I already told Gollum we'd clean up the campfire area during our free time, so you pick, Lauren."

The group sighed. Piper loved volunteering us for the most heinous jobs in the name of saving Mother Earth.

My eyes lit on an activity we'd never tried before.

"Let's do dance." Since joining the cheer squad last year, I'd taken lessons and loved it.

Jackie laughed. "You're kidding, right?"

"No. Why?"

"Because Hannah's group always does dance." Trinity's voice sounded muffled as she pulled off her hemp cover-up in the warming morning air.

I shrugged. After Texas, I could handle Hannah's crowd. "So? We'll ignore them."

"Like they'll let us." Jackie wrote our names on the sheet. "But if Lauren wants it, then we'll make it work. We'd better get changed if we want to make the rope course."

As I turned to go, I nearly ran into Matt. His eyes were wide, his jaw tense.

"Who is Seth?"

I stepped back. "Can we talk later, Matt?" I stepped back and lowered my voice. "When we're alone."

"Later? Are you kidding? Some guy takes off because of you and all you can say is *later*?" His shoulders bunched and a twitch appeared high in his cheek.

So much for not taking this public. Although, to his credit, at least he cared that I'd had a relationship with someone else. Enough that he wanted to talk about it. Seth, on the other hand...I hated that we hadn't figured out anything. That he'd taken off instead.

I searched for the right words and drew a blank in the sorry-for-effing-up-your-summer department. I should have been cruel to be kind and now it was too late.

One of the Warriors sauntered up to Matt. "Dude—whitewater rafting starts in like ten minutes. Let's go." He gave me a once-over. "Looking good, Lauren."

I ignored him. "Matt, go ahead. Please. We'll talk tonight."

Matt shook his head and followed his friends outside.

I bit my lip and watched him go.

I was 0 for 2.

Chapter Five

As we trekked from our beach volleyball practice, I made a mental list of all the ways my camp experience had fallen sucked so far.

1. My friends seemed frustrated with me for upsetting Seth, letting Matt treat me like that. (They'd said that *Seth* wouldn't have gotten in my face like that in a million years.)

2. I got stuck in the "spider web" portion of the low ropes course and stayed there for a long time, since no one seemed in a great hurry to untangle me. See #1.

3. Gollum called me into his office during lunch for an interrogation about Seth. He was not happy to have the owner's grandkid ditching camp on the first day, and seemed convinced that I knew more than I was telling.

4. I hadn't eaten lunch. See #3.

5. Since I still sucked at volleyball, I hadn't won any points with my friends there.

6. Seth wasn't here.

7. Matt had glared at me both times he saw me during the day.

8. My friends were grumbling big-time about the dance class.

I didn't know how to fix anything, either. At home at least I knew how to keep the peace between Kellianne and my mother, acting as mediator when they got mad each other or at Dad for his long absences from the family. Here, I was out of my element for the first time in all my years of summer camp. I was starting to feel like I didn't belong. I'd hoped to talk about Macbeth essays and science projects with Siobhan in between helping Trinity paint and Piper save the earth.

Damn it, what was happening to everyone?

Arriving at the theater and dance studio on top of a hill behind the girls' cabins, I braced myself for a far bigger round of confrontations. Hannah and the other girls from the Divas' Den cabin were already in the studio. Of course, they'd all brought cute dance outfits from home, while the girls from our cabin still wore shorts and T-shirts from volleyball.

"Nice shirt, Jackie," Hannah remarked mildly from her spot at the barre in front of the mirror. "Although the jean shorts kind of make you look like a truck driver. No offense."

Jackie stretched her long legs and volleyball-toned arms in her white tank top. "Nice leotard, Hannah. It makes you look like you're shrink-wrapped in Pepto-Bismol. Oh wait, that's probably what you're going for since you make everyone sick." Jackie then kicked off her shoes and stood in the back of the studio with her arms crossed. My other friends did the same.

"Maybe we should warm up a little," I encouraged them, taking off my shoes, too. "Loosen up."

I really wished they'd just give dance a try and stay open-minded. Sitting down on the floor, I ran through some of my normal stretches, hoping they'd follow suit. Siobhan joined me, perhaps spotting that a few of the moves were yoga.

"Hello class!" The dance instructor, Leslie Kim, padded in on silent, bare feet. She was all of five feet tall and a former gymnast. I'd seen her around camp other years and had always wanted to take a class with her. She looked energetic and fun.

And wasn't I here to have fun? At least I wasn't settling arguments about lipstick shades for the wedding.

I faced forward and kept my focus on Leslie while she led us through some basic moves. We did some chassés and pliés and worked on our posture. Very basic. Very easy. Except that Alex had a hard time being still and focusing on her breathing. I thought she'd lose it when the instructor asked her to take out her gum. After the first twenty minutes, we turned on some music and did the Thriller dance, which everyone knew. Even Jackie made a half-hearted attempt to do the zombie hands and make like the undead. Or maybe she just wanted to strangle Hannah.

Things were looking up until Piper stepped on another girl's toes.

"Do you not know your right from your left?" a Divas' Den member huffed, her high ponytail flouncing around her ears.

"Now ladies," Leslie Kim warned, turning down the music since we'd all stopped to watch the confrontation anyhow. "This is a beginners' class."

The girl fisted her hands and put them on her hips. "Only because no advanced classes are offered the first week. But you know us. Why do we have to do the same moves as the geek squad who don't know a plié from a scissor kick?"

Piper's face flushed. My blood boiled, since I'd assured my friends we'd be able to avoid dumb confrontations like this. But our cabins had a history. Hannah and the other Divas' Den girls burst into laughter while our teacher's brows drew together.

"I'll see you after the activity period is over. For now, I need you to wait for me outside so you can cool off and think about your rudeness."

I was somewhat soothed by this. But when Leslie moved toward the windows to crank them open more, the Divas took turns high-fiving each other in silent mode. They seemed to smack hands in slow-motion, deliberately goading us as their friend sashayed her way out of the studio.

Dance class went downhill from there. My friends glared at me while we slogged through the cool-down workout ten minutes later. I was doing my neck rolls when Kayla, a Divas' Den girl obsessed with designer labels, poked me in the arm.

If I'd had any martial arts training, I would have gotten into a fighting stance. I was that on edge.

"You have amazing posture." Kayla wore a bright canary T-shirt off the shoulder with the words "Juicy" in glitter letters. She hitched at the strap of the turquoise dance leotard she wore underneath. "And your chassés were awesome."

"Thank you," I muttered, too surprised to think through any possible ulterior motives on Kayla's part. "I started taking dance last summer to help with cheerleading."

"She's a cheerleader now too?" Piper remarked darkly from somewhere behind me.

"Is that a crime?" Spinning on my heel, I faced her as Leslie Kim dismissed us.

"No," Piper shot back, her over-sized green recycling T-shirt almost swallowing her whole. "But you used to talk about science fairs and honor society instead of high kicks. Remember?"

She stomped to the back of the studio to retrieve her bag. It clinked with recovered cans which, for some reason, struck me harder than her words. Piper was passionately dedicated to a cause. Every year that I'd come to camp, she'd been saving the earth, whether by planting trees or convincing Gollum to offer a sustainable garden. Year in and year out, she was the same Piper.

Unlike me.

I'd come to camp a different person and expected everything to be the same.

"See you tomorrow," Kayla said out of the blue. I'd forgotten she'd been standing next to me. She gave a wave as she went off with her friends.

While her group filed out of the dance studio, my friends put their shoes on.

"I still like science," I said, to myself as much as anyone else. If Dad had gotten the letter of reference for me, I might have e-mailed my NASA Aerospace Scholars application early. When he hadn't come home in time to say goodbye, I'd left the file open on his computer. Hopefully he got my silent message.

"You still like science, but you liked Matt more. Maybe that's why a summer boyfriend is a good thing." Siobhan handed me my bag.

"What do you mean?" We walked out into the sunshine. Jackie had jogged ahead to catch up with Piper, who was halfway back to the cabins.

Trinity and Alex stayed with us, although I think that was because the boys from Seth's cabin were playing lacrosse on the field outside the dance studio. Alex waved to Vijay, who was tossing the ball back and forth with Julian.

"I mean summer is a good time for having fun." Siobhan paused next to Alex to watch the guys. "It's one thing to date during the summer when classes are out. But during the school year, boyfriends steal focus."

"And how would you know?" Alex teased over her shoulder. She'd found her pack of gum by now, and was back to chewing with enthusiasm.

"I have eyes." Siobhan poked Alex in the shoulder. "I don't need to date to know my mom is right on this one. Guys are a distraction."

As if hearing her mother's voice in her head, she turned on her heel and headed back toward Munchies' Manor, perhaps remembering some homework she needed to tackle. I went too, sad to think about Seth missing these moments with his friends.

Alex and Trinity followed as a group of junior campers streaked by on a scavenger hunt. A few of them wore floral crowns, a craft I used to love. One year, all of my cabin mates and I made matching wreaths out of maple leaves instead of flowers. We wore them for two weeks until they were nothing more than twigs and Gollum made us stop.

"You've changed a lot for Matt." Trinity breezed ahead of me as we reached the girls' cabins. "We're worried." The screen door rattled shut behind her.

I flopped on the porch's wood-slatted rocker and fanned myself with a fly swatter. Alex leaned against the railing and crossed her arms.

"I didn't change for Matt." My fingers drummed on the chair arms. "There've just been a lot of changes in my life. Period. Like my dad is never around, and when he is, it's like he's not really there."

"But I thought you two were tight." Alex held up twined fingers, the friendship bracelet that matched mine sliding down her slim arm.

My laugh ended in a watery hiccup. Was I really this close to losing it? What was it about good friends that made it impossible to lie...to them...or yourself?

"Not anymore. The only people that notice me are my mom and Kellianne...and that's if my outfits aren't coordinated." My feet pushed the rocker back and forth, the runners squeaking.

"So no one really talks to you? Asks what you care about?" Alex lowered her sunglasses, her expression understanding.

My eyes slid from hers. She could see too much.

Alex gripped the rocker and stopped my momentum. "I know how you feel. All my parents care about is that I act like a lady at their promo events, dress like I'm eighty years old in their photo-ops, and attend our youth group meetings. They talk, but don't listen. Ever."

My breath caught. I so got that. Our parents might have different expectations, but they were still the same. They molded us into the people they wanted to be instead of helping us become ourselves.

"It sucks." I unwound my hair from its too-tight bun.

"Is that why you dated Matt? Because your mom liked him?"

My fingers froze as I combed out my tangled locks. "Maybe. Though my mom married a scientist, not an athlete."

Alex's shoulders shifted as she shrugged. "And I'm definitely not marrying a do-gooder who cares more about his Twitter followers than his family."

"I wanted to come back here and be with Seth... with all of you...and now nothing is the same." My calf stung and I swatted it automatically, leaving a squashed mosquito and a splat of blood. Gross.

Alex cocked her heart-shaped face and studied me. "So what are you going to do about Matt?"

"I don't know." I leaned my head against the high-backed rocker and stared up at our cobwebbed ceiling.

Alex flung her tiny self in my lap and wrapped her arms around me. "At least we've got each other."

"Ewwwww—get a room," Jackie hooted from the window beside us.

Alex put her hand over my mouth and gave it a passionate kiss before she leaped off of me and rushed inside. I smiled when I heard Jackie's shrieks as Alex chased her around the cabin. This was exactly how my summer was supposed to be.

Only it wasn't.

*   *   *

After dinner, I plodded back to the cabins with my friends and debated what to do that night. The camp was operating on half-manpower while Gollum took turns interviewing the counselors about Seth's departure. Apparently, he thought Seth's disappearing act might hurt his record as camp director. Another time, I might have found Gollum's freak-out funny. But right now, I still needed to speak to Matt privately. Apologize. Tell him I'd made a huge mistake by bringing him here, and that I loved Seth. Face the anger I deserved.

In the meantime, he had Hannah to comfort him. She'd been at his table so much that her counselor, Victoria, had twice roused herself from her normal state of spaciness to drag Hannah back to her cabin. Victoria was popular with the

Divas, probably because she usually let them get away with anything most of the time.

I tripped in the dark, lagging behind my friends. There was no bonfire tonight, just extended twilight free time. Emily was still back at the lodge for the counselors' meeting about Seth and the camp's runaway protocol.

"Are you coming?" Alex called, shining her flashlight in my face. With all the Seth drama, dinner had been served late.

Now dusk had fallen and I was blinded by the bouncing ray of light from Alex's Eveready.

"Yeah. Sorry." I jogged a few steps to catch up. Maybe I'd work on Kellianne's list, write all of her bridal shower thank-you cards. All eighty-five of them. My hand cramped at the thought. Why was this my job again?

At least that would give me something to do until I could sneak away and find Matt.

"I can't even believe we'll have free time without Emily." Alex squeezed my arm. "I'm totally going to find Vijay and convince him to make out with me."

She handed me her flashlight while she reapplied lip gloss. I hoped bears didn't have a thing for strawberry bubble-gum flavor.

"Sounds fun," I said, wishing my FKOC could have been happy and uncomplicated.

"No poaching." She pointed a glow-in-the-dark press-on nail in my direction. "Vijay is all mine."

I rolled my eyes. "I'll try to restrain myself."

"Do more than try." She slowed her step as we reached the cabin.

Ahead of us, a light flickered inside the cabin. A candle? That was totally against the rules, but nothing we hadn't done before. Still, it surprised me that our door was open.

Piper and Jackie waited inside.

"We wanted to talk to you about Matt." This was from Siobhan, who had stepped outside with Trinity.

"And Seth!" Jackie called.

This looked planned—like they'd been waiting for me.

What was going on?

"What about them?" Had they seen him hanging out with Hannah and gotten the wrong idea? I was sure he wasn't a cheater, not with how upset he'd been about his dad messing around on his mom.

Matt would break up with me before he did anything like that. But of all people...Hannah? As for Seth, he'd made the decision to leave. I hadn't asked him to go.

Trinity waved me inside the cabin. "We're going to ask the spirits about them."

I bit back a smile of relief as I spotted the Ouija board in the center of a lipstick-drawn circle. The peach color looked familiar...at least my cosmetics had come in handy. Good thing it was a shade Mom had chosen. It looked better on the floor than on me.

Siobhan nudged me in the back. "Come in already. We're having an intervention."

"Is that what we're calling this now?" Asking the astral world to weigh in on deep philosophical questions, like the first letter of our future husband's names, how many more times they'd serve green Jell-O for dessert, or if Rob the Hottie was into younger women, was a long-time Munchies' Manor tradition. It wouldn't have been camp without it.

As we all piled into the cabin, Siobhan locked the door behind us. My closest friends since forever stared at me with a mix of expressions, from Trinity's apologetic smile to Alex's grin and wink.

I looked from one to the other. "We're just having fun, right?" An uneasy feeling rolled through my stomach.

Trinity dabbed patchouli oil on her wrists. "This is serious, Lauren. One guy's mad at you. Another's disappeared. I'd say a little intervention is exactly what you need."

"It's for your own good." Piper sat inside the circle with Jackie.

"We decided at lunch." Alex wound around the suitcases and bunks to pull the shades on the cabin windows. "We knew Emily would be gone, so we thought now would be a good time to talk to you."

"I thought you were going to find Vijay tonight." I wondered if she'd just said that to throw me off-track.

She inhaled a popped bubble. "I can help you, then find Vijay after. It shouldn't take you all night to realize what is totally obvie to the rest of us."

The others nodded.

Alex cleared her throat. "Do you think Matt could have tried to, you know, scare Seth off?"

"Of course not. He didn't even know about Seth until breakfast."

Dead. Silence.

I could have counted down the seconds like on the last day of school. Now I knew how Piggy in *Lord of the Flies* felt. And look how it'd ended for him.

"That's why he was so upset afterward," I explained in a rush. Okay, I should have been more forthright about the boyfriend drama. But I didn't want to sound like Kellianne, gushing about two guys, poor me! Wasn't that such a problem? Who doesn't get annoyed by a girl like that? I'd hoped to figure it out on my own. Of course now that the spirit world was about to weigh in...I clapped a hand over my mouth to hold in a giggle that felt more desperate than funny.

Perhaps to cover the awkward silence, Siobhan got up to lay a sleeping bag open in the circle and Trinity arranged the board on top.

"Let's see if we can get some answers." Trinity sat on the sleeping bag and gestured us closer. "Though you may not like what you hear, Lauren."

Sighing, I settled beside Siobhan. Even writing 'Thanks for the toaster' eighty-five times would have been better than this. But as we squished together, the nostalgia of sitting in the dark, hand in hand, pulled at me. I wanted to connect with my real friends somehow. We joined fingertips all the way around Trinity as she rested her palms against the board and closed her eyes. "Spirits, we invoke your positive energy and seek your wisdom. If there is one among you with knowledge of Matt–"

She cracked open an eye at me.

"Butler," I whispered, pushing down my lower lip to keep my smile at bay.

"Butler." Trinity nodded and closed both eyes again. As we waited for a sign, pounding rattled the windows.

Everyone screamed.

We broke hands and backed away from the Ouija board, freaked.

"Oh God, oh God, oh God," Alex chanted, crossing herself. "I'll never touch that board again, I swear it."

Bang! Bang!

This time, the sound came from the window near Jackie's bunk on the back wall.

"What the hell?" I stalked over to the shade and pulled it aside.

Matt's face appeared.

"I need to talk to you."

The fact that I had to face him, say what needed to be said, was a whole lot more ominous than any banging spirits could have been. My gut clenched tight as a fist. My friends were going to kill me for leaving the intervention. An intervention that was supposed to help me with Matt and Seth. But I really, really needed to talk to him and I knew best where he was concerned.

"I'm sorry," I began, then stopped as I read the body language around the room.

Piper's back was turned. Siobhan's arms were crossed. I thought I saw some steam coming out of Jackie's ears.

But no matter how I wished things could have been different at camp this year, I was still officially Matt's girlfriend.

So, picking up my flashlight, I went out into the night.

Chapter Six

The screen door thudded behind me as I slipped down the porch steps. Matt stood with one foot propped on the base of our crisscrossed birch balustrade, his face pale in my flashlight's glare.

A breeze lifted my hair while the silver maples rustled overhead. The oppressive air felt like rain and doom.

I pointed over my shoulder at the cabin. "Do you want to go in and talk?"

"Not with all of them listening." He nodded to a window filled with my friends, their concerned faces pressed to the glass. My scowl made Trinity squeal and the rest stumble back, but at least they weren't chasing after us.

Privacy was definitely in short supply at camp. But now that Gollum was busy lecturing the counselors about protocols for dealing with kids who were having problems at camp, this was my best chance to catch some alone time with Matt.

"I know a place." I led him down a river path toward the top of a small waterfall called Highbrooke. As we approached, the sound of gurgling, tumbling water rose. It was a guarantee we wouldn't be overheard. And what I had to say was for Matt's ears only.

I paused and looked back at Matt, waiting for the words to come. *Whenever you're ready, brain...*

He took off his flip-flops and sat on a riverbank log. Did that mean he was willing to listen? I kicked off my shoes and sat beside him. Before us, the moon briefly appeared behind a thick cloud and shimmered on the expanse of calm water before the falls. A startled turtle splashed off a boulder and into the depths. Mist rose from Highbrooke, droplets gathering like crystal beads on Matt's dark hair.

"Matt, I'm so sorry." The words rushed out as fast as the water streaming down the mini-falls. He peered at the juniper-lined opposite shore while I gazed at his rugged profile. He was as perfect as a statue, and just as stony. "I should have told you about Seth. I never meant for you to hear about it from Hannah."

"Then why didn't you? Do you have any idea what you put me through today? All day I've been imagining you and that guy." His accusing eyes flew to mine, a twitch appearing under his left eye as the moon ducked for cover.

Guilt pinched at the memory of being with Seth, alone for those stolen moments. Rain began to drizzle softly. Then, a moment later, the wind kicked up and the rain came down hard.

I barely felt it since it didn't compare to the storm inside my gut. How could I blame Matt for being mad? I'd been so focused on Seth, I'd ignored how Matt would feel when he found out about my old boyfriend. He'd been there for me while I coped with my mega-stressful year in Texas, taking me out for pizzas on the nights when my dad was working late. Giving me something to think about besides the stuff I used to share with my father. I owed Matt better than this, even if Seth held my heart.

"I'm sorry," I repeated, wishing I could conjure the words I needed to say to end things in a way that wouldn't hurt Matt. Maybe the Ouija board hadn't been such a crazy idea.

Matt stood, the rain plastering his T-shirt to his chest. "Sorry doesn't cut it. It's all I hear at home. Sorry, Matt, I'm leaving your mom. Sorry, Matt, I can't forgive your father. Sorry, Matt, your life totally sucks now."

I caught his wrist as he turned to leave.

"I should have told you sooner but I was— afraid." My throat closed around the truth. "You were already so upset that I didn't want to make things worse. You were so busy fitting in visits to the lawyers' offices for the custody thing, and I kept thinking I needed a time that wasn't so hectic but..." I ducked my head and felt a raindrop run down my nose and plop onto my chest. "Yeah. I guess I was mostly afraid of upsetting you."

Matt reached down and tucked my damp hair behind my ear, tipping my face up to his. The water-filled air turned his eyelashes into long wet spikes. "Afraid? After nine months, you should have trusted me. I would have understood."

I swallowed, thinking hard. Since my life had imploded and Dad had gone AWOL this year, I'd found it difficult to trust anyone. But Matt had been good to me. I might not have liked the way he acted around his friends sometimes, but he'd always been considerate with me. A gentleman.

"You've gone through so much lately."

"But I needed to know." Matt spelled it out simply. Clearly.

It was such a clear-headed, wise thing to say. He'd hate me for thinking this, but at that moment he reminded me of Seth.

"You're right. I should have let you know about Seth—that we'd dated in the summer." I shivered as the rain fell in heavy sheets, and geared up to tell him my true feelings. Only suddenly I wasn't so sure. Seth was with his grandparents while Matt had stayed here with me, in the rain, trying to straighten this out.

"You swear it was just a summer thing?" He towered over me.

I nodded, knowing now that it was the truth even though I wanted so much more.

"Be honest, Laur...do you still want to be with him?"

My will wavered like a candle flame, then strengthened. I owed Matt the truth.

When I nodded, Matt's rigid shoulders lowered and his breath whooshed out. He sat down again, surveying my face with little flicks of his eyes in the slackening rain.

"When were you going to tell me?"

"The night at Turtle Creek." I pushed back on the slippery log and felt Matt's arm wrap around me, anchoring me in place.

Water flew sideways when he shook his head. "And I told you I was crashing your summer camp instead. Surprise." His short laugh didn't sound funny at all.

My heart pounded. God, oh God. This was worse than I imagined. Why wasn't Seth here? This was devastating and I needed him, damn it.

"I...I don't want you to feel like you have to leave camp. Like you're crashing my summer."

Matt's eyebrow shot up and his jaw squared. It was the expression I'd seen him wear on the field when he was all that stood between his team winning or losing. "Oh, I'm not leaving."

Relief washed over me. It was going to be okay. He liked it here. Maybe even saw a few girls he could date. We'd still be friends and—

"You're my girlfriend. I'm not giving up on us that easily."

I blinked at him. "What?"

His hands cupped my face, his green eyes earnest. "You're the best thing that's ever happened to me, Lauren. Remember that time we skipped school and sang karaoke at my cousin's honky-tonk bar?"

I nodded, remembering that country dive and the mischievous day. Matt had a way of getting me to do things I'd never dare on my own. He'd also sounded amazing on those Keith Urban songs.

"That was the first time I ever sang in public. Funny, three-hundred-pound linebackers don't scare me, but I would never have taken that microphone if you hadn't been there. You make me the person I want to be, Lauren. Give me these four weeks before I leave for football to convince you that good times like that aren't a fluke. We'll be as good here as we were in Texas, as right for each other. I know it."

Confused, I shook my head. "I don't want to risk hurting you.

He matched his broad palms to mine and curled the tops of his fingers over my smaller ones. Something about that gesture tugged at my heart. "It's *my* heart, Lauren. Let me decide what it can take."

And just like that, I knew my answer. "Yes." I held up a finger when Matt's smile grew so ecstatic I thought it would break my heart. "But just for the four weeks. When you get ready to leave for strength training, we'll talk."

Matt's green eyes darkened. "And no Seth, either. Right?"

My heart dropped. An anchor in a bottomless sea. "No Seth."

"That poor son of a bitch." Matt crushed me to him.

My eyes welled and my chin rested on his broad shoulder. Right now, it felt good to have his arms around me. To have him care. At least Matt wasn't afraid to show me how he felt.

Seth had always steered clear of emotionally deep waters. Suddenly, the fact that he'd disappeared seemed more self-centered than noble—more like me, in a way. I'd been selfish like that too. Matt stuck around to face the facts— good or bad. And he deserved more than I'd given him in the past months. I owed him better and I could give him four weeks to see if...if there was more between us than what I'd thought.

Footsteps sounded behind us. My eyes flew to Matt. If anyone caught us out here together, we'd be shipped back to Texas. In spite of all my good intentions with Matt, my first thought was—if that happened—I'd never see Seth again.

"Quick, in the river," Matt whispered, tugging me down the small bank. I hesitated, then followed. I was drenched from the rain anyway. In seconds, we submerged ourselves up to our noses, our feet slithering through underwater plants as we treaded water.

A flashlight bobbed along the shoreline. I held my breath, ready to sink completely under the surface if one of the counselors appeared. But to my surprise, Hannah's friend Madison loomed into view, an umbrella shielding her low-cut tank top, short skirt, and impractical heels. I smiled in relief, knowing all too well where she was headed.

Once she disappeared, Matt's wide hands gripped my waist and pulled me against him.

"What's she doing out here?"

I tried to ignore the electric brush of his muscular thighs and rippling abs. I had thought, once I saw Seth, my attraction for Matt would disappear. But I'd be lying if I said his closeness didn't affect me. His touch warmed me inside and out. And now that I'd decided to be with him...

"She must be meeting someone." My voice became breathy when Matt wrapped my legs around his waist to keep us both afloat. "There's an abandoned hermit's cabin about a half-mile from here. Kids go there to hook up."

Matt swung us in a slow circle. At six foot two, his toes had to be touching the river bottom.

"Who needs a cabin, when we can be alone like this?"

He cradled my face and lowered his mouth. His lips began to move incrementally along my jawbone. We were very alone out here, more so than we'd ever been before. Back at Turtle Creek, there'd always been friends nearby and a curfew hanging over our heads. Now? The possibility of being together was all too real.

"Matt," I breathed around the catch in my throat, knowing we shouldn't complicate things between us. Especially when I'd only promised him four weeks.

That was tough to remember when his hungry lips met mine. His arms tightened around me and his fingertips ran through my hair. My lips parted under his, my hands trapped between his chest and mine. Underneath my palms, his heart drummed.

His hands moved forward until he cupped my face, then pulled away. He made a soft, ragged sound as he gazed down at me.

"God, you're beautiful," he murmured, eyes more intense than I'd ever seen them. My pulse raced when his lips drifted down to my clavicle and along the neckline of my shirt. His hands skimmed across my back, making me shudder in a way that had little to do with the water temperature. When his strong fingers circled to the front and rubbed my ribcage, my body tingled in pleasure.

And yeah, I was sending out the wrong message. Trying to shake off the feelings, I grabbed his hands and nudged him away. I treaded water and tried to slow my breathing. Matt looked like he'd run wind sprints.

"Too much?" he asked, still the southern gentleman despite the wicked gleam in his eye.

I nodded, wanting to say more but needing time to puzzle things out. We stayed out as long as we dared, and we needed to be in our beds before our counselors got back from their meeting.

Back at my cabin, I just barely beat Emily when I slipped inside. My friends might have given me the third degree, except that our counselor was right behind me and we all had to fake sleep since it was well past curfew. Grateful this once for the early bedtime, I dried off, put on sleep shorts and a tank, and snuggled under the covers in record time. I turned over and pounded my pillow, Matt's face intruding every time I tried imagining Seth's.

Who knew I'd have a First Kiss of Camp with two boys? Or that they'd both confuse me so much? I'd thought my feelings about them were clear before I came here. But Seth had surprised me, by letting me go so easily that it hurt. And Matt had given me a few surprises too, forgiving me when I didn't necessarily deserve it and fighting for me like I was more than a nerd masquerading in designer clothes.

As my eyes drifted closed, Seth's sun-tipped curls and lightly freckled face finally came into focus. He'd want to know what I decided when he came back and wouldn't like my answer. I'd done nothing wrong tonight, but I couldn't stop feeling like I'd betrayed him—us.

I might have had a FKOC with both guys. Now I needed to figure out which one would have the last.

Chapter Seven

"Who wants me to do their eyeliner?" Emily flitted around the cabin with a shiny tube of liquid make-up in one hand and a can of hairspray in the other. "I'm an expert at the cat eye. Jackie?"

It was our first Friday night at camp, the traditional night for a get-to-know-you dance. Our cabin was in an uproar, with discarded outfits on the beds, flat irons plugged into every free outlet, and a mob at the tiny mirror in the bathroom. The whole place smelled like vanilla after we'd chased each other around with perfume and scented body glitter.

For a little while, it felt like old times, partly because I knew Seth was back at camp. He'd walked into Gollum's office with his grandfather on Wednesday morning and apparently been welcomed back with open arms. I'd seen him in passing at meals since then, and at evening activities when Matt sat beside me and held my hand.

But we'd avoided each other. Waiting, I supposed, to talk at the dance as we'd planned.

Only I was sure he'd guessed my decision. It was getting a awkward between us and I hoped we could make some kind of peace tonight. I didn't want us to grow so distant we'd never find each other again. Just because I'd agreed to try things with Matt for a month didn't mean my feelings for Seth had disappeared.

"Don't come near me with that thing." Jackie leapt from one bunk to another, avoiding a persistent Emily.

"Just a little eyeliner won't hurt," she wheedled, launching into an explanation of how makeup could transform a duckling into a swan, or something like that. Considering Jackie was more of a swan than any of us even without makeup, it was an argument Emily was bound to lose. Jackie smudged the eyeliner on top of her cheeks like an athlete and pronounced herself perfect, startling Emily quiet. A first. Meanwhile, I helped Alex twine a clip-on pink hairpiece into a braid through her dark waves.

"What if Vijay doesn't ask me to dance?" She lost half her lip gloss to the bubble she blew. It popped before I could answer.

"Ask him." My fingers worked faster and faster as the braid neared the end. "He was watching you at lunch today."

"Get out!" She smacked my arm with a little quilted makeup bag that only had lip gloss and eye shadow inside. I'd given her one of my eye glitter wands because her parents were super strict about clothes and makeup.

"I'm serious," I insisted while Emily started flashing the lights.

"Check it out, girls!" she squealed. "A strobe light. Maybe we should have a dance right here!"

We tried not to trip over anything while we headed toward the door.

"Why didn't you say anything?" Alex hissed as we all gave each other the last minute "stray bra strap, lip gloss on teeth" check.

Because I was too busy freaking out that Seth had been hanging out with another girl over the last few days. She was a year older than me and in a different cabin. We didn't hang out in the same crowd, but I'd heard she was nice and volunteered a lot with the youngest campers. It didn't help my anxiety that she was also really, really pretty.

But I couldn't share that with Alex. This was her time, not mine. Instead, I shrugged. "I thought you saw."

She scrambled over to Trinity and Siobhan to share the news, breathless and talking in an octave that would make Hershey howl in pain. I was happy for her even if I was worried for me. I smoothed my high-low hem and slid into lace-up ankle boots. I wanted to look nice tonight, although I had no clue who I wanted to impress. Officially, my date was Matt.

My friends—except for Alex—had been a little distant toward me since the failed intervention. I'd heard that Trinity asked the Ouija board if Seth and I were meant to be together. Apparently, the answer was yes, and Trinity had lain in bed crying and writing in her journal for an hour. But even though I was good at feeling guilty this summer, I refused to feel bad about that one. My friends controlled the Ouija board more than any mystery spirits and, as smart girls, we all knew it.

They must have thought Seth and I belonged together. Did I?

A male whistle of appreciation got our attention, stopping my group just outside the main lodge.

"Thank you!" Alex called out to the admirer I couldn't see in the dark.

As I got closer, I spotted Seth's bunkmates outside the lodge. It definitely hadn't been Seth, who hung at the back of the pack. Julian and Vijay led the group, Julian in full *Lord of the Rings* regalia, including a cape, a cool-looking metal chest plate, and a wooden sword at his side. He was usually a quiet guy, but his warrior gear gave him serious swagger. Plus, I had to admire someone who didn't change his look for anyone else. Julian liked a cape, so he wore a cape.

He winked at Piper, and I was surprised to see her smile at him. Not wanting to get in the way of any flirting, my eyes accidentally gravitated toward Seth. He looked great in khakis and a pin-striped button-down. My heart sped up against my will. I needed to tell him what I'd decided about us...and Matt...but I didn't want to do it with all our friends around. And hello? I shouldn't be ogling him, let alone fantasizing about tripping the girl he'd hung out with this week as I watched him return her wave.

I really needed to learn how to deal with seeing those two together because...I swallowed hard. The reason I couldn't be with Seth was my fault. He had a right to be happy with someone else. Still, I stomped when I headed toward the lodge to find Matt.

Emily followed, her fingers clutching my elbow and slowing me down as we walked into a transformed lodge. Silver stars hung from the pine rafters, and glitter coated the floor. A popular song blared from the speakers, and the dance floor was already full of junior campers getting their groove on. They got to arrive earlier than the senior campers, but they'd have to leave earlier too. Staying up late was a perk of being in the last two years of camp.

"Wait up!" Emily called into my ear. Her short-sleeved, rhinestone-covered pink sweater dress was a serious throwback, but her pink boots were cute. "I forgot to tell you Matt will be late."

That got my attention.

"He will?"

Emily nodded, blond curls jiggling along with her dangly earrings. "I practically fell over him coming out of the arts building when I was on my way back from a counselors' meeting about appropriate dress code. I mean, have you seen some of the trampy outfits around here?" She adjusted her butt-skimming hemline. "Anyway, I saw Matt, and he told me to tell you he'd be a half-hour late."

"Thanks," I told her, wondering what he'd been doing in the arts building. He'd surprised me once by playing the piano in the music room, just fooling around after school. I thought it had sounded great, but he'd dismissed it as no big deal.

I didn't want to make things awkward for my friends by hanging around them when they were flirting with the guys in Seth's cabin. Especially when the sight of Seth talking to that girl he'd befriended made me ready to draw blood. She looked prettier than ever with a jeweled headband I wanted to rip out of her waist-length, light-brown waves.

"Lauren!" someone called before I could commit a felony.

Turning, I saw Kayla and Hannah by the refreshments table, their cocktail-length dresses upping the sophistication factor of an Appalachian camp dance. They looked like a page out of *Seventeen* with Hannah's perfect auburn updo and Kayla's sleek blond layers caught in a glittery butterfly clip.

Junior campers admired them from afar, whispering enviously behind their hands.

"Hi," I returned nervously, not sure what they'd want from me. Back home, I understood how to deal with the mean girls of the world, wearing the bitchy armor at all times, ready to do battle.

But this was camp, and I didn't act that way here. I'd spent weeks dreaming about ditching my inner bitch.

"Come here." Kayla waved me over, smiling.

Was I really going to cross the lodge to the land of the camp's most popular girls? It felt like a defection from my old crew, but I needed space. Anything was better than standing awkwardly in the middle of the dance with no one to talk to.

"Great dresses," I murmured as I scooped punch into a cup.

"Thanks." Hannah's smile seemed genuine, but then she was so egotistical she probably took compliments as her due.

"Our guys aren't here yet so we thought you'd want to wait for them with us." Kayla gestured to the empty chairs near their perfectly coiffed friends.

"Our guys?"

"Kayla's dating Cameron," Hannah volunteered, taking out a tiny bottle from her gold metallic purse and dabbing a little of the contents on her wrists.

"They don't call him 'Hands' for nothing," Kayla whispered in my ear, making me laugh.

Cameron, a member of Warriors' Warden, could secure any kind of banned items at camp, from extra candy to alcohol. Not that I'd ever been the recipient of contraband, being a rule-follower for the most part. They'd called him Hands ever since he'd slipped into Gollum's office as an eight-year-old and come out with the camp director's coveted whistle. He'd gone into business for himself the next day, and I heard he'd made five hundred bucks his first summer.

While I congratulated Kayla on the new boyfriend, Hannah passed her the little bottle with a fragrance I could now smell.

"What is that?" I asked, trying to ID the label.

"Kayla made it," Hannah said proudly. "It's an essential oil she had blended for all the girls in Divas' Den."

"I have extras." Kayla pulled two more bottles from her bag. There was a double D in purple script on the front. "Want one?"

"Thank you." Warmed by the generosity, I took the one Hannah gave me.

"I think your friends want you." Hannah nodded past my shoulder.

I turned to find Alex and Siobhan waving me back to "our" side of the lodge, the spot we'd always claimed for the Friday night dances. Seth was gone and the only one from his cabin still hanging out was Garrett, so it seemed safe to return.

"Bye." I gave a wave. Camp would be more fun if we could all cross sides of the room now and then. Why the great divide between camp cliques? I expected that stuff in high school, but here...we could do better than that.

Walking past the dance floor where a few junior campers tested out the Cupid Shuffle, I opened the bottle of scent.

"What's that?" Alex hauled the bottle to her nose before I could answer. "Mmm. Smells great."

"Try some," I offered, wanting to share the generosity.

Alex dabbed some on her neck while Siobhan tried to find everyone else's pulse point. I grinned at Siobhan's precise, scientific approach. While they shared the oil and asked why I'd been hanging out with Divas' Den girls, Alex talked over them.

"Seth wants to see you. He's outside now."

My mellow mood evaporated, my heart beating staccato against my ribs.

"Excuse me?" Did this mean he was anxious to get this talk over with...get some closure so he could fully move on to be with Head Band Girl? My heart thumped louder than the DJ's corner.

"Seth." Alex pointed to the door. "He's out by the picnic tables."

My friends looked at me expectantly. They hadn't said much when I'd hung out with Matt this week, which I'd appreciated. On the other hand, I knew they'd be happier if I smoothed things over with Seth so it wasn't weird when our cabins hung out together.

Slipping out the back entrance of the lodge where it faced the lake, I saw a few other kids sitting at the picnic tables with drinks.

I passed the groups of kids talking and laughing and a couple sneaking kisses off to one side. At the last table before the beach, a lone figure sat in the shadows. I'd know the curls anywhere. It was the new height and broad chest that still surprised me. By any girl's standards, Seth had turned crush-worthy this year. Certainly I wasn't the only one who thought so.

"Hey." I took a seat at the table beside him, closer than I'd intended.

Some habits were hard to break.

"Hey." His mouth lifted at the corners, left-side dimple appearing. Something in his cupped hands pulsed.

"That's a—" I began, racking my brain for the name he had taught me last summer.

"*Photouris pyralis*," Seth finished for me. He held out his glowing hand.

"A firefly," I breathed, closing my fingers around the elusive insect the instant he laid it in my palm. I smiled in delight, watching my fingers shine then dim as the bug tiptoed across my flesh. From a biology enthusiast like Seth, this was a precious gift.

He turned toward me, familiar and somehow different. He smelled like the woods in spring and freshly mowed grass. It reminded me of other times I'd rested my head on his shoulder while we sat around the bonfires at night. His eyes searched mine before dropping in that shy way of his.

Confused, I fought the melting feeling inside me. He was a nice guy—warm-hearted. So the firefly didn't necessarily mean anything. But the butterflies in my stomach told me that, despite my promise to Matt, I wanted it to. Seth had said he'd give me space. Did that mean he'd wait another month?

"Thank you." A warm breeze blew off the water and tossed my hair in my eyes. "I'm glad we can still be—umm, friends." For a moment I wished for the impossible, that we could be more.

"Is that all we are?" His fingers smoothed back the strands and lingered.

Just then, it felt like old times. A shiver danced up my spine. My brain was sending my heart so many mixed signals I felt like I'd short circuit. Or was it my heart messaging my brain? Either way. This sucked.

"I'm not sure—"

His mouth landed on mine.

Seth.

His lips were warm and gentle, familiar and foreign at the same time. My heart exploded. He still cared.

I had thought about him so often this year. I'd spoken his name out loud before I went to sleep, dreaming of this moment. I guess that's what paralyzed me now. I was half-stuck in the past, back when it was okay to kiss Seth. But until I stopped being Matt's girlfriend, this was dead wrong.

"Seth." I broke away, my heart pounding, lips tingling. "We can't. I told Matt I'd give our relationship a try. We're going to give it another month."

He dipped his head, then lifted large amber eyes to mine. "Didn't you already have eight months together in Texas?" He shook his head. "Never mind. I knew you cared more than you admitted. I knew I shouldn't have left to give you space. Should have stayed and forced the issue."

"Then it wouldn't have been you. It isn't what the guy I fell for would have done."

He closed his eyes for a moment and a shudder ran through him. "Nice guys finish last. I'm going to lose you."

I rose on shaky legs and released the firefly. It blinked twice, then disappeared.

"Not necessarily. You were right when you said I cared about Matt. I do. As my oldest, closest friend, of course you'd know that. But I still have feelings for you too. I won't ask you to wait...so for now, can we go back to being friends?" My heart recoiled from the blow I'd just delivered. How had I come so far from my plans for this summer?

Seth shook his head. "I'm sorry, Lauren. But seeing you with Matt the past couple days just about killed me." He stood, his voice rumbling between us. "Maybe once I find someone else, we can go back to being friends."

My eyes followed his to the curvy girl leaning in the doorway, the flashing lights behind her reflecting off her headband.

Ohmigod.

My heels sank in the sand and I felt like the rest of me was going down too. The finality of hearing him say he'd move on hurt me more than I had ever imagined. Pressure built in my chest, making it hard to breathe.

"I've got to go." I bit my lip, trying to stifle a sob.

I backed away and bumped into a picnic table.

"I probably shouldn't say this." Seth's voice hovered a notch above a whisper. "But for what it's worth, Lauren, I wish we could be together this summer. I'm sorry we didn't work out."

He was sorry? I thought I'd break in two right in front of him. But this was my decision.

Mine. Somehow, knowing that didn't make it any easier.

I stumbled back to the lodge, desperate to get away from him and everything I still felt. I would find Matt and tuck myself against him for the rest of the night. I'd hold his hand and dance with him. Be the best girlfriend in the world.

My eyes burned. I hadn't cried much this year, burying my fears and worries to keep them hidden from a family in turmoil. But now, all the crap of the last twelve months threatened to spill over in a wailing sobfest if I didn't get my head on straight. Fast.

Seth wasn't trying to hurt me. He was being honest. Dealing with the fact that I'd picked another guy over him. I should be relieved, but instead I felt sick. Tucking my hair behind one ear with trembling fingers, I sidled past a couple of boys playing a card game near the back door. Inside the lodge, I scanned the crowd for Matt until my friends came toward me. Circling me.

Scowling at me.

"Finally," Trinity huffed. "I thought you were never coming back in."

"What's the matter?" I asked, scared that Trinity had seen Seth kiss me. "It wasn't my fault," I blurted, ready to defend my actions since Seth had kissed *me*, not the other way around.

I stopped myself from saying anymore when I realized they all looked a little funny. Piper's eyes were red and swollen. Siobhan's neck was red. Alex's shoulders were splotchy and broken out. It was like they'd all caught some kind of weird rash while I'd been outside.

"Thanks for the perfume, Lauren." Piper's throat sounded scratchy as she pointed to the place where Siobhan had carefully applied the Divas' Den signature fragrance. "And the case of hives."

On the other side of the room, I noticed Hannah laughing so hard she had to hold herself up using her friend's shoulder. Her cabin mate ducked her grin behind a napkin. I didn't see Kayla, but I decided I'd strangle all six of the Divas' Den girls in their sleep for this.

What had made me think they'd changed?

"I didn't do this—" I started, but Siobhan stepped closer to me, madder than I'd ever seen her.

"What. The. Hell?" Her hands fisted at her sides.

"I didn't—" I tried again.

"Tell it to your *friend*, Hannah." Jackie dropped a protective arm around Siobhan's shoulders while she nodded toward the laughing audience across the room.

I noticed Jackie didn't have any rashy skin, but then again, I couldn't picture her trying out a new scent.

What the hell had the Diva girls put in that fragrance?

Fuming, I went to confront them while my cabin mates stormed away toward the door.

"Wow." A familiar voice said in my ear, stopping me. "You look hot."

I turned to look up at Matt and got distracted. His blue dress shirt turned his green eyes a shade darker. He was handsome, and he'd travelled a thousand miles to be with me this summer. As much as my heart broke for what Seth and I had just lost, Matt deserved this chance. Maybe we both did. He had a little crowd of admirers a few steps behind him, reminding me that, if I didn't want to be with him, there were plenty of girls who would give their right arm for the chance.

"Thank you," I said lamely.

"Dance with me," Matt urged while I gathered my scattered emotions.

"Okay," I whispered, hoping his arms would steady my world right now. I wasn't ready for a confrontation with the Diva girls. Not right now.

Tucking my head into the crook of his neck, I let the music take me away. My friends were upset and didn't seem to even trust me. Seth couldn't move on fast enough.

Except for this moment with Matt, the dance was an epic fail. He hummed a tune I didn't recognize, a melody that relaxed me until I could draw an easy breath again.

If I could just get through this week, my dad would be here for next Saturday's Parents' Weekend. It'd always been our time together in the summer, away from my sister and mother. I couldn't wait to have his attention. Finally. I half-wished I could ask him to take me home, but as soon as I thought it I rejected the idea.

I needed to stay and figure out who I belonged with—Matt or Seth. Instead of letting life guide me, I had to dig deeper and decide that for myself.

Chapter Eight

Zoo-zoo-zeeee called a blue-colored bird on a branch outside my window. I groaned, wrapped my pillow around my head taco-style, and burrowed further under the covers. Today was the start of Parents' Weekend, something I normally looked forward to since it meant a hike or raft ride along the Nantahala River Gorge with Dad. Except this year, he'd bailed.

Zoo-zoo-zeeee. I pulled my comforter over my pillow-encased head and tried to ignore the knot forming in my stomach. In a couple of hours, my mother and Kellianne would descend on me for their first weekend visit in eight years. And I was pretty sure it had more to do with needing input on wedding problems than whitewater rafting down Patton's Run.

By staying in during free periods this week to avoid Seth, I'd had time to make Kellianne's seating chart. I'd also written her place cards and the bridal shower thank-you notes. Though the one to Aunt Flo had been a bit of a challenge. Possibly some of my frustrations at the world and Kellianne in particular had leaked through.

I think it went something like this:

Dear Aunt Flo, Thank you so much for your thoughtful gift of a fertility basket. I'll be sure to wear the fertility tracking bracelet every day. Andrew was especially pleased with the oak bark virility supplements. We are excited to use the economy-sized package of pregnancy tests. See you at the wedding and don't forget the Tarot cards! Love, Kellianne.

I have to admit, it felt good to lick that one closed. Score one for the wedding slave. And it served Kellianne right. She should have written her own thank-you cards— something I would have pointed out if I hadn't been so committed to keeping the peace in the Carlson house.

Matt did his best to cheer me up and was more attentive than ever. He'd gone with me to Movies Under the Stars Night, which sounded romantic but was really just a grainy old film projected on the side of the Rec Room. The cool thing was that he'd agreed to sneak out and watch the stars for real. We'd held hands on the beach and I'd taught him how to locate the Big and Little Dippers and some of my favorite constellations. Without other kids trying to get his attention, he'd focused totally on me. After a while, he could identify each sky pattern and knew its story. Even better, I impressed him without landing a tumbling move or wearing lip gloss.

Since my bunkmates had grown more distant, it'd been easy to use my wedding to-do list as an excuse to stay back when they left to hang out with the Wander Inn guys. I didn't want to see Seth and his new girlfriend any more than I had to. I'd spotted them together around camp, but couldn't tell if they were just friends or more than that. Trinity, however, had complained about how fast Seth seemed to be moving on. Her real issue with Seth, I guessed, was that he couldn't be with *her*. She'd burned up a lot of journal pages after returning from a visit to his cabin during free time.

"Wake up, home girls!" Emily shouted. I inched down my blanket and peered at her. With her side ponytail, pink tights and a blue sleeveless shirt tied at the waist, she could have stepped out of a vintage Olivia Newton-John video—an impression she cemented by holding an old-fashioned boom box over her head that blared the '80s song "Let's Get Physical."

She set down what amounted to the worst alarm clock in history and pranced around to the beat, swatting at us as she passed our bunks. "Time to clean up Munchies' Manor before the 'rents get here and start ragging on us, right?"

Arrrgh. I threw back the covers and shivered as the early morning air wafted through our screened front door and slid along my bare arms and legs. Siobhan hopped down from her bunk, her eyes darting away from mine. Trinity muttered something about her horoscope warning her to stay in bed today while Jackie threw a pillow at the boom box and missed.

"We're supposed to be cleaning up this mess, not adding to it, Jackie," Emily teased, spreading her arms wide and doing a few waist-bends and squats before jogging over to Alex and pulling her out of bed. Alex stumbled a few paces and walked right into my bunk ladder.

I reached out a hand to steady her. "Are you okay?"

She jerked away and began piling wet towels to hang outside. All right, then. It looked like the silent treatment would still continue after the skin rash prank. Maybe Kellianne and Mom's visit wouldn't be so bad after all. At least they still talked to me.

I slid down my ladder and felt something crunch underfoot.

"My dream catcher!" Trinity wailed. Four pairs of accusing eyes flew to me.

"Nice," Alex mocked, the screen door bouncing closed behind her as she returned from the porch. "It's okay, Trinity. Maybe it's time to get some new dreams instead of chasing after Lauren's. "

Pain stabbed in my gut and brought tears to my eyes. Is that what they considered Seth? Old dreams? Thankfully, I was already bent over, scooping up the pieces of birch wood and feathers. At least they couldn't see how much the comment hurt.

"I didn't mean to break it," I muttered.

"Like you didn't mean to play your little prank on us?" Piper scratched a lingering red patch from the rash. Alex and Siobhan nodded, narrowing their eyes at me.

"Ummm. Hello," Emily interjected. "I think Lauren's apologized enough for the perfume. It wasn't even hers. So let's move on and get this cabin cleaned up. Who's up for Madonna?"

That got everyone going, though not without plenty of grumbling. Piper even threatened a sit-in protest until she noticed there wasn't a clear spot on the floor to sit. Reconciled to our fate, we put the first item back in its place...Emily's radio.

I studied Trinity out of the corner of my eye as I swept the sand from under our bunks. Her fair skin had turned pink at Alex's comment about Seth. A part of me wanted to tell her off for lusting after my guy.

Only he wasn't my guy. But the fact that Girl Code meant Trinity couldn't do whatever she wrote about in her journal didn't make me feel better. Seth was available now. I'd worked hard to avoid him this week, but that didn't mean I hadn't thought about him. Did he really *want* to be with someone else? Or was he just trying to make me see that I'd made a mistake by not being with him?

Thirty minutes later, the floor was visible, our bunks made, snacks tucked out of sight. Glad to be done, I grabbed my toiletries basket and headed for the bathroom.

"Not so fast, Lauren." Emily blocked my way. She held a big medieval-style goblet over her head, pink glitter covering its pewter sides. "It's time for a little something I like to call Kindness. Something Munchies' Manor seems to have forgotten."

Siobhan plopped on her bed and sighed. "Emily. No disrespect, but if I don't get my calculus homework done before my parents get here, they'll drag me home."

"I can help," I spoke up. Science and math had always been my thing and I'd taken the advanced class with juniors this year. Siobhan gave me a tight-lipped smile as she slid over on her bunk and put the textbook between us.

Emily dropped a poker chip in the cup as she rested it on the bureau I shared with Trinity and Alex.

"That's one kind deed." Emily's gums showed in a toothy smile. "Every time someone does something kind, we drop in a chip, and when it's full we'll do something special—like go into town for a real dinner, my treat."

Everyone smiled at that. We were Munchies' Manor again.

Emily crossed her thin arms and tapped her foot. "So who's got something else they can share from this week? Something about Lauren, perhaps?"

I looked up from one of the four-step problems I was checking. Dead silence descended on the cabin.

"Come on, Alex," Emily wheedled. "We all know Lauren kept Mr. Woodrow from catching you and Vijay the other night."

I remembered Gollum's bobbing flashlight and the smooching couple directly in his path. I'd raced out of the cabin, cut through some bushes, and stumbled into him. When I told him I was lost, he'd pulled out a pocket Breathalyzer, then escorted me the four hundred yards back to our front porch.

Alex dragged her feet as she picked up a poker chip and dropped it with a ping in the cup. Her eyes met mine, softer than they'd been all week. "I didn't know Lauren did that on purpose."

Emily pursed her fuchsia lips. "After eight years, I think Lauren knows her way around, don't you? Though I'd have thought, Alex, that you'd know the safest make-out spot. Highbrooke Falls. Right, Lauren?"

I flushed. Emily was like a CIA agent.

"Lauren used recycled paper to write her sister's thank-you notes." Piper marched over to the Kindness Cup, dropped in a chip, and smiled at me for the first time all week. "The rainforest thanks you."

Not that Kellianne would have...but I'd picked out the cards in the nearby town of Waynesville with Piper in mind, knowing she'd kill me if I used anything else.

I smiled back and continued working on Siobhan's homework. I'd done three problems to her five. The left side of Siobhan's mouth curled. It was her game face. My pencil flew. Game on.

Jackie clomped over to the cup. "Lauren hasn't missed a volleyball practice yet. Unlike some people." She glared at a squirming Alex, who popped in a piece of gum and began chomping. We all knew where her free and not-so-free time was going.

Jackie's closed hand appeared before me. "Your serve has come a long way, Lauren." She gave me a quick fist bump. I blinked back tears, amazed Emily's crazy idea was working.

"Anyone else?" Emily called, then put her hand over her mouth and coughed, "Trinity."

Trinity dropped the pieces of her dream catcher in the cup, then sat beside me. I looked up from Siobhan's last calc problem and met her glistening eyes. "Thanks for being cool about me liking Seth. We'll never go out, but..." Her eyes shone with hope—wanting me to say, "No problem. Go for him."

But I couldn't. The light in her eyes died as I gave her a quick hug and said thanks.

I walked over to the cup, counted out five chips and dropped them into the goblet. I swallowed, all eyes on me. "I know I've been acting weird but it's because I've had a...a confusing year. For months, I wanted more than anything to come back here and hang out with you guys. So thank you for sticking by me because I really need you while I figure stuff out this summer."

"Group hug!" Emily shouted while the girls rushed me.

I wiped stinging eyes on my T-shirt, arms around everyone. My weekend from hell had transformed into two days I could survive with a little help from my friends. All because of Emily.

If I could avoid boy disaster for the next two weeks, Matt would head home for football practice and I'd decide if we were meant for each other as he insisted, or if my nagging heart had it right from the start...and Seth was The One.

Maybe Emily had another miracle up her sleeve?

*   *   *

"Surprise!" squealed Mom when I reached her rented black Mercedes. Kellianne sat in the passenger seat. She nodded, then flipped a page in a magazine.

I squashed the disappointment that Dad hadn't changed his mind and come after all. I hadn't even realized I'd held out a little hope until right this minute.

"Ummm. I kind of knew you were coming, Mom."

She hugged me briefly, her flowery perfume clinging longer than she had.

"Yes." Her perfect pink lips parted in excitement. "But I bet you didn't know Matt's father and his dad's new girlfriend were coming too. We heard the news before we left."

My eyes darted around, panic filling me despite the fact that Mr. Butler was nowhere in sight. Did Matt know about this? The last I'd heard, he thought his mom was going to visit. Solo. Watching Matt jog up felt like watching a train wreck in slow-mo. I glared at my mother, trying to tell her how insensitive she was to spring this on us.

"Hello, Mrs. Carlson. You look nice today." Matt smiled politely. I, on the other hand, found little to admire about my mother's outfit—a pink Polo dress and heels better suited for one of her charity benefits than camp.

My mother gave Matt one of her few genuine smiles. "Thank you, dear. So do you." I glanced over at Matt's crisp beige pants and a blue and white button-down that brought out the green in his incredible eyes. He could have stepped out of the local country club or the pages of GQ. In the meantime, I looked like I'd just rolled out of my cabin...which I had.

Mom eyed my wrinkled tank and booty-skimming shorts. "I'm sure Lauren was eager to come greet us, but we'll excuse her now to get more properly attired. Matt, we're going to bring you into town with us so you can meet your father in Waynesville for lunch." I noticed she left out the girlfriend part, perhaps feeling a bit guilty for the surprise attack after all.

If Matt was disappointed that his mom hadn't come, he did a good job of hiding it. Only the twitch beneath his eye gave him away.

"Lauren looks great to me, but I'm happy to wait with you, Mrs. Carlson. Maybe Kellianne can tell me about the wedding. I know Lauren's been working hard. I haven't seen as much of her as I'd like lately." Only Matt could make my avoidance tactics seem noble.

As if on cue, the tinted Mercedes window rolled down and Kellianne's French-tipped fingers dangled outside. "Did you bring the thank-you notes?" she demanded.

"Hey, Kellianne." I passed her a medium-sized cardboard box. "The seating chart and the place cards are in there too."

"Thanks. And this is for you. It's from Dad." She handed me a creased, letter-sized envelope. I turned it over in my hands, but the sealed enclosure and lack of outer markings kept it a mystery.

There'd been a time I would have been thrilled to get something from my dad, but now that he'd ditched me—again—in favor of work, and epically failed on helping with my NASA application, this felt like a weak bribe for forgiveness. It was way too light to hold the letters of reference I needed. So what was it? An apology note? No thanks. It'd feel as empty as the envelope.

"I'll be right back." I dashed up the sun-dappled path, eager to change and return before Mom spilled the news about Matt's dad's girlfriend. Matt was still furious at his father for cheating. Meeting the object of Mr. Butler's affections would set off serious fireworks. As for reading whatever Dad sent, that could wait. It'd make me angry, and I had enough bad feelings to deal with.

A brown hawk wheeled in the blue sky, ready to strike. I thought of the oblivious animal about to be its meal. Matt and I had that much in common at least. One minute our lives seemed perfect and the next—*wham*—everything went to hell. I didn't want Matt to lose himself the way I had when my parents upended my Ithaca life. At the cabin, I tossed the envelope up to my top bunk. It hit the wall and slid down between the bunks to the floor. I left it there for later, grabbed a white eyelet sundress and sandals, swished on some silver eye shadow and pink lip gloss, and brushed my hair free of its ponytail, securing my long bangs off my forehead with a small plastic clip.

My headlong rush out of the cabin skittered to a halt at the sight of Seth and his father walking toward Munchies' Manor.

"She's not here, Dad. So let's go rafting, okay?" Seth didn't glance up.

Seth's father, a ruddy man with a neck as thick as his shaved head, pointed at me. "If she's not here, who's that, then?"

Seth's eyes widened. A part of me thrilled at his appreciative look. Any time I'd seen him this week, his attention had been glued to Headband Girl—Breyanna, I'd since discovered.

I trotted down the stairs, nervous that Mr. Reines would treat me differently now that Seth and I were broken up.

"Hi, Mr. Reines. How's Indiana University wrestling?"

"Division One champions," boomed the coach, his voice, like everything about him, larger than life. "So are you going to get changed for our rafting trip? We don't have all day. And where's your father? Our Geology chair resigned, and I wanted to mention it to him. He'd be perfect."

My eyes flitted to Seth's. Did his father still think we were a couple?

Seth's sheepish look gave me the answer I needed. He hadn't said anything to his dad. Did that mean he still thought there was a chance for us to get back together? Suddenly I wished I was in my tank and shorts, about to go on our traditional rafting trip. If Dad had come, he'd know about the geology job. Maybe we'd leave Texas and relocate to Indiana where I could be with Seth full-time. I'd spend every second of my one hour of phone time tomorrow telling Dad about the job.

"My dad couldn't make it this year," I said, not wanting to reveal Seth's secret. "My mom and sister came instead."

"Well, it's good to see you anyway, Lauren." Mr. Reines caught me in a bear hug that crushed the air out of me. "You're all this kid here talks about."

My eyebrows rose. I never knew Seth mentioned me outside of camp. I'd always figured I was out of sight and out of mind for him. Interesting.

"Guess I'd better get going." I untangled myself and headed back down the path. "Mom and Kellianne are taking me to lunch."

"Lauren," Seth's father thundered, stopping me in my tracks. "Aren't you forgetting something? I'm sure I'm not the only who wants a hug."

I looked from his wriggling eyebrows to Seth's apologetic look. He confused me so much. Did he really want to be with me? Or was he serious about moving on with Breyanna? Not wanting to argue with Mr. Reines, I stepped into Seth's arms. Just for a second. The delicious outdoor smell of him filled my nose as his strong hands spread across my back. A lick of warmth flickered in my stomach.

"Goodbye, Lauren. I'll miss you." His breath was soft against my ear.

"Bye." I backed away until I bumped into something hard. I whirled around. "Matt!"

"Just came to see what was keeping you." Matt's eyes were two ice chips in a frozen face.

Seth's father hiked up his shorts and strode forward, a smile creasing his face. "I didn't know

Lauren had a brother. I'm Coach Reines, her boyfriend's father."

I cringed. Matt dropped Mr. Reines' beefy hand the second he shook it. "Funny, you don't look anything like my dad." He held out his hand and tugged me down the path.

I didn't turn around when Mr. Reines let out an indignant huff. Matt turned toward me the minute we were alone.

"What the hell was that?" His brows were knit together, his shoulders tense.

I gripped his arm. "It's not what you think. Seth hadn't told his dad we'd broken up so—"

"So you thought you'd be his girlfriend again for old times' sake?" Matt jerked out of my grasp and strode down the path.

I jogged to keep up, cursing my heeled sandals.

"Matt. It wasn't my place to tell his dad. Seth had to speak up."

"That's always how it is with you, Lauren. Letting other people do the talking. How about we hear from you once in a while?"

It was tough to know what to say when I hardly knew what I wanted.

Matt's jaw tightened as he paced down the path. Before we reached the parking lot, he turned and grabbed my hands. "I can't stand seeing that kid's hands on you. Okay?"

I could feel the adrenaline coursing through him...or maybe it was his pulse throbbing. It hurt that I'd made him feel that way.

"Okay. But you don't have to worry. He's into someone else now."

"Don't kid yourself, Lauren. He still wants you." He glared at me for a minute, but then he leaned over to plant a hard kiss on my temple. "You didn't see the way he looked at me while he had his arms around you."

That didn't sound like easygoing Seth. But I didn't want to argue about it when my own eyes told me that Seth was with another girl in all his spare time.

"Whatever," I grumbled. I took his hand and squeezed. "Let's not fight today. My mom chickened out on telling you back there, but your dad brought the new girlfriend."

"No way." Matt stopped in his tracks, cursing under his breath. "I can't believe that bastard would bring her here when he knows..." He trailed off, fuming.

"Sorry. I just thought you deserved a warning." I smoothed a hand down his arm, hating that he had to face so much crap today. His dad was a jerk. Maybe his father should hang out with mine...give each other tips on how to ruin our lives.

"Thank you." Matt's arms shot around me, pressing me against his chest so hard that I could feel every flexed muscle. "What would I do without you?"

"Matt." I tipped my head back and felt his lips graze my cheek. My bones loosened and my body melted against his.

I wanted to stand by Matt. But I also wondered when it would be time to put myself and what I needed first. All my life I'd followed someone else's lead—first Dad, then Mom. Seth, and now

Matt. Maybe Trinity could tell me when my stars would align.

We returned to the parking lot hand in hand. Matt and I climbed in the back seat, his fingers toying with the scalloped hem of my dress. With the help of Mom's GPS, we soon zoomed by a sign that read "Waynesville, Population 9,841." As we drove down Main Street, we passed rose-colored brick buildings, flowerbeds overflowing with petunias, and carefully pruned oaks. Campers and their families crowded the pristine sidewalks.

I nudged Kellianne and pointed at a colorful restaurant sign. "Big Mountain BBQ. Wonder if they cater weddings?"

"That'd be much too upscale for you, Lauren, don't you think?" She gave me a saucy glance in the rearview mirror as we passed checkered-cloth-covered picnic tables beneath a red and white striped tent. Barbecue pits sent plumes of smoke into the hazy air.

Matt patted my knee. "Nothing but the best for my Lauren. Right, babe?"

If there was an Olympic event for synchronized eyebrow lifting, my mother and sister would have won gold. I could almost hear my mother humming *"dum dum dah dum"* in her head, imagining her daughters married to the most eligible guys in Dallas. Hopefully Matt was teasing, because although he'd been groomed to enter his father's car dealership business out of high school, I was definitely going to college and hopefully, someday, to the moon.

We'd never really talked about a future. Maybe that's why I hadn't thought it was a big deal to break up at the end of the school year. Well, at least until Matt had been hit with the divorce news. If Matt and I somehow weathered this summer from hell together, we'd need to talk about what we wanted after high school. For that matter, if Seth was in my future, I wondered what he had in mind after he graduated. He'd be applying to colleges this fall.

We pulled up to a mammoth beige-stone mansion, its square turrets giving it a gothic feel. In all the years I'd come to Camp Juniper Point, I'd never made it to the Dutton Estate, a large hotel that had once been a private home. It had 250 rooms, an indoor swimming pool, and its own bowling alley, according to Siobhan, who'd gone there with her family last year.

A lot of the land in the Nantahala Forest near our camp had been donated by the Dutton family. We parked beside a sleek, red Lamborghini. Matt's father leaned against it, rubbing noses with a petite redhead, her diamond earrings flashing in the midday sun.

Kellianne leaped out of the car and greeted the young woman with a hug. My mother followed more sedately. The redhead looked familiar, but it wasn't until Kellianne stepped away from her that I put it together. She and my sister had been college roommates, making her just a few years older than Matt and me. And she dangled a diamond ring the size of a walnut from her left hand. My breath rushed out. Poor Matt. Ambushed on so many levels.

I touched his rock-hard shoulder. "Are you okay?"

Matt put his fingertips over his eyes and leaned his head back against the seat. A bitter laugh escaped him.

"Matt. I know this sucks. But we'll get through this."

He squeezed my hand and tugged me out of the car on the side opposite our chattering families. I followed his lead, ducked behind a swan-shaped hedge, and then scrambled after him down the oak-lined driveway.

"Where are we going?" I demanded. I was prepared to comfort Matt, not go all *Bourne Identity* with him.

His eyes met mine as we broke into a jog.

"Big Mountain BBQ, of course."

Chapter Nine

We'd barely sat down with menus when we were busted.

Mr. Butler and the trophy girlfriend spotted us at one of the picnic tables before we'd ordered. They were circling us in moments with my mom and Kellianne in tow. Kellianne glared daggers at me the whole time she wasn't pointing meaningfully at her shoes. Sister telepathy told me she blamed me for scuffing the heels of her designer pumps.

As if I cared. I had real issues. Like Matt's life going to hell and my father going MIA for his first parents' weekend ever. Just thinking about it stung.

"Laurie, so good to see you," Mr. Butler said in his chummy Texas twang while the redhead linked arms with my sister and compared manicures. "Would you mind if we steal this boy away for an hour or so? Lots of news to catch up on, and he needs to get to know Sherry."

"It's Lauren, Dad." Matt corrected his father through clenched teeth. "And we were just about to order."

"Nonsense!" My mother ganged up on us now. "Lauren promised us she'd go shopping while we were here. Lots of things to do when there's a wedding to plan." She squeezed Kellianne's shoulders.

The blushing bride shook off Mom like a bad cold. Definitely some tension there. Before I could protest, Mom tugged me to my feet while Matt's dad took my place at the picnic table.

"We haven't even eaten," I protested once we were out of earshot. I was practically salivating for ribs and slaw. "We might as well have something while we're here."

"Do you remember how form-fitting the maid of honor dress is?" Kellianne eyed my waist like I'd put on ten pounds at camp.

"Fine. I'll starve myself. I'm sure a cadaver will be an attractive addition to the wedding party." Stomping down the sidewalk away from the Big Mountain, I braved a glance back at Matt. The discussion at his table was already animated. The redhead had disappeared, leaving Matt and his father in a heated talk. I felt for Matt. I really did. But I had to put in my time on the wedding and it was parents' weekend. I might as well spend time with the only parent who had shown up for me.

"If there even is a wedding," Kellianne muttered as we followed Mom to the stores.

"Everything okay?" I whispered out of the corner of my mouth. Mom hated public scenes.

Kellianne shrugged, the bones of her shoulders protruding even further. How much weight had my already slim sister lost, and why?

"It's fine." She lifted her long hair and fanned the back of her neck. "Forget it."

And with that, her heels clattered on the cement as she caught up to Mom. Hours later, we'd been in every store in the tiny town and I had a whole new list of wedding jobs. Lunch had consisted of a low-carb chicken wrap that tasted about as good as the food at camp. I tried not to think about the pizza and wings Dad and I would have been wolfing down if he'd come.

I hadn't seen any sign of Matt or his father since we'd parted ways at the restaurant. The sun was setting when I hurried to join Mom and Kellianne at some frou-frou girl store with so much pink in the window I'd require an insulin shot before we were done.

"Lauren." Kellianne stopped me on the sidewalk while Mom exclaimed over retro eyeglasses on a display table outside. "Who are you taking to my wedding?"

The question was completely unexpected. As was Kellianne's serious expression.

"Matt, of course." My heartbeat sped up, as if she could see my doubts and worries.

"Are you sure?" she pressed.

No.

"Yes." I fought the urge to fidget. "Why?"

"Because I noticed that seating chart you gave me has you sitting next to some guy named Seth Reines." She followed Mom into the shop, leaving me to scrape my jaw off the floor.

Had I written Seth's name in by mistake? I was tempted to run out to the car and look for myself, but I didn't want to seem as pathetic as

I felt. Besides, Kellianne would have no way of knowing Seth's name otherwise. I'd made Dad promise not to tell Mom and Kellianne about my camp boyfriend, and as far as I knew he never had. Plus, Dad had been as MIA to the rest of the family this year as he had been for me.

"Sorry about that," I mumbled behind her as we wound our way through an overpriced tourist trap dressed up like a French boutique. "I must have been overtired. I can take the chart back and proofread more carefully."

"That's okay," she chirped in a sing-song way that put me on edge. "I'll be anxious to read over it and see how many more people are attending that I've never heard of."

I buried my nose in a display of body scrubs and sea salts, hoping she'd drop the subject. Especially when two Divas' Den girls came into the shop. Hannah and Brittany, the vampire-obsessed airhead. She was so pretty that boys didn't seem to care about her fake fangs.

"Sooo," my sister continued, sidling up next to me to check out a mud scrub packaged in a bottle shaped like a poodle. "Who's Seth?"

"No one," I whispered. The last thing I wanted was for Hannah to get word I'd been seen ditching Matt and talking about Seth. She'd convince Matt our relationship was over before I returned to camp.

"He doesn't sound like no one," Kellianne huffed. "But if you want to keep your secrets, go right ahead. Like I care about your love life."

Right. She never had before. So why had she asked me about it today?

While Mom and Kellianne studied the display of earrings, I headed outside to avoid further catastrophe. I breathed in the mountain air that grew cooler as the sun slipped lower on the horizon, savoring the scent of pine needles as a soft breeze blew in off the lake.

It was so pretty here. I slipped away from the crowded streets where half my camp congregated to buy ice cream cones and spend the new influx of cash from their visiting parents. Heading closer to the lake, I stopped short at the sight of a dark-haired football star on a stone bench.

"Matt?" I felt a little uncertain approaching him, because something about his posture seemed off. Hunched over, head in hands, he didn't look like the confident boy who had all of Jefferson Davis High wrapped around his finger.

Slowly, he picked his head up and met my gaze. His green eyes were darker than usual. His tie was loose, and the top button of his shirt was undone. His hands fisted on his knees.

"He gave the girlfriend a ring." His voice was flat. Almost unrecognizable.

"But he's not divorced yet," I said stupidly. "He can't do that."

"He says it's not an engagement ring." Matt glared out at the water. "But you know that's how the girlfriend sees it. Worse, that's how Mom will see it."

I sat beside him, hoping Mom and Kellianne didn't come looking for me for a while. Matt and I watched a few families push paddleboats into the lake, and I slid my hand into his.

"When my dad took his new job, he abandoned me too," I confessed, surprising myself.

"Seriously? I don't know what surprises me more—that your dad is a bum too, or that you're actually sharing something about yourself."

"He's not a bum," I said automatically. "But hey, you said you wanted to hear more from me, and my dad has been on my mind a lot today. Usually, he comes to this stuff and we spend the day on the water instead of eating rabbit food and trying on jewelry."

Matt's hand tightened on mine.

"Right. You'd usually be hanging out with your old boyfriend, too."

"You know, I should have told you about him. I apologized for that. But I'm not going to apologize for dating someone before I even knew you."

"Wow." Matt's wry laugh surprised me. "I ought to be careful what I ask for. I wanted you to share stuff with me, and now you're *really* letting me have it."

I smiled too, glad to have something to enjoy for these few minutes. Actually, the breeze off the lake was just right too. I loved dusk when the sky turned pink and purple and the soft light made everything a little more beautiful. Down by the water, a toddler in a pink dress lost her grip on a yellow kite she'd been flying. I watched the spot of color zigzag in the breeze, caught in an updraft while a father chased the string.

"I'm glad you're here," I whispered, wondering if Matt understood me better than I understood myself these days. At least he was here, sharing something important to me. And he cared.

"That's good. Because I'm going to be here longer than I thought."

"What do you mean?" I blinked as I turned away from the little girl, who'd burst into tears.

"There's no way I can go home now and pretend like I give a crap about football, the most important thing in the world to my dad."

"You're quitting football?" I tried to envision Matt not leading the team this fall, and my mind drew a blank. Our friends back home wouldn't believe this.

"I'll miss the rest of strength training and the first two weeks of summer practice. If they want to boot me off because of that...then yeah. I'm done. And you should have seen the old man's face when I told him." A dark grin stole over his face. "He thought he'd come here with big news, but I topped the ring with a whopper of my own."

"Matt." I turned to him, my eyelet dress catching on the rough stone. "Don't risk your place on the team just to hurt him." Not attending summer practice meant being a benchwarmer at best, even for someone as talented as Matt.

"I don't care. I'm pissed I played all these years just to make him proud of me."

Was that true? I never would have guessed that Matt didn't love football. Was that because he was a popular kid and I just saw what I wanted to see when I looked at him? Had I dated Matt for eight months without really knowing him at all?

I'd thought I didn't understand myself. But apparently I didn't understand him either.

"Anyway," Matt continued, his tone gentler now. "That means there's no need to go back home in the middle of the summer."

"Really?" My mind whirled at what that meant. With Matt here all summer, where did we stand at the four-week marker? I'd said we'd stay together until then, and knowing there was a potential end point had made it easier to deal with missing Seth.

And that stung. I remembered the way Seth had looked at me when I left with Matt this morning. I hated hurting him, and in the process, I had hurt me too. If Matt was staying, I'd spend the rest of the summer avoiding Seth. And I'd never know why I scribbled his name in beside mine on Kellianne's seating chart.

But there was a whole lot more to Matt than I'd realized and it didn't feel right letting another great guy slip away.

"Yeah. I told my dad to sign me up for the rest of the summer at Camp Juniper Point." He seemed to be waiting for my reaction.

I felt it was important to give him one too, since he'd told me I needed to speak up more often.

So I threw my arms around him and hugged him hard.

"We're going to have a great summer," I whispered in his ear.

Trouble was, I crossed my fingers when I said it. Not because I didn't mean it or anything. But just because I wanted it to be true so very badly.

Chapter Ten

Gravel crunched under the wheels of my mother's rental and I waved...and kept on waving as if I could physically push the black Mercedes around the bend and out of my camp life. Phew.

It'd been a long parents' weekend, and this Sunday afternoon's goodbye couldn't have come fast enough. Last night I'd barely slept, my mind replaying my conversation with Matt. For the past couple of weeks, I'd held on to the hope that Seth would forgive me when Matt left, and that Matt would be strong enough to handle a break up. But now things were worse than ever. Seth was spending time with another girl while Matt was going through a crap-storm at home.

What a mess.

In all the drama, I'd even forgotten to ask Mom about my letters of recommendation for NASA. I was so mad at my father I barely cared, but I should have asked.

Was I really going to throw my future away with both hands just because my dad didn't care anymore? My hands balled at my sides. I had to do something. Matt was grieving, and I'd promised him and myself that we'd have a good summer together. But I'd be lying if I said that it'd be easy.

Seth and I had history, feelings that had been and would always be. Yet I was starting to see Matt as more than the perfect sports hero. His trophy of a life might have been tarnished, but it was only adding to his appeal. I'd always cared, but now my feelings were changing, growing, and it scared me to think I might fall for two boys. Who did that? Cheaters. That's who. And I so didn't want to be that person. Wouldn't be that girl.

I fanned myself with a plucked oak leaf, grateful for any breeze in the sticky air. I tucked my frizzing ends behind my ears and hurried up the path to the cabins, ready to plop in front of our window fan. The sky was a flat grey with dark clouds that threatened rain. I picked up the pace, not wanting to get caught in the downpour.

Thwack! The familiar pinging sound of a ball hitting a bat stopped my homeward rush. I squinted through our 'Field of Dreams' chain-link backstop and spotted a shirtless Matt standing next to home plate. An involuntary sigh escaped me.

He was gorgeous.

His V-shaped back rippled when he tossed a baseball high in the air, biceps flexing as he twisted his lean waist to smash it toward the outfield wall with an easy swing. *Thwack!* He pulled his shirt from the back pocket of low-riding jeans and mopped his face, his dark hair so wet it looked like he'd already been caught in a rainstorm. How long had he been at this? I hadn't seen him at breakfast with his father and the girlfriend—Sherry. We didn't follow a strict camp schedule on this weekend, and from the sheen of sweat glistening on his muscles, I'd say he'd been here for hours.

"Hey." I ducked around the fence. "What's up?"

His face was an open wound, his eyes bleak, mouth in a narrow line.

"Did your mom and Kellianne leave?"

My breath caught at the flash of his elongated, six-pack abs as he threw another ball in the air, then smashed it with the bat. *Thwack!* I tracked the orb until it disappeared over the fence. I wanted to say "home run", but Matt hadn't exactly scored this weekend. Guilt twisted my gut. Ogling a boy in the midst of a crisis? It was wrong on too many levels to count.

But I admired Matt's drive and determination, something that always came out when he played sports.

"They left a couple of minutes ago. I was on my way back when I saw you."

Matt dug in a bucket of balls for the next victim of his bat while I crept closer.

"What are you doing?" I put my hand on the bat and waited for him to pay attention to me.

He snorted. "Having fun."

I put the bat down while a noisy family surrounding a sobbing younger camper walked by, a counselor hovering behind them. It was the perfect reminder of how hard goodbyes could be.

"Doesn't look like it."

Matt's powerful shoulders shifted in a shrug. "At least it gets my mind off things."

"Do you want to talk?"

He shook his head, sweat droplets flying. "Just got to work this out."

I put my hand out, then pulled it back. "I get it. So I'll see you later?"

But before he could nod, the first drop of rain slid down my neck and rolled along my spine, followed by another and another. Within seconds, the sky fell apart as easily as my life had. Matt and I raced for the dugout when thunder boomed followed by a fork of lightning that touched down beyond the tree line.

"Wow. It's really coming down." I looked out at the green-black forest and the thick rain. I hoped none of my friends were out in this. And yes, I hoped Seth and his dad were okay. I hated to think of anyone out on the river.

Matt's square jaw was clenched so tight I wasn't sure he could open it. He nodded and stared without seeming to focus at the sheets of water making muddy ruts in the pristine field.

"So your dad left last night." I touched his slick forearm.

He cleared his throat and the voice that emerged sounded as thick as the rain. "He took off without saying goodbye."

My breath caught. What a jerk. How could he treat his son like that? While I struggled for an answer, the rain drummed on the metal roof, a background bass line to our mini soap opera.

"He doesn't deserve you."

Matt's laugh was bitter and short. "Funny, after he dropped me off last night, he said I don't deserve him. Said I was worthless without football and he wouldn't pay for the rest of camp."

"Worthless without football?" My stomach dropped like a jerking elevator. How cruel and totally untrue. Matt was so much more than football. He was...was...well, he played other sports. I shook my head. I had to do better than that. How much about Matt, the *real* Matt, did I actually know? He was more than a pair of shoulder pads.

I should have felt relieved he wouldn't be able to stay at camp for the second half of the summer, but instead I felt let down. Was there a part of me that really wanted Matt here? I knew I cared about him, but how deep did my feelings go?

"So what will you do?" My voice came out in a breathy rush.

His warm hand enfolded the one I'd placed on his knee. "My mom already called and said she'd pay for the rest."

"That's awesome." I squeezed his hand, a lightness overtaking me. I thought I'd stayed with Matt out of loyalty, but now I wasn't so sure.

He brought my palm to his face and pressed it against his damp cheek before letting it go. "I don't know what I would have done back home."

"Played basketball?" I shifted my sticking thighs on the wooden bench, wishing the rain would cool things down a little more.

"I meant without you." Matt lifted the slipping strap of my tank top, his fingers lingering on my bare shoulder, his touch making me shiver in spite of the heat.

"Oh," I looked at my swinging sandals and toyed with the frayed ends of my skirt. My heart was a nation divided on itself, one half expanding in pleasure at his words, the other shrinking, not wanting to lead him on. To betray the part of me that had always loved Seth.

Matt's voice deepened and echoed in the cramped space. "Would you have missed me?"

My eyes flew to his. I could at least give an honest answer to this question. "Yes."

"Then it's just you and my mom," Matt said after we'd sat in silence, watching the raindrops hanging like lace from the dugout roof's overhang. "You're the only ones who like me for real—not for the quarterback with the division champion title."

I blinked at him in surprise. Wasn't that exactly how I felt? That Matt cared about the parts of me that didn't matter as much to me, the girl who could land a basket throw toss and performed on a competitive cheer team?

"If you don't play football, what will you do this fall?" Thunder rolled through the camp, sending the last of the families scurrying indoors, leaving Matt and me alone in the narrow, shadowed space.

Matt cupped the back of my head and he lowered his nose until it touched mine. "This," he whispered, then captured my lips in a kiss more electrifying than the war nature was waging outside. His mouth was gentle at first, but the pressure grew more insistent until we both gasped for breath. My head whirled and I thought I'd black out until he lowered me to the bench.

The warmth of his bare chest seeped into my soaked tank, the drumming of his heart faster than the clattering rain. His lips left mine and travelled along my jaw to my earlobe. I shuddered when he lightly nibbled, the shock of pleasure intense.

My hands slid along his back, the muscles bunching beneath my touch. I traced the ridge of muscle above his hip and felt him tremble, his breath growing ragged. But when his fingers tugged up the hem of my shirt I was the one who sounded winded. His palms skimmed upward against my ribcage until they cupped my flesh, driving me crazy. Only another kiss kept me from making a noise. The storm was loud, but I didn't want to risk alerting others that we were behind the water curtain flowing in front of the dugout.

"Matt," I gasped, loving the feel of his hands on me, the pressure of his hips against mine. I was as hot as a stoked furnace, heat sizzling everywhere at once. My fingers buried themselves in the thick hair at the nape of his neck and I pressed my lips to his, wanting more of him.

He pulled me up and onto his lap. My hair dripped down my back as my head lolled, his mouth leaving a trail of fire along my neck before dipping lower to my clavicle and lower still. I kissed his brow, his temple, and his square jaw while his mouth explored. I wanted it to go on and on, but suddenly he pulled back, his chest rising and falling like one of those old-time bellows I'd seen on a school field trip.

His face was fierce, intense, every handsome feature sharpened. His hungry eyes were backlit with fire as they roamed over me. Why had he stopped?

"Lauren," he said when it seemed he'd finally caught his breath. I'd never seen him this winded, not even after the endless sprints of football practice. "If we go any farther I won't be able to stop." His eyes searched mine, willing me to understand what he was saying.

"Oh." My cheeks went up in flames and scrambled off his lap. Thank god the heavy waterfall had obscured us from view. I repositioned my bra and tugged down my tank top. I pinched the bridge of my nose, feeling a headache coming on.

"Hey." Matt lifted my chin until I was forced to meet his warm blue-green eyes, the color as inviting as a Caribbean vacation brochure. "There's nothing to be embarrassed about. You're my girlfriend. I love you."

My heart seized. He'd dropped the L-bomb. We'd skirted around the word for months, saying things like, "I love that about you" or just a casual "Love ya" that sounded like something you'd say to a friend. But this. It was huge. What to say? The obvious answer was no answer, but a fierce need to return the words clawed to the surface and fought its way out.

"I love you too."

He crushed me against his chest, his hands twining in my frizzing waves. I did love him, I marveled. His warmth. His sense of humor. His strength of purpose and conviction. But was I *in* love with him? That was the bigger question. One I had no clue how to answer.

"God, you're beautiful. You should wear your hair like this again." Matt held up a crimped lock and grinned, all tension gone, his eyes aglow. "Like a wild girl."

"Hardly." My hands smoothed down my tangled locks. "And thanks for not pushing the sex thing. I'm sorry I'm not ready."

Matt gently straightened my glasses. I'd forgotten that I'd woken too late to put in contacts. "Don't apologize for that." His broad hands spanned my waist. "I want to wait until you are."

I pressed my lips to his, then ducked my head. So sweet. And he'd never seen me with frizzy hair and glasses. Only Seth had ever complimented my real looks. Seth, and now Matt.

The rain tapped a few more times overhead, then stopped. Matt laced his long fingers in mine. "Thanks for stopping to talk to me. I was feeling pretty bad."

"I'm always here for you, Matt," I said, and meant, it. Whatever I figured out, I'd be by his side as a girlfriend or a friend. He was such a great guy. Any girl would be lucky to have him. So why didn't I feel like that deserved to be me?

Seth.

Until I figured out my feelings for my ex, I'd never be free to give my whole heart to Matt. No matter how much he deserved it. But that was the thing. Seth deserved love too. How the hell would I choose?

Matt held his hand out the dugout entrance. "What is it about us and rain?"

I wrapped my arms around his trim waist, loving the feel of his back muscles against my cheek. "It's almost time for electronics hour. We still get it on Parents' Weekend."

Matt whirled around, held my face and swooped in for a quick kiss. "I challenged Eli to Mario Kart. Are you ready?"

I looked around the dugout, then back at his beaming face. I'd made him so happy. What power I had over this beautiful, strong boy. How strange that I'd dated Matt for months without ever really knowing him. Maybe it was time to start.

*   *   *

"Lauren, phone!" Emily called, handing me my cell when I returned. I blinked in surprise. Since my mother and sister had just left, who'd call?

"It's your father," Emily added, then passed out the rest of the electronics. It was all I needed to hear. Finally. A chance to tell him about the Geology position at Indiana and something else... what was it? I bounced off the cot and flew across the cabin, my anger at him disappearing now that he'd remembered me.

"Hey Dad," I sang, shutting the screen door behind me and flopping into a slatted rocker that had been protected from the rain. "I've got news." I watched as a few campers kicked at mud puddles and shook water-logged tree branches at each other, enjoying the outdoors more than the plugged-in time.

"That's great, honey." His voice sounded farther away than the thousand miles between us.

I stopped rocking and leaned forward. "Aren't you going to ask me what it is?"

"Huh?" I heard a lighter flick and three short puffs.

"Are you smoking again?"

He'd quit five years ago after he'd helped me with my science fair project on the effects of nicotine on the body. My plan worked, because he'd thrown out his pipes the next day.

"Work is crazy right now. That's why I couldn't make it to Parents' Weekend. Sorry about that." He exhaled.

"I'm more upset that you're smoking. Dad, you've got to quit. And that goes for your job, too. It's making you miserable." A yellow chickadee landed on our porch and pecked at leftover Cheetos bloated from the rain.

He inhaled and was silent a moment. I imagined him blowing the giant smoke rings I'd once poked with toddler fingers.

"It's not that easy when you're a grown-up, Lauren," he said, voice low and defeated.

The chickadee took flight when I stood to pace the slick, wooden floor.

"Maybe it can be. Seth's dad told me about a Geology Chair position that just opened at Indiana University. You'd be perfect for it." My heart pounded, imagining us moving there, being close to Seth every day. My dreams of a year-round relationship with him, and getting my old dad back, began to take shape. My confusion about Matt magically disappeared.

Dad's pipe pinged against something— an ashtray, most likely. "Lauren, your mother's happy here. She's back with her family and she loves her new job. I can't drag her away from all that again."

The way they'd dragged me from my old life in Ithaca? I ground my sandal into the Cheetos until I reduced them to a squishy pile of orange.

"How are things going with Matt?"

I flinched at the abrupt change of subject.

"Um. Fine. He seems to be having a good time." My mind flashed to our dugout hook up and I flushed. Thank God Dad didn't know about that. "He's playing lots of volleyball and has his team in position for division championship."

"Sounds about right," Dad mused. "But his father's complaining about him staying at camp. He just sent me a text asking me to see if you'd convince him to go back early for football practice. Guess he thinks you're to blame."

A bitter laugh escaped me as I pictured his stepmother-to-be's new diamond ring. "He's on the wrong track there, Dad. Matt stayed for himself."

"What about Seth?" It wasn't like my dad to get involved in my dating life, but he'd known Seth for a long time.

I tipped my head back and stared at our porch roof. In a corner, a spider wrapped strands around a fly. One of the fly's legs stuck out from its silken trap and wiggled. I knew exactly how it felt.

"He's okay. I think he might be seeing someone else." Each word felt like broken glass in the back of my throat.

"Sorry about that, honey."

"It's fine," I said, my voice thick. The sun broke through a cloud and lit up the spider web, water droplets hanging from it like diamonds.

"Lauren, why stay with Matt if you still care for Seth? I haven't been around much, but I've seen enough to know that Matt's not your type."

I closed my eyes, wondering how he had any idea what my type was. He didn't even know me anymore. And I understood my true feelings even less. "Like you said, Dad, life's complicated."

"But I don't want you growing up that way. Giving up." His words rushed out like I'd knocked the wind out of him.

He had a point, but I was too mad to admit it. What a classic case of "Do what I say, not what I do." I used to think my father was better than that. "You've compromised on everything. Why shouldn't I?"

"Lauren, did you open the envelope I sent you?" Suddenly his voice sounded urgent. Did he really think I would be placated by some lame note full of excuses? None of it was a substitute for having my old father back.

"No." In the background a door opened, and voices murmured.

I tapped my foot, waiting until Dad came back on the line.

"Lauren, I've got to go. An emergency's come up at one of the refineries. Just open the envelope, okay?"

I swiped my eyes. Like I even knew where it was. I remembered having it when I'd returned to the cabin yesterday, but hadn't seen it since.

"Whatever, bye." I held my breath, tamping down the emptiness that rose when he chose his job over me—especially on a Sunday when he shouldn't have been working anyway.

"Goodbye, Lauren. We'll talk soon." The phone went dead.

Now there was an empty promise if I'd ever heard one—and I'd heard a lot from him this year. Should I be grateful that he was sacrificing to make Mom happy and bring home a bigger paycheck? It cost us more than it paid. Maybe there was something to be said about doing what he said and not what he did.

Chapter Eleven

There is a lot of great stuff about camp. Some things are fun but embarrassing, like the talent show at the end of the summer. Some things are fun but end in tears half the time, like the dances.

And then some camp activities are just one hundred percent awesome. The overnight trip for the older kids was always one of them. After riding an emotional roller coaster for the last few days, I was ready for a good time. My cabin mates and I had packed Monday at dawn while Mr. Woodrow stomped back and forth between the girls' cabins and the boys' cabins, complaining about anyone who tried to bring a bag that was two pounds over his predetermined weight limit. I'd had to repack once, leaving my flashlight at the cabin since it was heavy and the only thing I could think of to ditch. One hour into our canoe trip, poor Trinity was still recovering from abandoning her Ouija board. As if Tarot cards and rune stones weren't enough fun for one night. I had to hand it to her, though; she liked that stuff because it brought our cabin together.

We forgot about some of the weirdness between us while we pretended to read fortunes.

"Come on, home girls!" Emily shouted, splashing me with a sweep of her oar. "Dig deep! Do you want the boys to get there ahead of us? We'll never live down the humiliation if we don't catch up."

Our cabin was split between two canoes, and I'd ended up in Emily's. Jackie led the rest of our cabin in the other, and they were already closing in on the boys. Then again, Jackie played competitive volleyball and lifted weights during the off-season, so she had serious upper body strength.

"I went on this trip last year," I reminded Emily as I kept a steady pace. "And was part of the last group to reach the island. But no one humiliated us. In fact, they clapped for us when we arrived." All except Hannah's group, I added silently. They'd been too busy claiming the best lean-tos to notice our arrival.

"Probably because they assumed you were goners!" Emily dipped her oar so far down in the water she nearly went over the side. "Don't worry. I won't let you be subjected to that again. The guys from Warriors' Warden are going to hear the mighty roar of Woman Power."

Sure enough, Matt and his friends cruised along at a lazy pace just ahead. No doubt they thought they had the race to the island locked down. Their counselor, Rob the Hottie, was messing around in his canoe and standing on one foot. From the looks he shot Emily, I wondered if he was doing it to impress her.

Leaning into the oars, I felt Piper and Emily do the same. Beside us, Jackie, Trinity, Alex and Siobhan all seemed as thirsty for a win. Luckily, the guys were too busy shouting some kind of he-man chant for Rob, so they never heard us coming.

"The island is right there," I said softly to Emily as the nose of our canoe reached the back of Matt's.

I expected her to be happy as we shot past the boys. I hadn't anticipated the blood-curdling war cry she belted out, lifting her oar in the air like she was hoisting a trophy. I braved a glance back to see the guys' expressions since there was no way they could catch us now. We had too much momentum.

"Take that, suckers!" Jackie called from the canoe beside us just as the wake of our boat hit Matt's and toppled Rob.

And tipped the whole canoe.

Matt, Eli and Rob all went into the water. Backpacks and oars bobbed to the surface around the blue canoe.

"Matt." His name was on my lips as we rammed into the sandy shore of the private island owned by the camp.

"He'll be fine," Emily shot back, jumping out into the shallow current to drag the canoe ashore. "Don't get sucked in, Lauren. Men are far more independent when there are no women around to do their work for them."

"That's sure as hell the truth," Bam-Bam spoke behind us. Emily turned and flashed him a blinding smile. "Our unit commander was a woman. She was a damn good soldier and the best leader I ever had." Bam-Bam grinned, rubbing his jaw stubble while Emily shot him a warm smile.

Vijay and Garrett splashed to shore and heaved the front of their canoe out of the water. Seth, I noticed through narrowed eyes, helped Breyanna out of her canoe. When she complained that her pink glitter sandals—the ones that matched today's headband—might shrink in the water, he carried her to the beach. My breath rushed through clenched teeth at her girlish squeals and the way he held her when he set her down.

It was selfish to expect Seth to mope around camp, pining for me. But I'd be fooling myself if I pretended to be over him.

A couple more Warriors leapt into the water behind Rob's crew, rounding up the backpacks of the tipped canoe. Far behind them, Hannah's canoe rounded a bend.

"We'll get the best lean-to," I said, hardly daring to believe it. I'd gotten the worst one—the smallest, the leakiest, the one with the most angry chipmunks—last year.

"Only if we get a move on!" Emily led the charge as we all scrambled up the shore and onto the island, lugging our backpacks.

"I want this one!" Alex squealed, pointing to a shelter with a white bark roof and a funky woven grass mat hanging over an opening like a window curtain.

The lean-to was built around a tree and it looked like you could climb up through the middle of it to access wooden rungs nailed in the trunk. Following the steps upward with my eye, I spied a little lookout platform about fifteen feet up.

"Cool." I didn't put my bag down though, not sure if Alex would want me to room with her. My friends and I had only recently patched things up.

"You want to share?" Alex lifted an eyebrow. "That is, unless I can convince Vijay to pay a visit." She winked and snapped her gum with enthusiasm as she dropped her backpack on the ground outside the lean-to.

"Umm..." I hesitated, not sure if she was serious about the Vijay thing. But looking around, the other good shelters were all being claimed. "That'd be great." I concentrated on the positive aspects of fixing a friendship, rather than the potential downside of getting bounced at midnight for the sake of a booty call.

"Excellent!" Alex tossed her sleeping bag inside the little hut, and then pulled out a glittery pink letter "A" that she always brought to camp to hang on her bunk. Now, she tied the pink ribbon straps to one of the wooden rungs up the tree, identifying the place as hers. "Vijay will know where to find me in the dark. Too bad he couldn't share a shelter with Matt...or Seth. You could just switch places with Vijay after lights out and end up with whichever guy's on the menu tonight."

Her tone sounded teasing, so I ignored the jibe about Seth.

"You're serious about Vijay?" I lowered my voice while an argument broke out between Piper and one of the Divas, who'd apparently just arrived on the island. I could tell they both wanted the same lean-to, but I couldn't get involved in that while Alex was talking about giving it up to Vijay after dating him for all of a week.

"Duh?" She tugged on her midriff-baring T-shirt that, now that I thought about it, barely met the dress code. She was wearing earrings too, and some makeup, but then she liked to enjoy the girly stuff at camp since her parents were super strict at home.

"Alex, you only just started dating him." As much as I wanted to get along with her, I also knew I couldn't let a good friend make a big mistake. "Are you sure you want to get that serious with him already?"

"Have you *seen* how hot he is this year?" She didn't seem to pay attention to the Munchies vs. Divas showdown either, her gaze wandering past them toward the boys' camp.

Back at camp, the distance between the boys and girls involved several buildings, tree roots to the tenth power, and Gollum's private residence. Here, there were only a couple of birch trees. We had a prime view.

"Alex, get real." Damn it, I knew she wasn't the kind of girl who made decisions about sex based on a guy's abs.

At least, I thought I knew that. But what if I wasn't the only one in Munchies' Manor who'd had a rough year at home and was exploring a new role at camp? I'd been so focused on my issues...how much time had I spent checking in with my friends to see how things were for them beyond volleyball and bonfires?

I ducked out of the way of a Frisbee that someone sent sailing into the common area. Jackie was breaking up the lean-to squabble by spraying them both with Silly String. Luckily, all that chaos meant no one overheard Alex and me.

"What?" She frowned, her gum stilled, her arms crossed. "You already have a hot boyfriend, so don't deny me one. Besides, how long did *you* wait before you slept with Matt?"

"For your information," I returned hotly, "I have not slept with Matt. Not that it's anyone's business." My cheeks heated when I remembered our dugout hook-up. How close we'd come to scoring.

"Okay, fine, it's no one's business. So neither is it any of *your* business if I sleep with Vijay." She glared at me, not backing down. "But who is going to believe you haven't done it with Matt? He's the hottest guy at camp. Every girl in Hannah's cabin has offered to hook up with him. And you expect anyone to believe you're not putting out?" She shook her head, her sneer punctuated by a gum snap.

Had Matt really been hit on by all those girls, or was that just the latest camp rumor? I'd never thought about what he must be giving up to be with me. I still couldn't believe he'd sacrificed his starting football position by not going to summer practice...if they'd even let him on the team at all. As for sex, he said he'd wait. I cleared my throat. "Actually, we haven't—"

"Look, maybe we're not as close as we used to be, so you don't want to talk about it." She cut me off. "Maybe you think because my parents write blogs about raising wholesome kids that I'd disapprove." She jabbed a finger at me. "But I would never judge you, and I hope you'd never judge the person who helped you cheat to pass the swim test for three years straight. Someone who kept all the Friends Forever lanyards we made in Weaving. Not all of us got to go to pep rallies and beach parties like you this year. This is my only chance at fun and I'm taking it."

She stalked away before I could explain that even though I'd been surrounded by 'friends' and a boyfriend at those parties and pep rallies, I'd always felt alone. Kind of like now.

Alex joined Trinity and Piper as they draped a daisy chain around the front door of their lean-to. Apparently Piper had won the battle for the place. Across a leaf-covered path, Siobhan picked Silly String off Jackie, who had obviously gotten a taste of her own medicine after settling the dispute. Siobhan was laughing, using the purple goo to shape a necklace and matching bracelet.

Everyone was having fun except me. Even Emily was happily distracted from her ongoing war with Rob. She stood between the girls' huts and the boys' shelters with Bam-Bam, the two of them looking cozy. She'd chosen the clever outdoorsman over the hot jock, even though every other Juniper Point female thought Rob was gorgeous. Maybe she knew better than to get tangled up with a guy all the girls wanted.

A sharp whistle cut through the chatter and laughter. I turned to see Rob jogging past Emily, flexing his muscles in a not-so-subtle display. He cupped his hands to his mouth now that he had everyone's attention.

"Cliff diving!" he shouted. "Anyone who wants to jump, follow me!"

A chorus of cheers answered him as a handful of boys and a couple of girls raced toward the shore. The terrain was high on one side, providing a perfect spot for cliff jumping. Not that I'd try it. Way too scary. Besides, I was too unsettled by Alex's comments. Did the whole camp think Matt stayed with me for sex?

God. Was that what Seth thought, too? He hadn't said anything, but knowing him, he wouldn't.

When I had sex it would be with someone who loved the real me and was in it for the long haul. Matt knew the cheerleader better than the astronomer, and Seth called our relationship quits at the end of every summer. Neither one had what I needed for such a big step. Feet dragging, I followed Piper and Trinity toward the water's edge. The rest of the campers would play games down by the shore. I noticed Hannah walking down toward the shoreline too. She must have gone to the boys' shelters first, because she matched her pace to Matt's. He'd changed into dry clothes, his gray T-shirt tight around his wide shoulders. Hannah ate him up with her eyes while her long auburn braid swung in time to her steps.

Jealousy rose up and bit me. I felt an ugliness that I wouldn't have dreamed of feeling until Alex had stirred the beast inside me. What if Matt was staying at camp for more reasons than just me?

What if Hannah was one of them?

Just then, Alex and Vijay jogged past, chasing each other around the trees and sneaking kisses while the counselors were preoccupied. When they got around me, they slowed down and held hands the rest of the way to the beach.

"You got a great hut," a voice beside me said suddenly. Kayla and Brittany joined me. They were wearing matching pink T-shirts that said Divas' Den BFFs on them in purple.

Somehow, the sight of the T-shirts brought to mind Alex's dig about not lying to someone who kept every Friends Forever bracelet.

"Yeah," I agreed. "It was a miracle we got to the island first this year."

"We heard Emily wanted to show off for Rob," Brittany volunteered. "Is that true? It looks like she's trying to make him jealous now." She pointed to the beach where Emily had stolen Bam-Bam's fishing hat and wore it on her head while dragging wood into the fire pit.

"I have no idea what anyone's thinking anymore," I answered, too tired to play the games necessary to keep a social life afloat.

This was camp, damn it. I just wanted to sing a song and eat a freaking marshmallow. Was that so much to ask? Besides, I hated gossip and I wasn't going to start it. I'd been bitten in the butt by it myself with this new rumor about Matt's sex life.

"So true," Kayla agreed, surprising me. "Take the dance, for example. I had no idea that Hannah had adding itching powder to one of my essential oils just to play a trick on you. I don't know why she did it, but I'm sorry."

"Really?" I hadn't confronted Kayla or anyone else from Divas' Den about the incident, but I appreciated the confession. "Hannah needs to grow up."

"Totally." Brittany adjusted the strap of a tiny backpack decorated with a full moon and a winged purple fairy. "But Eli tricked Hannah with the itching powder a few days before and she was dying to pass on the torment. I kept waiting for her to sprinkle it in my sheets."

She gave an exaggerated shudder while we stood around the beach. Hannah worked on an elaborate French braid while openly staring as Matt and some of the guys from his cabin threw the frisbee. I was shocked he hadn't gone cliff diving, but then Matt's behavior continued to surprise me. Whenever I thought I had him figured out, I realized again I didn't know him at all.

Seth, on the other hand, must have gone to the cliffs. His bunkmates Garrett and Julian had gone too, as I didn't see them on the beach. Eli was missing from Matt's cabin.

"What a crappy thing to do." I thought about confronting Hannah right now, but I was afraid that, if I opened my mouth to speak to her, I'd end up accusing her of sleeping with Matt instead. My thoughts were all over the place ever since that conversation with Alex.

A whistle blew, and I turned to see Bam-Bam standing at full attention like he was back in the military. Ramrod straight, he held his hand up.

"Quiet!" he commanded in a voice that made me wonder if something was wrong.

We all shut up instantly. Sometimes you can just tell when you need to fall in line. Even Emily quit dragging her dead branches to see what he wanted.

But then, as one, we all heard a faraway sound that made my blood run cold.

"Help!" a man's shout echoed over the island.

Bam-Bam took off at a sprint up the beach and we all followed. Emily, Vicki, and every last camper left the Frisbees and the footballs to race toward the sound.

"Help!" the hoarse shout came again. Closer. Louder.

"It sounds like Rob," one of the boys said from nearby.

I looked for Seth, needing his reassuring strength. Could he be the one in trouble? My heart picked up speed. I spotted Matt at the front of the pack with another one of his friends and Bam-Bam. Whatever made a counselor shout for help like that had to be serious.

The trip to the cliff diving spot was a high climb and I was out of breath by the time I got there. Matt and Bam-Bam were in the water. Emily stood at the edge of the cliff, peering down into the river.

"What happened?" Brittany shrieked.

And for once, her words spoke for every last one of us. Someone squeezed my hand. Someone else gripped my shoulder. I swallowed hard as all of us seemed to hold our breath.

"It's Eli," Emily said, her voice raspy and her face snow-white. "He didn't resurface."

Chapter Twelve

I froze as Emily's words sunk in, terrified for Eli. Hannah's friend Rachel reacted first, her feet kicking up dirt as she sprinted to the cliff's edge and dove. Her strong arms flashed toward the river's center. "Eli!" she shouted, then plunged underwater. Several campers followed, including Seth. In seconds the deep blue water roiled with campers and counselors alike.

Amazing that it took an accident like this to make everyone put aside petty differences for the sake of a camp mate. Not all of us got along at Camp Juniper Point, but we *were* a family. Losing Eli would be like losing a brother, the one that put frogs down your wet swimsuit and ate all the cherry popsicles. My heart clenched at the thought of anything happening to him. The possibility was too horrible to imagine.

Brittany swiped at her damp cheeks. "He's dead!" she wailed.

I put my arms around her, as did Kayla. "They'll find him," I said, feeling much less sure than I sounded. How had such a fun day dissolve into a nightmare? I looked away from the river, blotting out the image of an unconscious Eli lying on its bottom.

As I led Brittany down the cliff to the beach, I caught Alex's questioning look. Siobhan, Trinity, and Piper stood beside her, eyes glued to Jackie who surfaced and dove with the other would-be rescuers. Alex's face spoke volumes. She was surprised to see me with Hannah's group instead of them. But as Eli's girlfriend, Brittany needed me—needed us all—more.

"Oh no!" Hannah blurted suddenly.

Shocked at her uncharacteristic emotional display, I rubbed her shoulder. "It'll be okay."

She held up her messy French braid. "Okay? Do you know how long it took me to fix my hair? Now I've got to start over. Be right back, Brit." She sprinted toward her lean-to without a backward glance.

What a friend. "Call 911." Anger bubbled inside. "Hannah's got a hair emergency."

A half-sob/ half-giggle escaped Brittany. She pulled back. "Thanks, Lauren. Sometimes Hannah can be such a, a..."

"Bitch," Kayla finished, though she looked over her shoulder before saying it.

Funny. Before this year, I'd always felt afraid of Hannah and the power she wielded over camp. I never knew her best friends felt the same way.

"No sign of him!" someone called from the river.

My heart rate picked up. What if they didn't find Eli? I couldn't imagine what Brittany must be feeling. If Seth or Matt was missing, I'd go crazy.

"It's going to be okay. They'll find him. They will," I murmured. Kayla squeezed my arm. When I met her eyes, they were warm with gratitude.

A sudden breeze carried a familiar, whining voice.

"It was just a joke! Ouch!"

Brittany, Kayla and I gaped as Bam-Bam hauled Eli into camp by the ear. The swimmers emerged, some bending at the waist, their breaths coming in hard, short gasps. Relief flooded me when first Matt, then Seth staggered onto the beach.

"Everyone out of the water. Eli's fine." Bam-Bam barked. "Head count in two minutes."

We surged toward Eli but pulled back as Bam-Bam marched him to his lean-to. Rumors leapt, eventually reaching us. Apparently, Bam-Bam had caught Eli hanging out downstream. After cliff jumping, he'd swum underwater around a bend, resurfaced, then hid.

"I'll kill him," Brittany sputtered. For some weird reason, that made me laugh. But before I could apologize, Kayla joined in, followed by Brittany.

Her friend Rachel stumbled over and flopped on the sandy ground, chest heaving. "What'd I miss?"

Brittany shook her head. "Thanks, Rach. But it was just a prank."

"Are you freaking kidding me? I'll kill that kid." Rachel's frustration turned into surprise when we burst out laughing again.

"Join the club." Kayla rolled her eyes and smiled in my direction. But some of my happiness melted away when I spied my Munchies' Manor friends hugging each other in relief. I wished I could have shared this moment with them. They were as happy that Eli was safe as we were. So what was up with the invisible wall separating us? I'd crossed into the popular world in Texas and survived. Maybe my friends needed some of the same experience...minus the itching powder pranks. We'd never bothered getting to know the girls in Divas' Den, assuming they were the enemy. Some were actually nice, like Kayla and Brittany and possibly even Rachel. All this time I thought they hadn't given us a chance. But the truth was, we hadn't give them one either.

I hugged Brittany and stepped back. "Will you be okay?"

Hannah strolled up, hair restored, and draped a possessive arm around Brittany.

"I think we can take it from here. Why don't you go back where you belong?" I looked from Brittany to Kayla to Rachel, waiting for one of them to disagree. But their expressions were neutral and Kayla avoided my eyes. Did they agree with Hannah or were they too afraid to speak up? Either way, the queen bee had returned and I was dismissed from her royal court.

My flip-flops stirred up pine needles as I crossed toward my Munchies' Manor gang. A few campers gathered wood for the fire while others laid out potato chip bags, rolls, hamburger patties and hot dog packages on the picnic tables. The counselors lit charcoal in grills raised on cemented pipes, the hickory scent making my stomach growl in anticipation.

Now that the Eli drama had passed, the counselors took a quick head count, then the Frisbee game resumed while sunbathers looked on. Hannah, outfitted in a white string bikini that would have never passed Gollum's dress code, waved at Matt when he joined me.

"Hey, babe." Matt ruffled my hair.

"Hey. That was really brave of you, looking for Eli like that." I slid my hand in his, enjoying Hannah's pout. For today, I wasn't going to worry about conquering my inner bitchy side. At least not where Hannah was concerned. How could she have been worried about her hair during that scare with Eli?

"Were you worried?" Matt's lazy smile turned my senses up to sizzle.

I nodded, eyes drifting over the cut torso revealed by his wet T-shirt. He was hotness personified. For a moment I fantasized about pulling him behind one of the lean-tos and stripping off that clinging shirt. Alex was planning a night with Vijay after a week of dating. And I was a big-time hold out, apparently, for remaining a virgin after months of dating.

Seth strode by, his sidelong amber glance grazing over me. Matt jerked us to a stop. He pulled me close and gave me a passionate kiss that left me breathless. But when I opened my eyes, it was Seth he was staring at, not me.

Seth pulled a towel over his head and stalked away. Obviously, he'd received the message loud and clear— "Lauren Carlson, property of Matt Butler."

Annoyed at Matt's possessive move, I strode away. I didn't appreciate being branded like a Texas Longhorn. Maybe I should have paid more attention at that damn intervention my cabin mates had tried to give me.

"Yo, Butler!" one of his friends called behind us. "Help us with the volleyball net."

I kept walking.

"See you later," he called to my stiff back.

"Much later," I muttered under my breath, wondering how he could seem so different when we were alone.

I jogged to catch up to my friends who headed toward the forest.

"Hey. Where are you going?"

Trinity turned. "I spotted sage and wanted to pick some so I could smudge everyone's lean-tos. Want to come? Ouch!" she exclaimed when Jackie tucked a daisy chain in her dreadlocks. I remembered that smudging meant waving burning sage to get rid of bad energy. It sounded like we could all use some sage.

"Wouldn't you rather tan with the Divas?" Siobhan put in, her safari hat obscuring her delicate face. There was no meanness in her tone. It was the matter-of-factness that killed me.

I linked arms with Alex. "I would if my friends were about to catch some rays instead of poison ivy. Come on, you guys. I was just comforting Brittany. Eli's her boyfriend."

Piper plucked a candy wrapper off the ground and stuffed it in her recycle bag. "We were worried about him too. But they don't want us around. Remember the rash they gave us the last time you hung out with one of them?" I stumbled over an exposed root as we tramped through the brush, the thick canopy of oak, pine, and maple trees blotting out most of the sunshine. My forehead beaded with sweat in the humid air.

"One of them? You make them sound inhuman."

Siobhan tipped up her hat. "Sometimes I wonder."

"I am Hannah, the Demon Queen from Planet Hades," Alex intoned.

"Some of them are cool. And Hannah's the one who put the itching powder in the body perfume. The other girls didn't know about it," I insisted.

Alex snorted. "I believe that just like I believe you and Matt have only gone to first base."

Technically, it was farther than that...but still, why wouldn't they give these girls a chance? "We should hang out with them sometime."

Jackie snorted. "Like that will ever happen."

I dodged a fat toad hopping past. "What? Is there some kind of law against it?"

"Look. We didn't make the rules, okay?" Siobhan slapped a mosquito on her shoulder.

"So why follow them?" Hadn't my friends always prided themselves on their uniqueness, refusing to join cliques to fit in?

An uneasy silence descended as we trudged along, the path narrowing so we passed single-file. Bickering forgotten, we charged into a real-life Monet painting with navy, sun-dappled water swirling behind a field of rippling lavender sage, white Queen Anne's lace, and yellow buttercup wildflowers.

"Try not to pull up the roots," Trinity cautioned, ever worried about damaging the ecosystem. Without a knife, it was hard to cut through the stalks. Alex and I twirled the green branches until they came off in our hands while Siobhan and Piper bent them back and forth, making them break. Jackie glided from one plant to the next, snapping plants like they were toothpicks.

"Thanks guys. That's enough," Trinity called after fifteen minutes. I flopped on a boulder next to Siobhan and Piper and admired the sparkling water. Downstream, Trinity plucked petals from a daisy and threw them one at a time into the water.

"Hope she's going to smudge our hut." Alex tickled me behind the ear with a bouquet. "I want to get lucky tonight."

"What?" Siobhan exclaimed. "Don't you think you're moving way too fast?"

"Yeah." Piper lifted her head and frowned at Alex. "Your parents wouldn't approve of your 'unwholesome' thoughts."

Awesome. Help from unexpected allies. Maybe Alex would pay attention if more people stood up to question this rush to ditch her virginity.

Alex pouted. "I'm so sick of them writing about me and their perfect life. I want to do something spontaneous and not care if it's wholesome or not. Besides, I've known Vijay for, like, ever." She kicked off her Keds and dipped her toes into the rushing water.

"But not as BF/GF," Trinity put in, joining us. She gathered our sage and tied it together with string from a fraying friendship bracelet.

Alex kicked a small spray of water at the group. "Hello. We've been dating for seven days. Camp time is different. That's like a year in the real world. And what's the big deal? It's just sex."

"Do you love him? Because you have to be in love to have sex," Siobhan announced as though stating a mathematical fact. She dried her splattered glasses with her shirt.

Jackie laughed. "Please. That's what I thought until I slept with Rick, my teammate. He said he loved me, then bragged to everyone about going all the way."

I quickly shut my mouth and watched the rest of the group do the same. Jackie had never talked about her love life. Now we knew why.

Jackie stared down Alex like she was sizing up an opponent. "Have you even DTRed?"

"No." For the first time, Alex's confident expression wavered.

Trinity pursed her lips. "Sweetie. You have to define the relationship. Make sure he wants more than sex."

"I'd have sex with Julian." Piper kicked off her shoes and combed her toes through the grass. "But only if we were going out."

Now it was Jackie's turn to look surprised. The rest of us froze in shock. How many more secrets were about to be spilled? Clean-up on aisle twelve.

Unable to stop myself, I stood and held Alex by her thin shoulders. They felt so small. Fragile. "Relationships are more than just sex. They're about sharing."

Alex shifted out of my grip. "Have you shared with Matt how much you love Seth?"

I opened my mouth and closed it. What could I say? She had a point.

"So if Vijay and Alex's one-week camp thing equals a year, then what would that make Seth and Lauren? Married and divorced?" asked Piper.

"Trinity never saw a breakup on their chart, remember?" demanded Jackie. Five pairs of questioning eyes met mine. I pulled the bottom string from a honeysuckle flower and tasted its sweet nectar, mind reeling. Did the stars see a future I couldn't?

Technically, I didn't believe in stuff like that. But a wishful heart isn't subject to the rules of science.

"Yeah. What happened to that?" Siobhan's hazel eyes assessed me from beneath her hat.

"The charts aren't as reliable long-term," Trinity said in a rush.

A bee buzzed lazily among us and then settled on the yellow bush. Lulled by the tinkling water, and drowsy under the sun's warm rays, my protective walls tumbled. I was tired of my friends' confusion over my Matt/Seth situation.

"Honestly, I planned to break up with Matt before camp. But then he told me his parents were getting divorced and I just couldn't." Relief warred with guilt at my confession.

Alex snapped her gum. "Seriously?"

"Heavy," murmured Piper.

Trinity smiled at me as she plucked a honeysuckle flower. "You did the right thing karma-wise."

Siobhan and Jackie looked unconvinced.

"You should have been honest with Matt." Siobhan pulled off her hat and waved it in front of her flushed face. "You're only leading him on if you still care about Seth."

"If she cared about Seth, would she treat him this way?" Jackie drawled. "The boy is in pain. Julian said he stopped playing Dungeons and Dragons. And he's a level thirty ranger. He's got like a hundred and twenty-five hit points."

Wow. The Wander Inn's old-school D&D games were legendary and lasted for weeks on end. They'd spend every free minute huddled in a circle, rolling their twenty-sided dice, using their imaginations instead of electronics to wage war and win gold. If Seth wasn't playing, he hurt more than I thought.

"He's fine." Trinity gathered her dreadlocks and secured them with a rubber band. "He hardly ever talks about her when we've hung out."

Hardly? That meant they talked about me sometimes. The two of them. Alone. I knew they weren't more than friends, but... My face started to burn from more than the sun. What happened between Seth and me was private. *How could he?*

Alex sucked in a popped bubble before asking, "Who do you like more, Matt or Seth?"

I flopped back in the wild grass and threw an arm over my eyes. "I don't know," I groaned. The long blades scratched my shoulders and tickled me through the thin fabric of my tank top. I was still miffed at Matt's caveman tactic, kissing me in front of Seth. It reminded me of the immature way he'd behaved with his friends that last day of school and his anger in the mess hall. Sometimes we seemed alike, and other times worlds apart.

Dad said things were complicated in the real world. But this was camp and my last chance to figure out my feelings. For Seth. For Matt. And maybe...about a whole lot more. What if—instead of worrying about what Seth deserved or Matt needed—I thought about myself for a while? I'd been spinning in circles for weeks without figuring anything out. Perhaps what *I* really needed was some space to get perspective.

"I could do another chart for you and Matt. Maybe you guys are a perfect match." Trinity peeled back my arm, her hopeful grey eyes meeting mine.

"I think I've got to figure this out on my own."

"Just don't take too long." Jackie pulled me up at the sound of the dinner bell. "This is Seth's last year."

Right. If I wanted to be with him, this was my last chance. For so long, I had seen myself in terms of who I dated. First it was as Seth's camp girlfriend, and then as Matt's cheerleader girlfriend. Maybe I needed to be on my own to see who I was and what I really wanted.

Until I resolved my confusion at camp this summer, I'd keep hurting both guys. It was time for a clean break from both of them. I trembled at the thought. But overriding my fear was a feeling of certainty that I'd stumbled on the right path. I'd never know who I was until I walked that road on my own.

When we reached the picnic area, I searched for Matt. He'd told me to catch him later. Little did he know I was about to let him go instead.

* * *

"Heads up, Lauren," hollered Devon, one of the Warriors, right before he plowed into me. We landed with a thud. I spit out a pine needle and brushed sand off my shorts. Devon was already on his feet, a football held above his head.

"Woo-hoo!" he shouted, his flag football teammates high-fiving each other. "Touchdown."

Matt grabbed me around the waist and spun me around. "That was the win. Lauren, you're my lucky charm."

I grimaced. He'd always called me that after his football games. According to him, he'd had the best season of his life with me cheering him on from the sidelines. Unfortunately, I'd gotten too comfortable watching the action instead of being a part of it. It reminded me of my dad—denying himself, who he was, to avoid confrontation. It ticked me off how easily I'd followed in his footsteps. I'd drifted for too long.

"Matt, we need to talk." I tugged my fingers from his sweaty grip.

He pulled his shirt out of his back pocket and wiped his wet face. "Sure. What's up?"

I pulled him toward my lean-to, ignoring his friends' whistles and catcalls. Matt hauled me close when we reached the structure. "I think I'm going to like this 'talk.'"

My worried glance flickered from his happy expression to my shuffling feet. Was I ready for such a huge game-changer?

Matt peered inside. "We're alone." He leaped onto the rough pine flooring, then reached out a hand. I ignored the help, hesitating, scared of taking my first lonely step toward independence. My eyes stung as Matt lowered his arm and watched in confusion as I crawled up onto the platform myself. This was going to be so hard.

Once inside, we sat on my sleeping bag. I kept my distance, ignoring Matt's crooked finger as he stretched out.

His eyes darkened, his eyebrows nearly meeting over his nose. "What's up, Lauren? When we're together lately, you're distracted, mad, distant or..." He shrugged. "Different. You're not yourself."

I couldn't have said it better. "You're right. I'm not myself. The problem is I don't have a clue who that is."

Matt sat up and held my hands. "You're the most gorgeous girl I've ever seen, and you're my girlfriend."

He'd spelled it as clearly as a skywriter. My identity revolved around my looks and my boyfriend, about as deep as a plastic kiddie pool. I rubbed my aching stomach. There was so much more to me. Or at least, there used to be. How could I bring all the pieces of me together, know my true self, with Matt and Seth clouding the picture?

"That's about to change." I dropped Matt's suddenly cold hands.

His smile faded. "What's about to change? Us?"

I nodded, a lump blocking my constricted throat. *Ohmigod.* This was so much worse than I'd thought. My heart raced. Tears stung my eyes.

Matt brushed my wet cheeks, comforting me even when I was hurting him. To get through the breakup, I focused on his jealousy, his temper, and the streak of selfishness that had made him jeopardize football to spite his dad. If I thought about his sweet, tender side, I'd never go through with it.

"Is it the physical thing? I meant it when I said I wanted to wait until you were ready." So much for ignoring his sweet side. God, he'd been so understanding about that even when I'd been carried away and... I shook my head, trying to make out his face through the waterfall flowing from my eyes. "No, you've been great about that." And he had. Matt had definitely DTRed... but he didn't love the real me. How could he? *I* still hadn't met her.

Matt rubbed his eyes, hard. "Then what is it? Did I do something wrong? Is it Seth?" His eyes searched mine, then widened. "It is Seth."

"No," I finally managed, knowing it was one hundred percent true. "This is about me."

"You don't love me." Matt ducked his wounded face.

"No. I mean yes. I do love you." I'm just not sure if I'm *in* love with you, I added silently.

Matt exhaled. "So what's the problem?"

"I just need some space to figure things out."

Matt scuttled backward as if stung. "That's what my father said before he moved out."

I flinched, but I couldn't keep putting Matt's feelings first. It wasn't fair to any of us. "A lot of things changed for me this year. I need to know how much of what's different is me."

"And how long is that going to take?" His eyes slid closed for a long moment.

I sat before him. In the distance, campers shrieked and laughed, their happiness a discordant note in the midst of our drama. "I don't know. But if you want to go to football camp now, I wouldn't blame you."

My breath caught as Matt opened his eyes and studied his new friends playing beach volleyball. Was he about to agree and go? As much as I needed to break up with him, I wasn't ready for him to leave.

"You just want to get back with Seth." His fingers clenched the end of my sleeping bag.

"No." My problems went deeper than Seth. "This is about me. I need to be on my own, to figure out what is going on."

Matt faked a grin and waved when one of his cabin mates signaled for him to join them. He stood and looked down at me, his face so raw and sad he might have been a stranger.

"Then you might as well get started now." He hopped outside and gripped the ledge. "But, I'm not going anywhere as long as we've still got a chance. Football can wait. When you figure things out, I'll be here."

I squeezed my eyes shut and dug my nails into the slippery nylon of my sleeping bag. I fought my usual impulse to run after him and make things better. Every instinct told me I'd made a huge mistake. I shook, feeling exposed and alone now that I'd stepped out of the shadow of someone else's life. Whatever happened from this moment forward, it wasn't because of Matt or Seth. It was because of me. No more hiding.

A moment passed, then another, and another until I felt strong enough to release my death grip and open my eyes. In the distance, Matt had already joined his team. His body rippled as he leaped up for an impressive net spike. He fist-bumped his bunkmates and crouched again, looking upward, ready for the next blow to fall from the sky.

*   *   *

"*Pssst*. Lauren," a male voice whispered above me, waking me from a sound sleep. I bolted upright and blinked into the blackness late that night. It was so dark I could have slept with my eyes open. Was this just a dream?

"Seth?" I felt around the narrow space, my hands sliding over Alex's empty sleeping bag. Guess she and Vijay were having their lucky night after all. For her sake, I hoped it didn't go too far.

"Up here." Seth's voice drifted down, confirming this was all too real, *and* too dangerous.

My eyes adjusted enough to make out the ladder that led to the rooftop platform over the lean-to. Oh God, this was crazy. But I couldn't tell him that I needed space from down here. If I shouted my plan, I'd wake half the camp.

"Coming." I shivered as I slid out of my sleeping bag, hoping no one else had heard him. My spaghetti-strap tank top and sleep shorts were little protection from the cool mountain air.

I climbed the ladder but slipped on the last rung. Seth grabbed my waist, pulling me up and over the ledge.

"Okay?" His concerned eyes met mine as he steadied me against him.

Breathless at his proximity, I nodded, ignoring the thrill at his touch. But I was supposed to be on my own now. *On my own, on my own, on my own.* I chanted it like a mantra so I wouldn't move from one guy's arms to another.

His impish grin appeared, slightly a chipped canine and one-sided dimple giving him a pirate's smile. Or maybe it was more like Peter Pan's. Either way, it reminded me of old times and got my heart thumping in spite of my good intentions.

"You look pretty good for a girl with bed head." His hands shook slightly as he smoothed my hair.

Great. Just what I didn't need to hear. I pointed to the stairs. "Seth, you've got to go. This is wrong. Besides. What will your new girlfriend think?"

Seth raked his fingers through his curls so half of them stood on end. "Breyanna's just a friend."

I crossed my arms and stared him down. Seth shrugged and looked sheepish. "Fine. Maybe a little more, lately. Nothing's happened..."

I didn't need him to add the implied, *yet.*

Seth continued to grip my hand. "Please hear me out, Lauren. This will only take a minute."

"Fine. But just for a minute. That's it." I plunked down on the rooftop and swung my legs over the edge, back hunched, arms crossed.

All around us slept campers in lean-tos. By the moon's low position, I guessed it was well past midnight. An owl hooted from a nearby pine, then took flight in a blur of white and grey.

"*Strix varia*," Seth breathed behind me. "Must be after a frog. Look at him dive."

I tracked the bird to the river. The current made a soft *shhhhh* sound as it flowed over and around rocks and boulders. I'd forgotten how much I loved this time of night—the peaceful, natural feel of it.

Seth's shoulder brushed mine as he lowered himself beside me. Goosebumps broke out on my skin, every molecule in my bloodstream screaming to life. I took a steadying breath.

He wrapped an arm around me. "Cold?"

I shook my head and edged away. "You said this would take a minute, so...?"

His finger pressed against my lips while the other hand pointed. My eyes widened at the sight of a portable field telescope set up to our left. Stargazing. As science geeks, it'd always been one of our favorite things to do together. I couldn't believe he lugged the collapsible apparatus on the trip. Given the limited gear we were allowed to pack, he'd made some sacrifices to have this moment with me.

"C'mon." Seth scrambled across the roof, peered into the eyepiece, and focused the lens. He looked up. "Last year we talked about seeing the Perseids and Swift-Tuttle together and tonight's a good clear night for viewing. I didn't want you to miss it. Have a look."

He remembered this rare comet pass and our promise to watch it together. After everything we'd been through this summer, he'd remembered. My heart leaped. *Say no,* I told myself.

"Okay," came out instead.

My eyes flew to the sky. I hadn't forgotten about our plan and our promise to watch the skies together, but I'd put it out of my mind when I brought Matt to camp. But now...this was science, right? We could be nerds for a few minutes without acting on our hormones, couldn't we? This was exactly what I needed. To rediscover my passion for astronomy, a part of me that I'd ignored all year, mostly because my dad had checked out of my life.

And didn't that make me a lot like Matt—spiting myself to get back at my dad for ignoring me? I felt ashamed of myself and my pettiness.

Now, I knelt behind the telescope and looked down into the eyepiece. My breath caught at the otherworldly view. A streak of white light shone against an onyx sky dotted with twinkling stars. Behind it blazed another stream of periwinkle and azure blue.

Wonder filled me. I was transported, aware of the vastness of life and my tiny place in it. The familiar, otherworldly feel brought back my Aerospace Scholar ambition and memories of planetarium trips with Dad.

I grabbed Seth's hand, wanting him to share this amazing moment. But then his arms wrapped around me and he stared into my eyes, the stars reflected in his gaze.

Our breaths synchronized. He exhaled against my temple, making my chest flutter. I turned to tell him I had to go. But before I could speak, his lips captured mine. I was a comet burning in a fireball of emotions.

My feelings for Seth rushed back with a pull as unstoppable as gravity itself. We tumbled against the roof, every nerve ending awakening at his familiar touch. My body softened into his, as if it were meant to fit there. Even the extra muscle he'd put on felt good- a solid and satisfying weight that crushed me in the best way possible. I traced the ridges of his biceps, cupped his broad shoulders, and stroked the back of his neck before burying them in his soft, springy curls. He was fantasy come to life. A forgotten dream remembered.

Seth pulled back and looked down at me with his expressive eyes. "I've missed you so much, Lauren."

"Me too," I admitted.

He rolled us over so that I was on top. My hair hung down like a curtain, the dark strands blotting out the world.

His lips curved toward his eyes, making his whole face sparkle. He was gorgeous, I thought, slightly dazzled.

"I heard you broke up with Matt and thought maybe you wanted to give us another shot." He heaved a long sigh. "I didn't want to spend my last summer here without you."

I closed my eyes, hating our camp's rumor mill, but hating myself more for sending Seth mixed signals. My emotions for Matt and Seth had grown, but they were all mixed up. I needed distance to straighten those feelings out. Tonight proved that more than ever.

"Lauren?" Seth ran his fingertips across my cheek. "Say something."

"I'm sorry," I whispered, sitting up and sliding away. "I can't."

Seth's brows came together.

"Can't or won't?"

I looked at the stars, wishing they held the answer.

"Both," I admitted, taking deep breaths of the cool air and hoping I could get my head on straight. "I need to be on my own." I crossed my arms over my thin camisole.

"Then why did you kiss me like that?"

"Because looking at the stars made me remember the past. Remember us. And I got distracted. But mostly because I'm a jerk." I started to stand, but Seth tugged me back.

"Don't say that. You're mixed up."

I pulled away. "It doesn't matter. I shouldn't confuse you."

"I'm not exactly innocent in all this myself." Seth shook his head. "Besides, my head's already screwed up. It's so hard seeing you every day when I can't hang out with you, talk to you...hold you."

I knew exactly how he felt, but I had to stay strong.

"That's how it has to be until..." I bit back the rest of my sentence, not wanting to give him false hope.

Seth's shoulders slumped as he stood and began collapsing his telescope.

"Until what? What are you looking for, Lauren?"

"I wish I knew."

"Me too." He sighed and stepped down the ladder, telescope under his arm. With a last wave, he slipped into the darkness.

I flopped onto the roof, brushed away my tears, and stared up at the stars, no trace of any meteors visible. Had Seth and I burnt out just as fast?

Chapter Thirteen

I thought about that parting a lot over the next week. I thought about it now, when I was supposed to be getting psyched up for the volleyball playoffs. My cabin mates stretched and joked while we waited for the match before us to finish up. Since I had no interest in watching the younger kids battle it out on the court, my mind wandered back to that night with Seth under the stars. I hadn't been avoiding him since then, exactly, but I also wasn't going to rush back into a relationship with my camp boyfriend.

For one thing, Matt was still here and I respected him too much to jump into Seth's arms after our break-up. Also, I missed Matt, even if my feelings for Seth were still strong. It wasn't fair to date anyone while I was a mixed-up mess. I had to fix myself before I was girlfriend material.

Hannah certainly agreed with that assessment. She'd moved in on Matt so fast it was laughable. I swear she'd cut all her jean shorts another inch shorter in the last week to get him to notice her.

She flounced past now in her gym shorts and tank top, her purple tennis shoes matching the lettering on her shirt that spelled out Divas' Den. None of the other cabins had team uniforms, but rumor had it that Brittany's rich father had sprung for the group's gear.

"Will you look at that?" Alex hissed in my ear between butterfly stretches. "Even their eye shadow matches."

I pressed my knees to the floor with my elbows and noticed that all the Divas wore purple eye makeup.

"A little much for a volleyball game, but we did the same thing on my cheer team. Everything matched, from the lipstick to the hair ribbons to the charm necklace with a megaphone." I'd loved that stash of goodies greeting me in my locker when I'd made the team. The megaphone even had my name on it, an expense financed by our booster club. "We wore gold eye shadow to match our red and gold uniforms."

"Well la-dee-dah," Alex laughed, decidedly unimpressed. "Would they kick you out if your skirt pleats weren't straight?"

I don't know why I ever discussed cheerleading with my friends at camp.

"All I'm saying is that it doesn't make them awful people because they wanted to coordinate."

I stood as the junior kids finished their game and the coaches waved us onto the court.

"Riiight." Alex gave an exaggerated nod as she walked onto the court with me. "And it's totally normal to choose a team based on how well they wear a miniskirt. Just saying."

Instead of thinking about how I was on the outs with Alex or that I had no one to hold hands with at the bonfire tonight, I focused on my competition. Peering over Siobhan's head to check out our opponents, Madison looked half-asleep and Brittany flirted with Eli who watched from the stands. Their team as a whole didn't look like much competition. But from experience, I knew that Hannah could whip these girls into a frenzy during the heat of battle. Never underestimate the motivating force of a mean girl threat. Once, Hannah had told Brittany that Trinity stole her poster of Edward Cullen even though the whole camp knew it was Hannah, fed up with the vampire fetish. Brittany believed it and won the final point for Divas' Den with a serve that nearly took Trinity's head off.

"Are you ready to win, girlfriends?" Emily asked as she set up our water bottles on one side of the court. Her T-shirt had been modified with a green magic marker so that it said "Munchies #1" over the logo. "If we beat the Divas we move on to play for the championship, and you look like champions to me!"

Jackie pumped her fist, and Siobhan nodded. Emily might tread on our privacy and say ridiculously inappropriate things sometimes, but she meant well. After she'd gotten us onto that island for the overnight trip in first place, Jackie seemed to have forgiven her for all the times she'd chased her around with a makeup brush.

We put our hands in for a team cheer and Jackie gave us a pep talk, reminding us of all the times the Divas had screwed us over the years— throwing our clothes in the lake, spreading rumors that weren't true, pranking us with itching powder. Once she had everyone fired up, the whistle blew and the Divas served. It was a weak effort and we scored the first point. But after that, things got tougher. Every point got harder to win. The stands filled with spectators. All the Warriors' Warden guys came, including Matt. They must have their next match on the indoor court.

"Go girls!" A deep voice barked from the stands. I looked up. A muscle-shirt-clad Rob stood beside his charges, hands cupped to his mouth. He turned to the boys in his cabin. "They play harder than you fellows, and they're just a bunch of females."

Emily practically choked Gollum by grabbing his whistle and blowing it hard. We froze.

"Time out! I want this—this—Neanderthal ejected from the game." Emily marched over to Rob. His dimples deepened at her advance.

"On what charge?" Rob's azure eyes swept over the girls, all of us sighing when his gorgeous gaze touched us. Jackie propped up Piper before she hit the ground.

"For your information, their gender has no bearing on how well they play. Your put-downs are a distraction and so are..." she waved her hands around him, "you. Put some clothes on, for God's sake."

Rob pointed at Emily's cherry-red booty shorts with the words "Go For It" scrawled in green marker across the back. "And what the hell is that?"

"Encouragement," Emily shot back. "Something you'll never get. So beat it."

Rob shrugged and grinned.

"My lady's wish is my command." He waved to his crew and sauntered away. "Stop checking me out, Emily," he called over his shoulder.

Emily's cheeks flamed. "That was to make sure you were really gone," she yelled.

"But I'll be back." His eyes gleaming at our flustered counselor. "Depend on it."

Gollum blew his whistle. "Enough. Let the game resume."

We took our positions. When Hannah waved at Matt between serves, I fought the urge to dive under the net and gouge her eyes out. Was that how Matt felt when he saw me talking to Seth?

Distracted, I nearly missed an oncoming ball at the end of the first game. I got my arms under it late and sent it backward instead of over the net, but Piper was right behind me and hit it in the right direction, scoring another point for us.

"Get with the program, Lauren!" Emily called, even though we had won the game.

O-kay. I wasn't sure why the volleyball contest had started feeling like a life or death situation. In theory, I knew we always wanted to beat the Diva girls. But did we need to confer on strategy between every point? The matches were a best of three series, with games played back to back. We only played up to 15 in our camp rules.

The Divas won the next round, in spite of Madison making mistakes every time she touched the ball. For a moment, I remembered her sneaking off the night Matt and I hung out at Highbrooke Falls. Was she overtired from another late-night escapade?

That forced us to game three and frustrated everyone on my team. Trinity bit her lip while Emily tried to give her pointers on the side of the court. Siobhan rehearsed her serve even though she didn't have a ball, her arms going through the motions.

As we got ready, I wondered if there'd always been this level of animosity between our cabins or if there was a new edge to the rivalry this year. While I waited for the next serve, my feet in a ready position, my gaze roamed the crowd again. Still no Seth. But Matt sat next to his friends on the top row of the bleachers. Out of nowhere, Matt looked up as if he sensed me watching him. For a moment, it felt like that first day that I'd cheered at his football practice, because he caught my eye and winked. In all of our months together, it was the first time *he'd* cheered for *me*.

Butterflies tickled my insides. *What was up with that?* Flustered, I barely got my hands under the ball again when a volley came my way. I made the play, but Jackie glared at me.

"Come on, Lauren, we need you."

Crap. I must have imagined that wink anyway, right? The next few points were evenly distributed—Divas, Munchies, Divas, Munchies.

On the opposite side of the net, Hannah shouted reminders to Rachel that Piper had stolen her lean-to on the island during the overnight canoe trip. She antagonized Brittany about the stolen Edward Cullen poster for the third year running, and amazingly I saw Brittany's eyes narrow at us yet again.

In other words, the match turned ugly in the last few minutes as the score tied up at 14. We rotated spots and I ended up on the front row, right across the net from Kayla. She looked as exasperated as I felt, her ponytail slipping sideways and an uncharacteristic shine on her forehead. Her cheeks were a shade of red that didn't come from the latest high-end blush.

"Good luck, Kayla," I stage-whispered to her through the mesh webbing.

She grinned while Rachel called out last-minute instructions to their team. "You too," Kayla called back.

"No fraternizing with the enemy," Emily trilled from the side of the court. "Get ready, girlfriends!"

It bugged me that everyone else thought of the Divas as the Evil Empire. I guess it had been bothering me ever since the canoe trip when we'd all been scared together and holding hands. Well, except for Hannah, but there's one in every crowd. But seriously, Kayla was a nice person and I didn't understand why we couldn't approach the match with a sense of sportsmanship.

In the bleachers, some of the boys from the Warriors' Warden started a chant for the Divas, rooting them on. But it was our turn to serve and our point to win. Plus, Jackie was doing the serving and she was our ace.

Focus.

I knew this game meant the world to the girls in my cabin, so I watched that damn ball volley back and forth so many times I had a headache. I even made a diving set for Piper, who pummeled it into their court and nearly won it for us. But Rachel made a terrific save, getting the ball back into play.

Then Seth walked into the athletic complex. With Breyanna. His hand was on the small of her back as he guided her up the bleachers to a space too small for just friends to sit in. The let-down was crushing.

"Lauren!"

Six people called my name at once, all my teammates and Emily shouting at me. Startled, I looked up in time to see the ball coming toward me too late. I stepped back before it smashed me in the face.

Losing the point for my team. Giving the win to the Divas on a silver platter.

On the other side of the net, squeals and cheers broke out as Kayla and her friends ran to the center of their court for a group hug. My teammates stood frozen in their places for a long moment, as stunned as me that I'd just lost us the game.

Oh. Crap. Guilt sucked me under like a riptide current.

"I'm sorry," I offered lamely, knowing it was inadequate.

What was the matter with me? They'd told me to pay attention but I hadn't. I deserved their wrath.

I expected them to yell at me. Berate me. Wail and gnash teeth. I didn't expect them to storm off the court in a cold, tense fury. But that's exactly what they did. They were too mad for words.

"Wow. What's their problem?" A lone voice came from behind me while the next set of players took the court.

I turned and spotted Brittany as she straightened from where she'd been sorting through a big, floral gym bag. She hauled the straps over her shoulder, her lavender track jacket embroidered with silver scrolling letters that spelled out Divas along one shoulder.

"Everyone thinks I'm an idiot for getting distracted by a boy," I grumbled.

"Well, your timing was perfect for us." She said as we left the volleyball court. "The next team we play for the title is easier to beat than you guys."

"I may never be forgiven." I dodged a junior camper running past me with a butterfly net, a pair of hand-made paper wings attached to her back.

"Well, it would have been nice of you if you *did* let us win because Hannah was going to have a total bitchfest if we lost this one." She pointed wordlessly toward a butterfly on a tree branch, and another circling camper with a net squealed in delight.

Apparently the little kids were having their insect collection day.

"Cool!" I watched the tow-headed girl carefully scoop up the prize catch. "I think it's a Red Admiral," I told her. "Don't lose it."

The kid was already tearing away with her treasure. I was remembering how much more fun it was to go on a bug hunt than play high-stakes volleyball.

"So will your friends forgive you?" Brittany's wide blue eyes blinked up at me as we walked.

"I don't know." I had the feeling I was running out of chances with my camp friends and I wasn't sure how to fix it. Instead of discovering who I was or what I wanted, I'd only managed to alienate everyone else so far. Way to go, Lauren. If I had my pom-poms I'd give myself a big L-O-S-E-R cheer.

"Well, if you can't convince them you didn't rig the game, you can always hang out with us." Brittany ducked under a low branch on the way back to the girls' cabins. "At least when Hannah isn't around."

I laughed. "Thanks. And to set the record straight, I swear no one from my cabin took the Edward Cullen poster."

"Really?" She looked skeptical.

"Honest." I lowered my voice as we neared the cabins. "I heard that Hannah was tired of vampires."

She was quiet as we stopped on the path right behind Divas' Den.

"I might be over vampires too." She'd lowered her voice so much that this was obviously a big-time secret. "Which wouldn't be a big deal, except I'm totally crushing on werewolves now." She gave a shrug that sent her ponytail swinging. "I know your friend Trinity has a cool wolf totem, in fact. Maybe I'll ask her if I can see it sometime. See you at dinner, Lauren."

I stared after her, trying to make sense of that conversation. It had been really cool except for the werewolf part. Was she joking?

But I was willing to overlook it for the sake of a friend. They were way too hard to come by, and Brittany had been nice when no one else would even talk to me. Maybe I needed to look at the rest of camp as a chance to get to know other people better, especially myself.

Chapter Fourteen

"Get going, girls!" Emily shouted from our cabin porch. We vied for a spot at the mirror, needing a last look at makeup and hair before heading to the bonfire.

"Yeah, hurry! I've still got to finish my economics homework when we get back," Siobhan added from outside.

"You should have let me help you," I called out the window.

Siobhan squinted at me through the glare of the porch light. "I couldn't risk you dropping the ball." She and Emily laughed. "Besides, if your calculations are as slow as your reflexes, I would be up till midnight."

Now Emily was howling. *Great.* That was, like, what? The hundredth joke about the volleyball blooper heard round the world?

I glanced up at the nearly full Kindness Cup. Emily had made them drop in chips for every shot and save I had made...but it hadn't really helped. Their joking around still hurt.

I tuned it out as I slumped back on Siobhan's bunk and buried my face in my hands while the rest of the girls in my cabin finished getting ready for the bonfire. What a crappy day. Week. Month, even... My summer of peace had turned into a cold war that felt chillier by the second. I knew my friends cared about me or they wouldn't tell me how they really felt. Or remind me where my loyalties should lie.

But still. We weren't in junior high any more. What had I done except act like a human being around the Divas' Den girls? Date a guy who wasn't Seth?

"All here?" I heard Emily call outside.

"Yes," the group chorused even though I wasn't with them. Used to our group doing everything together, Emily led them away without a head count. Their excited chatter grew fainter as they walked to the bonfire. Instead of racing outside, I stayed put. We all needed space tonight, although it hurt to admit that our tight-knit crew felt close to unraveling.

I stretched out on the bunk and threw an arm across my damp eyes. We should be past fighting about boys or childhood arguments. And if they'd give Matt or the Divas a chance, they'd see we weren't so different. Their fights were probably as ferocious as ours, outfits as carefully planned, and crushes just as painful.

Speaking of which...my eyes drifted across the room to Trinity's diary. She'd left it on her cot and I was dying to know what she'd written about Seth. I knew she was hurting that she couldn't be with him, even as it hurt me to see him with another girl. But I'd never break her trust in a million years.

But then I realized I was lying there, worried about my friends, worried about Seth, worried about Matt, worried about myself. Always about myself. But none of them deserved my self-absorption. It was all about me and it had to stop. Maybe some fresh air would help. I slid into my flip-flops, tugged down my striped tank to meet my jean cut-offs, and made for the door.

A flashlight blared on outside, illuminating a pale face.

"Ahhhhhh!" I stumbled back.

The flashlight clicked off and Brittany stepped inside wearing a periwinkle cotton sundress and white Keds.

"Relax," she laughed. "It's just me."

I drew in a ragged breath. "You scared me."

She smiled wide. "Did you think I was a vampire?" She sauntered to Trinity's cot and fingered the wolf totem hanging from a peg in her bunk railing. "I'm all about werewolves now. I thought I'd stop by and check this out. I saw Trinity bring it to the volleyball game and wanted another look."

I moved between her and the carving. "Trinity wouldn't like you touching her stuff."

Brittany's eyes grew round. "She doesn't like me?"

I swallowed the truth. "No. It's, ummm, she doesn't let anyone mess with her things."

"Oh. I get it." She let go of the totem and smiled at me. "And you look super cute, by the way. Matt's going to go crazy when he sees you."

My traitorous heart leapt at the possibility.

"I thought he was into Hannah now." I tried not to sound as jealous as I felt.

"Hannah wishes. She's totally crushing on him, but all he talks about is you."

"All bad, I bet."

Brittany tugged a few strands free of her ponytail, letting them fall along the sides of her face. "No. Totally the opposite. Hey. Do you have any hairspray?"

So Matt wasn't trash-talking me, *and* he missed me. In a fog of happiness, I climbed the ladder to my bunk and rummaged for the hair product. Maybe I'd pump up the volume on my look too. I twisted the bottom of my hair into ringlets and sprayed. After separating a few to give myself the "didn't-even-try" look, I climbed back down.

"Sorry about taking so long—oh!" I stopped on the last rung, surprising Brittany. She sprang from Trinity's bunk, guilt written across her face with a capital G.

"Oops. Sorry! That wolf totem is irresistible." She clasped her hands behind her like a kindergartener headed for time-out. She walked backwards to the door. "Don't tell Trinity, okay?"

"Sure. Hey. Are you going to the bonfire?" I didn't want to show up alone.

"I'll meet you there. I've got to run to my cabin first." The door swung shut behind her, the velvet darkness swallowing her whole.

I grabbed my flashlight and stopped cold. Trinity's wolf totem hung from the bed rail, but her diary was gone.

"Brittany!" I rushed outside, flashlight bouncing off shrubs and trees. Where was she?

Her cabin was dark. She must have taken the diary. Why?

Whatever the answer, there was only one solution. If I didn't get it back, my stormy friendships would hit Category 5 status. After missing the volleyball, I'd top their suspect list for the missing journal and any secrets it revealed.

*   *   *

A strong hand snaked out from a behind a pine tree, stopping my headlong rush.

"Ahhh!" My flashlight hit the ground and spun like a disco light.

"Lauren. It's me." Matt stepped out of the shadows, the moonlight glancing off his cheekbones. "Can we talk?"

"No time." I grabbed my flashlight and straightened. "I'm really sorry, but this is super important."

Pain flashed across Matt's face, shadows pooling under his eyes. "More important than me?"

Crap. I didn't want to make him feel worse. But Trinity's missing diary was a ticking time bomb. I didn't have a minute to waste.

"What's up?" I adopted a casual tone. Maybe if I kept it light, Matt would too.

I sidestepped Matt's touch and stuffed my hands in my pockets. It was hard to ignore the heady scent of his cologne—a subtle blend of musk and spice that drew me like the moth fluttering around my flashlight. Memories of us twined around each other in the dugout still made me blush.

"Do you miss me?"

I swallowed. "Sometimes." It was as close to the truth as I dared admit.

Matt hugged me. I let myself enjoy the smell and feel of him for a sec before I pushed against his chest. "Matt. Let go."

"I can't," he said, then released me anyway.

"This is hard on both of us. But it's necessary. Trust me."

Matt exhaled. "I'm trying, Laur. But everywhere I look you're there."

I opened my mouth, but Matt held up a hand. "I know I could have left camp for football, but I'm starting to figure out what I want for my future. The only problem is that every version includes you."

My heart squeezed. Ohmigod. That was beautiful. But it also made me more certain about our breakup. Matt needed space as much as I did, he just didn't realize it.

I touched his tensed arm, my fingertips lingering on his strong bicep before I forced myself to say, "If we're meant to be, then it will work out. Just give it time."

"How much time?"

"I don't know, Matt."

Raucous laughter erupted from the bonfire. Could it have to do with Trinity's diary? My panicked gaze flew down the dark path, then back to Matt.

"Just don't make me wait too long," he said and started toward the bonfire.

I jogged after him, unable to keep up with his long strides. "What does that mean?" I called to his disappearing back. Heaviness settled in my lungs, making it hard to breathe.

When I reached the smoky clearing, Matt was already beside Hannah. Was she the reason he didn't want to wait?

But my jealous heart seized when I spied what she held. Clutched in her red-tipped fingers was an all too familiar book.

Chapter Fifteen

"Hannah." I sprinted over. "That's Trinity's. Give it." I glanced at my Munchies' Manor friends who were engrossed in their own conversation. Thankfully, they hadn't noticed the diary drama. But how long could I keep them in the dark? I'd have to work fast.

Hannah tilted her head. "Trinity's? How do I know for sure without checking?" Her mouth twisted into to a smirk. "A journal in the wrong hands could be very damaging."

I lunged, but she tossed it to Eli. He caught it and did a touchdown dance beside the fire.

"Don't worry." Hannah widened her eyes, all innocence. "Eli will get to the bottom of it."

"You're the one who should be worried." I stomped toward Eli, already concocting ways to take my revenge on Hannah and Brittany. My friends had been right. These girls didn't deserve a second chance.

"Temper. Temper." Hannah said behind me. "You're so lucky to be rid of her, Matt."

Matt murmured something I couldn't make out, then Gollum's whistle blew. Silence descended on the chattering group.

The wind picked up the three strands of his comb-over, his expression serious. I shivered, reminded of our canoe trip panic attack. What was wrong now?

Alex turned and caught my eye. She glanced from me to Eli, shaking her head at our proximity. I knew what she was thinking. Once again, I'd wound up on the wrong side during an emergency.

"Madison Bechard has run away," Gollum announced abruptly. "She left a note sometime after dinner and hasn't been seen since." He cast a disparaging eye at the Divas' counselor Victoria, who at least had the good sense to look remorseful.

"Counselors, meet me in the parking lot for a search," Gollum continued. "She couldn't have gone far on foot."

The breeze died down and his hair strands fell beside his left ear. Despite the humid air, I trembled. Who exactly had Madison been meeting at the hermit's hut? The camp rumor was that she was seeing an older guy. Had she run off with him? Was she safe?

Nervous, I raised my hand. "Mr. Woodrow. I saw Madison sneaking off toward the hermit's hut a few weeks ago."

Hannah and her gang shot me a venomous look. I hated to tattle, but Madison could be in danger.

Gollum snorted. "Don't you think that's the first place we looked?" Horrified looks crisscrossed the clearing. How long had the counselors known about our hideout?

"Anything else?" Gollum reached for his whistle.

I raised my hand again. Most of the Divas' Den girls put their hands on their hips and glared. Only Kayla looked as worried as I felt.

"She was seeing an older guy," I offered. "Someone who doesn't go to this camp."

Gollum stepped close, a twig snapping underfoot like a gunshot.

"Name?"

I shook my head. "That's all I got, sorry."

Gollum grabbed his whistle and blasted it.

"All right people, this may now be a kidnapping. Counselors, assemble in the parking lot while I call the police. Victoria, you're in charge."

Victoria gave a nod, although she looked way too distracted to oversee anything. She paced around the bonfire, in her own world.

Gollum jogged away as Bam-Bam pulled a pair of goggles from his camouflage vest.

"Those have night vision," Emily announced. "If anyone can capture a runaway, it'll be Bam-Bam. He can see anything in those."

Hannah smirked. "Anything? Like what, Emily?"

"Well, there was this one time when we were—" Emily prattled before Bam-Bam cleared his throat. Red crept up Emily's neck. "Well, no time to waste with stories." She pulled Bam-Bam into the woods.

Rob shook off another female counselor's clutches and stomped behind them. The rest of the adults followed, leaving us with no one but Victoria, who'd already wandered twenty yards away in her pacing. I saw a light flash near her ear and got the impression she was on a contraband cell phone.

"Sweet. Freedom!" Eli punched Trinity's journal skyward. I rushed him, but he danced out of reach.

"What's the problem, Lauren?" Hannah sang. "Fair's fair. You blabbed Madison's secrets, so now we'll spill Trinity's."

A quick glance to my Munchies' Manor friends showed they'd finally caught the exchange. They gaped while Trinity sent me a death glare.

I looked at Matt for help. He shifted on his feet, his inaction reminding me of how he'd stayed out of Crash's science-project demolition. He lifted an eyebrow, as if waiting for me to fix this mess.

"Give it back, Eli," Seth's deep voice sounded to my right. My chest loosened. Finally, someone was stepping up to help me. But when I glanced over, Trinity clung to his arm. Was he aiding her or me?

A couple of Warriors stepped up and blocked Seth. The moment grew tense as both sides of the campfire eyed each other in a scene straight out of West Side Story.

"You're dead meat, Eli!" Piper shouted. The worst insult from a vegan.

"That's not yours," Siobhan growled, her tiny frame advancing on Eli.

"July 25th," Eli read aloud in a falsetto voice, Trinity's diary open. "Seth is sooooo hot. I know we'd make the perfect couple if only Lauren would leave him alone. She brought a boyfriend to camp but still wants Seth. Every time we're together I want to kiss him."

Eli made kissing noises, sending the younger campers into a giggle fit. Alex, Piper and Siobhan rushed to Trinity and held her as she cried. Matt glared, no doubt furious with the reference to Seth and me.

Jackie strolled toward the biggest Warrior guarding Eli. My breath caught. The boys might be taken in by Jackie's looks, but her body looked coiled and ready to spring. Oh, it was on now.

Jackie's white teeth appeared in a come-hither grin.

"What's up, Momma?" Eli raised his eyebrows and hitched up his slipping shorts. Neither boy saw the flash of Jackie's fist as she clocked the biggest boy, toppling him like a bowling pin.

Victoria circled us again, definitely holding one hand over a cell phone while she shouted over a vague order for us to "settle down" before returning to her call. No wonder Madison had gotten away with so much.

With everyone preoccupied, I seized my chance. Eli had a big personality, but his small body was no match for a highly conditioned cheerleader on a mission. A high kick sent the diary spinning out his hands and into the fire. In seconds, Trinity's incriminating words vanished into the flames. If only I could make the fall-out disappear as easily.

I rushed to Trinity. "I'm so sorry. You guys were right. They're all jerks."

Trinity's eyes were red and blurry. I reached out a hand but Siobhan stopped me. "Trinity doesn't want you right now."

"I'm her friend," I said, confused. "I got rid of her journal."

"But who let them have it in the first place? Friends don't give diaries to the enemy." Trinity nodded over at Hannah and Eli's bunch, who were still laughing and making kissing noises.

My mouth dropped. "I didn't give it to them."

"Right." Jackie shook her head in disgust. "And you weren't responsible the last time you screwed us over either, were you? We've heard enough excuses," Jackie fumed as Seth joined us. Trinity stumbled into Seth's arms and sobbed. His eyes were as stormy as the rest. I don't know what hurt more, seeing his arms around her or the anger in his face.

He—of all people—didn't believe me?

I stepped back and bumped into Kayla. She twined her hand in mine, an unexpected ally when everyone else seemed to hate me.

Strengthened by her support, I said, "If you believe I'd do something that low, then you don't know me."

"And *you* know who you are?" Piper cocked her head and studied me. "We loved you, Lauren. The old you. This new one, we don't even want to know."

I looked around, shocked to see them all nodding. Seth remained stony-faced. My cheeks were damp and my nose stung like I'd leapt from our pool's high dive and hit bottom.

"Lauren, you can stay at our cabin. Madison's bunk was above mine." Kayla put in. "Even if they catch her, Gollum's never letting her back at camp."

I glanced from the girls at Divas' Den to Munchies' Manor and shook my head. I might not know who I was, but I definitely knew who I was not. I wouldn't take up residence with people who stole diaries.

"Go, Lauren." Trinity's voice was muffled by Seth's damp shoulder. "You're more like them now."

A part of me curled up black and crisp at their collective nod. They were kicking me out.

Kayla tugged me away. I walked backwards, hoping someone would call out, stop me from leaving. But they turned away, closing ranks.

Numb, I followed Kayla up the path to my cabin. I sank to the wood floor and pointed when she asked me which stuff was mine. Drained, I watched her pack my gear, unable to process that this was really happening. I'd been friends with these girls for years and now they didn't want anything to do with me.

"Hannah's going to be jealous when she sees this." Kayla pointed at my Gucci bag, her side ponytail swinging in the same direction.

I shrugged, her words barely penetrating the fog of hurt that swirled around me. How had things gotten this bad? Was I about to become a Divas' Den girl? It was exactly the kind of mean, popular girl type I'd wanted to leave behind in Texas.

Except for Kayla. And hey, one friend was more than I had in the Munchies' Manor cabin at the moment. My hand trailed over Alex's bunk, my heart in my throat.

Kayla folded my tank tops in threes and matched the seams of my shorts before laying them in the suitcase. Outside, campers returning from the bonfire shouted things like, "Seth my love," and "Kiss me." Urgency had me kneeling beside Kayla, stuffing the rest of my things in the bag and zipping it up.

"You don't want to take a look around?" Kayla held out my pillow. "Make sure you're not leaving anything important?"

I shook my head, needing to get out of there before Trinity and the rest returned. I couldn't face their accusations again. Or Seth comforting Trinity.

Kayla stopped my headlong rush out of the cabin with a hug.

"It's going to be alright, Lauren. You're moving on, that's all."

She was right, I thought, my suitcase wheels making grooves in the ground behind me. But was I moving in the right direction?

*   *   *

"What the hell was Kayla thinking?" Hannah's voice poured from the screen windows as we approached Divas' Den. Something snuffled in a bush beside me and I moved closer to Kayla.

Bumps in the night woods could give you a lot more than chills.

"What's the dif?" I heard Rachel say. "We've got an extra bunk."

"Losers don't sleep here," Hannah's voice sounded final.

I dropped my bag and stood on the path. No way was I entering that lion's den. Kayla squeezed my arm, her lips straining upward in a failed attempt at a reassuring smile.

"She doesn't dance like a loser. We could use her for our talent show routine," I heard Brittany say. "With her fan kicks, we can't lose. Besides," she continued. "You owe me, Hannah. You promised the diary wouldn't go public. Why did you do that?"

"I saw Seth and Lauren together that night on the canoe trip and thought she would have mentioned it to Trinity. I thought, if it was in the diary, I could show Matt that Lauren was still into Seth."

"But it *wasn't* in the diary," Brittany practically shouted. "I thought you were going to sew it shut or put more itching powder on it or...I don't know. How could you do that to those girls?"

It made me feel slightly better to know at least that Brittany hadn't wanted to out Trinity's secrets to the world.

Still, Hannah's giggle made my fingers tighten on the handle of my suitcase.

"Either way it worked. Now Matt knows Lauren's been chasing Seth behind his back and Seth thinks Lauren stole the diary from their clique. It's a win – win," she crowed. "Now Matt will stop caring about the phony and be with me."

Kayla's horrified eyes met mine. She shook her head, and I understood what she was trying to say, that she had had no part of Hannah's plan. Kayla might be nice, but how could I share a cabin with someone like Hannah? I'd probably end up with a venomous snake in my bed.

"At least with Lauren staying here, Matt will be around more." Rachel's voice sounded muffled, like she was brushing her teeth.

"True." High-heeled sandals clicked across the cabin floor.

"Do you want to go back?" Kayla whispered in my ear. I shook my head. There was nowhere else to go.

The bush beside me shook again. I froze when a skunk waddled out and stopped before us. Kayla gripped my arm and squealed. Didn't she know we had to stay still in case the skunk got spooked and....

Foul oil skirted from behind his tail, coating us in its deep stench.

...sprayed.

I gagged as Kayla ran to the side of the cabin and retched.

"Fine," Hannah harrumphed. "I guess Lauren will have her uses so... Hey, what's that smell?"

My temper rose along with my stench. Grabbing my suitcase, I stormed up the porch steps and banged open the front door to their cabin.

"It's your new roommate, Lauren," I charged inside, dragging in the evil odor with me.

The girls dove for their sleeping bags, choking sounds erupting from beneath their pillows.

I smiled despite the throat-convulsing odor. At least Hannah wouldn't be the only rotten egg in here.

Chapter Sixteen

Cold water pelted my back the next morning, the hot water long gone.

"Lauren," Kayla yelled from the shower stall next to mine. A hand holding a tomato juice can appeared over the wall. "You want more?"

I grabbed the container and poured the thick red liquid over my head. Spaghetti and meatballs would never taste the same again. My scalp burned as I scrubbed it for the fourth time.

"Any luck?" Kayla called. Her shower turned off and the curtain rustled open.

I took a cautious inhale and gagged.

Yup. I stilled smelled like that old time Looney Tunes skunk, Pepé le Pew. Except Pepé always got the girl. As for me, I'd be lucky if either Matt or Seth was even speaking to me. Smell or no, they both thought I was rotten—Seth for believing I'd given Hannah the diary, and Matt for thinking I'd been after Seth while dating him.

What a ginormous mess.

I turned off the water and shivered at the icy flow running down my calves. Where did they pipe this water from, the Arctic?

Wrapping a towel around my body, I stepped into my flip-flops, then pushed aside the shower curtain. Kayla waited in the changing area, bedraggled hair hanging in her face. She sniffed as I approached.

"You reek."

I grinned. My first smile in—geez, I honestly couldn't remember. "And you're one to talk? Who do you think got us into this mess?"

Kayla giggled, pulling her underwear up under her towel, then fastening her bra over it before pulling the terrycloth away. I followed suit.

The door banged open. A group of pre-teens stared at us, sniffed, and bolted back down the path.

That got us laughing. By the time we were fully dressed, me in a blue and green tie-dye tank top and cut-off shorts and Kayla in a white polo and navy shorts, I was feeling a little more human.

Last night, we'd slept in our sleeping bags on the porch, Hannah waking us with complaints of our smell every time we managed to drift off.

"You want breakfast?" Light glinted off of Kayla's blond highlights as we stepped out in the dewy morning.

I shook my head. "Ugh. I smell so bad I'm making myself sick."

"Well, I didn't want to say anything..." Kayla slanted her blue eyes at me. I picked a pinecone off the path and threw it at her.

"Hey!" she laughed and chucked one back. In seconds we were in a full-on cone war, needles flying, hands filled with sap. I tugged a sticky missile out of my hair just as my former Munchies' Manor friends appeared on the path, heading for breakfast.

They held their noses as they passed. Piper looked me up and down. "Looks like someone pissed off Mother Earth."

Jackie peered over her shoulder. "Now she smells on the outside the way she is on the inside." The group turned and marched away, their heads close and whispers audible.

Kayla looked at me in sympathy. "Those are some mean girls."

I opened my mouth to protest, then closed it. She was right. They had their moments of mean just like the Divas had their moments of nice. Nothing was as black and white as it seemed.

"Wanna head down to the nurse? See if she has anything?"

"Are you kidding? The most she can give us is, like, baby aspirin. Let's go see my boy." Kayla jumped over a boulder in the path that led toward the boys' section.

"Cameron, right?" I scurried after her. He was a Warrior known for sneaking in camp contraband. An illicit thrill shot through me. I was now *officially* a rule breaker.

We sprinted up the path, following the long shadows that stretched before us. I pulled up short at Warriors' Warden, suddenly remembering Matt. Would I see him? My heart began to race.

Kayla cupped her hands and raised her voice. "Morning, Cam. Can you come outside?"

A moment later, Cameron appeared at the screen door, his arms gripping the overhead casing. A large hand loomed from behind and tousled his already-spiked hair. A second later, Matt's grinning face showed beside Cameron's. His smile faded when he saw me, his nose curling. I studied my chipped blue toenails.

"What the hell happened to you guys?" The door hinges creaked. I peeked up to see Cameron and Matt spill out onto the porch. Matt's shirtless physique drew my eye, muscles rippling in a way that made me sigh.

"We went to a spa. What do you think happened to us?" Kayla's hands fisted on her tiny hips.

Cameron narrowed his dark brown eyes and sniffed. "I don't know if I can fix this in time."

"In time for what?"

He motioned for us to come closer. It was a brave thing to do, considering our smell could strip paint. He lowered his voice.

"A bunch of us are sneaking out to the D&O tonight."

Kayla squealed. *"Ohmigod.* The Down and Out. Love, love that place. You are so not going without us." Kayla stamped her feet hard enough to lose a sandal. "Cam. You have to fix this."

"Alright. But it'll cost you. How much have you got? I could use a new shirt for tonight." Cameron plucked at his faded, olive-green tee.

"Excuse me?" Kayla picked her sparkly daisy sandal up from the bottom step and shook it at him. "You're my boyfriend. I shouldn't have to pay."

He backed into the cabin. "Business is business, babe. When you've got the cash, I'll see what I can do."

"But we didn't bring any," Kayla pleaded.

The screen door clicked shut in answer.

"Scrooge!" she yelled, then turned to me. "Wait here. I'll go get the money." With that she took off, leaving Matt and me alone. Awkward.

"So..." Matt stuffed his hands in his low-slung tan cargo shorts and leaned against a birch post. I tried to ignore the sun glistening on his six-pack abs and failed. God, he was gorgeous.

I met his emerald eyes. "So..." I trailed off. Super awkward.

"Are you hanging with us tonight, or with Seth?" He hopped off the porch, made a face, then jogged back up the stairs. "Wow. That *is* strong." He coughed, eyes watering.

"Thanks. I think I'll bottle it as a boy repellant."

I watched a pair of birds snipe at each other, flitting from branch to branch, fighting for territory.

Matt gave me a rueful smile. "Well. It's not exactly working on me."

I tried to fight the wave of pleasure rushing through me and failed.

"Matt. You know we're only friends, right?"

Matt's face darkened. "According to Trinity's diary, I guess we've been 'only friends' longer than I thought." He turned as if to leave.

"Matt," my soft plea stopped him. "It's complicated. But trust me. Everything I said, everything we did, I meant."

He turned, his long brown bangs falling in front of his expressive eyes. "Problem is that you meant it with Seth too."

I opened my mouth and closed it. He was right. I'd come to camp thinking I wanted Seth but was obligated to Matt. Now my feelings had grown for both.

"I also meant it when I said I needed time to work things out. I didn't appreciate the pressure you put on me last night."

Matt shrugged, broad shoulders bunching. "I'm only human. How long am I supposed to wait?"

"No one asked you to wait. Do what you want," I stormed off. It was wrong to expect him to put his life on hold while I figured out mine. But I couldn't help wishing he would.

Matt gripped the porch rail and leaned over. "Fine. I will. Starting tonight at the D&O."

A vision of Hannah and Matt snuggled in the corner of the backwoods bar gripped me.

"Fine. I'll see you there," I spat.

Matt's hair slid across his cut cheekbones as he tilted his head and studied me, a knowing grin playing on his full lips. My breath rushed out. I'd fallen neatly into his little trap.

Matt turned. "Yo! Cam. You got something for Lauren or what? She's going with us tonight."

"Relax, Bro!" Cameron came through the door. He held up a spray bottle that read "Skunk-Off." "It's my last one, so it's going to cost you."

"I've got it." Matt grabbed the can and tossed it to me.

"Matt. No. Kayla will be back in a minutes and—" I made as if to throw it back, but he and Cameron ducked inside the cabin.

"Are you going to be at the volleyball game?" Matt's eyes weren't any less green through the screen door. I nodded before I could think. Wait. Was today the day they played Seth's cabin? Crap.

"Good. Cheer me on." With a wink he disappeared in the darkened interior.

I turned at the sound of Kayla panting up the path. She jogged to a halt, her eyebrows knitting when she looked at my face.

"What's wrong? Did you get what we needed?"

I held up the bottle. "And then some."

*   *   *

Since our odorous condition meant we were excused from regular activities, Kayla and I spent the day at the beach. Between the fresh air, sun, swimming and spraying each other with Skunk-Off, we were finally odor-free. By the time the afternoon shadows had chased us halfway down the sand, the players arrived at the volleyball net on the beach.

Rob and his Warriors jogged onto the court. All were shirtless and had painted giant blue "W"s on their backs. Behind them sauntered Hannah, wearing little more than wedge heels, a sheer cover-up and a scarlet bikini. The rest of Divas' Den set up beach chairs. My heart lifted to see the two extra seats Rachel had set up beside her and Brittany. I'd forgotten how good it felt to be included.

When we reached Brittany, her face nearly matched her violet one-piece swimsuit.

"What's up with her?" Kayla flopped in one of the chairs and took the Diet Coke Rachel passed her under the chair.

Rachel lowered her dark sunglasses and leaned forward. "Smell's gone, Brit."

Brittany's chest heaved as she sucked in air. "*Ohmigod*. Was that smell disgusting or what?" She passed another soda to me, hidden in a towel. I nodded thanks to Rachel and snuck a peek to see if Rob or any counselors were looking. Campers were only allowed juice, milk, and water. I took a quick sip and sighed, loving the icy feel of the fizzy drink running down the back of my throat.

A soft hand landed on my elbow. I glanced up and met Brittany's eyes through her star-shaped sunglasses. "So sorry about the diary, Lauren. I never thought—I mean, I didn't think that— well, Hannah *promised* and I owed her a favor and—oh God. I'm so sorry." She spoke fast, her embarrassment palpable. She hadn't meant any harm.

I tried to smile, but failed. That prank had really, really hurt my friends.

"Maybe it all worked out for the best," I murmured as Seth's team wandered onto the court, Breyanna tagging along. Behind them were Alex, Jackie, Piper and Trinity. I supposed Siobhan must have stayed behind to do some paper on Shakespeare or work out the mathematical variations of calculus—something I would have helped her finish in time for the match, I thought with a pang.

"Go Seth," cheered Breyanna. Her polka-dot headband flashed as she twirled, arms wide. Seth ducked his head in that boyish way that made my heart leap and smiled at her. Emptiness gutted my heart. That smile belonged to someone else now.

"Are you cold? You're shaking." Brittany draped her towel across my shoulders.

My lips curled in gratitude. "Thanks. Have you guys heard what happened to Madison?"

Brittany leaned close. "They found her in a Motel 6 with some guy whose ID said he was thirty. So gross. And I know he told Madison he was only twenty-one."

I pulled the towel edges closed and shivered. "Glad they found her."

"I bet she's even happier." Brittany nodded solemnly. "Except now she's got to go home to her step-monster. Oh look. The game's starting."

"Let's go, ladies," Rob boomed. His team lined up, Matt in the front.

Bam-Bam jerked his thumb at the court. "Move 'em out, grunts." The Wander Inn gang took their places. My heart stopped as Seth stopped in front of Matt across the net. Matt leaned forward at the waist, his knees slightly bent. Seth stood with his legs wide apart, arms across his chest, death in his eyes. I couldn't see Matt's expression, but I was sure it wasn't any better. They looked ready for pistols at dawn rather than a volleyball match.

Emily sprang from a piece of driftwood and wrapped her legs around Bam-Bam's waist. "Kill 'em!" she shouted, then kissed him long and hard.

Gollum's whistle blast startled Rob, who'd stared at the spectacle with the rest of us.

"Yuck. Like, what does she see in him? Rob is way hotter." Brittany's gold bangles slid along her forearms as she lathered on tanning lotion.

"Totally. And Bam-Bam's worn the same shirt since we got here. Like, get a wardrobe." Hannah pulled her cover-up over her head, immediately gaining lots of male attention. Matt, I noticed with some satisfaction, kept his focus on his competition instead.

"I think that's his army gear. You know, from Iraq," I murmured, my focus still on Seth and Matt. If looks could kill... I couldn't finish the thought.

"Hello, the war is over. Read a paper once in a while. No offense," Hannah shot back.

"Sorry, I don't subscribe to *Popstar!* magazine. What does Justin Bieber have to say about world affairs?" I enjoyed the telltale red blossoming in her cheeks. Guess I hadn't ditched my inner bitch after all.

Kayla, Rachel, and Brittany's heads swiveled back and forth between Hannah and me. I sank back in my seat and took another sip of soda. Point, game, match. Lauren. Why was it easier to fit in with the queen bees than my former quirky friends? The possible answer frightened me.

A sharp whistle started the action. The Wander Inn, winners of the coin toss, served first. Vijay's overhand hit landed in the far left corner with a sand spray and a loud whoop from Alex. But his second serve initiated an intense, minute-long volley. It ended when Devon, a world-class flirt from the Warriors' Warden, got distracted by Emily's thong-baring sneaker tie. He completely lost track of the ball. When the guys in his cabin chided him, he shrugged it off and winked at Emily, earning a growl from Bam-Bam.

The next three points went to the Warriors and then another to the Wander Inn guys when Seth ate sand for a diving save. He set up an over-sized teammate for a hard spike that sent the Warriors scrambling.

After that, things seemed to settle in with both sides scoring in equal amounts. Before we knew it, the dinner bell rang and we were down to match point. Seth and Matt were facing off once more at the net, with Eli serving.

He smacked the ball to the far right where Garrett locked his forearms and crouched for a deep dig that sent the ball spinning into the stratosphere. When it finally remembered the laws of gravity and returned to earth, the ball came down toward the net, right between Seth and Matt. Both leaped at the net, Seth for the spike, Matt for the block. I half-rose out of my chair as their bodies collided. The ball fell between them, though it happened so fast I couldn't tell which team won the point and game.

"Yes!" Matt punched the air, lowered his arm, and pointed at Seth's red face. "Win!"

"No freaking way!" Seth hollered back. "The ball was over the net."

My knuckles grew tight around the arms of my beach chair.

Matt's jaw jutted. "It was on your side."

Seth crossed his arms, biceps tensing. "Then why's the ball over there?" He nodded to Matt's side of the court.

"'Cause that's where it landed after it hit your foot," Matt growled, his fist clutching the net and lifting it.

"That's bullsh—"

The whistle screeched.

"Enough!" Gollum's square body waded into the fray. "As the official, I make the calls."

"So make it already, Drama Queen," Hannah whispered, making Brittany giggle. I glared at her, knowing that, whatever the outcome, there'd be consequences. This wasn't a moment for jokes.

"Point and," Gollum drawled, "game go to..." All right. I had to give it to Hannah, he was enjoying the suspense. "The Wander Inn," he intoned. "Now everyone get to dinner."

Cheers erupted from the opposite side of the net. Bam-Bam crushed Emily in a bear hug. Rob drop-kicked his gym bag into the woods and stormed after it.

Alex kissed Vijay in a way that was more NC-17 than PG-13, while Breyanna wrapped her arms around a sweaty Seth. My eyes met his over her shoulder, his pained expression reflecting my feelings.

"Lauren," Matt called to my left. I broke eye contact and looked his way. He was bright red, chest heaving. "Can I have some of that soda?"

"How about Gatorade?" I hurried over to the team cooler and poured some into a plastic cup. As a cheerleader, I'd always done this for him, an old habit that died hard. Funny. It hadn't occurred to me to ask him to do the same at my volleyball game.

I met Seth's eyes as I handed over the cup. He looked from the cup to me and frowned. After giving the clinging girl a squeeze, he backed away.

"What an ass," Matt muttered when Seth led his team in a rousing rendition of "We Are the Champions" on their way to the showers. Since losers washed up last, some of Matt's teammates had jumped in the lake. The Divas' Den girls followed.

"You want to go in?" Matt nodded to the water.

I shook my head and looked down. "Sorry I wasn't your lucky charm today."

Matt lifted my face, eyes searching mine. "You being here was the lucky part."

My heart somersaulted at his sweet words.

Sand kicked at my ankles as he raced for the splashing group and plunged in. Mouth open, I watched the raucous crowd. I always thought Matt saw me as an accessory to his glory- filled life, the adoring cheerleader girlfriend straight out of a movie cliché. I'd never known he thought of me as the star.

Chapter Seventeen

Six hours later, I was wedged between Hannah and Matt in the back of a pickup headed to the D&O, the only bar around that was so backwoods that IDs were optional...possibly even discouraged, since most of the customers lived off the grid.

Cameron had arranged for one of the groundskeepers to pick us up at the edge of camp, a much longer walk when wearing a black micro-mini dress and a pair of four-inch platform heels, both borrowed from Kayla. Hannah kept leaning around me, chatting up Matt. Little did she know that his thumb was surreptitiously stroking the side of my bare thigh, sending shivers of excitement that had little to do with the air flowing over the cab.

"Your skin is so soft." His husky voice filled my ear.

"Stop it."

"Excuse me?" Hannah recoiled, her lips pursed tight enough to spit nails.

I widened my eyes innocently. "Nothing."

Hannah crossed her arms and flounced back. "Yeah, right," she whispered.

I leaned over her toward Kayla, the wind whipping my hair in Hannah's pouting face. "You look nice, Kayla." And she did. In a white lace tank top and low-slung jeans, the tan she'd acquired from our marathon beach time today glowed to perfection.

"You too," she shouted over the roaring engine. She turned toward Brittany, who was busy making out with Eli, then turned back. "How much longer?"

The truck swerved hard enough to make us tumble like bowling pins. I was a nauseous bundle of nerves at the thought of going to my first bar, and this roller-coaster drive was not helping.

"Looks like we're here." I spit hair out my mouth and accepted Matt's hand up. I pulled up the dress's plunging neckline, otherwise loving my sophisticated new look and the way it hugged my new curves.

Devon caught me around the waist, helped me off the flatbed, and whirled me around the gravel parking lot to a thumping country tune. A couple of plaid-shirted men leaning against the a truck whistled, their cowboy hats shadowing their faces.

"Girl, you are hotter than a shot of Tabasco sauce," Devon laughed. "Ooooh *weee*." He shook his hands like I'd burnt them, making me giggle with him. He might be a world-class flirt, but he was harmless. Not that Matt seemed to feel that way. The storm cloud hovering over his head had the other boy backing away fast.

"Guys! Come on." Cameron held the door of a one-story building that could have fit in my grandparents' pool house. A neon light in the single window glowed "Redneck Approved." Looking around the parking lot, I realized it was packed with pick-ups. Any cars that dared show their grills were American.

I hitched up my top again and followed the group, wondering if the jukebox would stop the minute we entered—a bunch of privileged camp kids out for a lark amongst hardworking adults. But the honky-tonk tune kept blaring as we closed the door. Guess we all needed an escape. That much, at least, we had in common.

"Want to dance?" Matt asked low and fast in my ear.

"Matt. Please," I protested, admiring the handsome picture he made in a brown suede cowboy hat that set off his eyes, a fitted plaid shirt, jeans, and scuffed cowboy boots.

He swung me in his strong arms.

"Well, you don't have to beg." He grinned, apparently thinking he'd outmaneuvered me. Over his shoulder, I caught Hannah's poisonous stare and let him circle me around the peanut shell-covered floor a few times before I broke free. I couldn't deny how good it felt to be in his arms again. But slipping back into a relationship with him was exactly what I didn't need.

"What's wrong?" His eyebrows rose, his hands reeling me back in. "I'm just being friendly. Isn't that what you want? To be friends?"

I jerked back and frowned. "Matt. Knock it off. If you want to dance, ask Hannah."

In the ladies room, I crowded beside Kayla and Brittany for an inch of mirror space as Hannah washed up in the sink.

"So what's the deal? Are you and Matt together again?" Brittany rubbed her crimson lips together before turning to me.

"No. Just friends." I gasped at the havoc the ride over had played on my hair. "Anyone have a brush?"

Kayla handed me a mini pink one. "That looked *super*friendly to me." She winked and snapped her bag shut when I handed back the brush.

"Seriously. I, I..." God. How to explain that I didn't want the hottest guy in camp? They'd be as confused as my Munchies' Manor friends had been about my rejecting Seth.

"Want space?" Hannah spoke up behind us.

I whirled around. "How did you know?"

She tightened the backing on one of her emerald-cut diamond earrings. "Like, when have we ever seen you without a guy, Lauren? It's about time." Her heels clicked away, and the door swished shut behind her.

Brittany, Kayla and I looked at each other, eyes wide. I hadn't thought the girls knew I existed before this year, let alone that I'd been dating.

"She's right," Brittany spoke up. "Why do we need guys anyway?"

"Ummmm...to kiss," Kayla put in.

Brittany shrugged. "Eli's breath smells like Pringles. Not to mention his stupid little pranks. I say we all break up with our men, enjoy a summer of freedom."

"Yeah, but Cameron totally saved our butts this morning by giving us his last can of Skunk-Off. Plus he got us the ride here."

Brittany fluffed her hair in the mirror and turned. "I heard Matt paid Cameron for the can since he wouldn't give it to you. Besides, didn't we all pay the driver like five bucks?"

Kayla looked confused. "Yeah. But—"

"But nothing. Kayla. He's cheap. If he's this way about bug spray—"

"Skunk spray," Kayla interrupted.

Brittany sighed. "Whatever. Imagine how he'll be at your high school graduation. 'Oh, here's a pen, Kayla, so you can write me.' Or at your wedding. 'Who needs a band when we can do karaoke?'"

Kayla's face grew more horrified by the second. A toilet flushed behind us and Rachel emerged. We made way for her at the mirror after she rinsed her hands.

"Brit's right, Kayla. Cheap is cheap. I say we make a pact. Let's make the rest of camp a no-boy summer." She held up a freshly washed pinky.

I grinned and curled mine around hers. "I'm in."

"So in. *Buh*-bye, Pringles breath." Brittany's finger wound around ours. We looked expectantly at Kayla. She shook her head, then extended her little finger.

"All right, but if I need a hug one of you is giving it to me."

We all piled in for one anyway. Something light bubbled inside of me as their warm arms wrapped around me. I'd felt so alone at camp these past few weeks. In the most unlikely places, at the strangest moment, I finally felt accepted. Who would have guessed?

Kayla and Brittany decided not to ruin the night, and would break things off on the ride home. So the rest of our time flashed by in a blur of sweaty line dancing, root beer pong (the only version the owner would let us play), darts, and a burping contest which Brittany won with a one-minute blast that grossed out Eli enough to break up with *her*. He was still shaking his head at her hysterical laughing fit—not the reaction he'd expected.

Kayla and Cameron argued on the way home when he insisted on her paying her share of the soft drinks. I couldn't help but notice Matt paid for all of Hannah's sodas and spent most of his time with her, his eyes wandering to me enough to let me know he hoped I was watching. Which I was. Damn him.

Back at camp, we piled out and stumbled wearily down the path. Since we'd closed the bar, it was well past three in the morning. I couldn't imagine the pain of hearing the opening notes of the camp wake-up call in just three and a half hours.

"Hey," someone called from the woods to our right. I'd know that voice anywhere.

"Seth?" I wobbled over to the bushes, my tired ankles hardly able to keep me upright after my long night, the rest of the group behind me. The shoes I'd borrowed had turned into torture devices shortly after midnight.

"You're drunk." Seth stepped into the walkway, his face shadowed and tense.

"Are you kidding?" I went to push him, but my blistered foot gave out and I stumbled forward.

Matt reached to steady me, holding me against his pounding chest. Hannah tried to pull him away, but he shook her off.

"What the hell are you doing out here, Reines? And why are you bothering Lauren?" The Warriors circled behind Matt. Kayla gave a nervous squeak.

"I'll talk to Lauren whenever I want to," Seth snarled, clearly unimpressed with the muscle massing against him. "I've known her longer than you."

Matt's grip on my arms tightened. "She's been my girlfriend for eight months."

Brittany crept closer to hold my other hand.

"Not anymore," Seth spit out, features sharpening.

"At least I wasn't the dumbass that dumped her every summer."

In a movement too fast to register, Kayla and Brittany pulled me away as Seth lunged. In seconds, fists flew. I stumbled back and barely kept my balance. My hand rose to my mouth. How could I stop it? It'd be like getting between a car and a metal crusher.

Matt took an upper cut to the jaw that sent him reeling back. But when Seth came at him again, Matt smashed his stomach with a punch hard enough to knock the wind out of Seth. By the time Eli and Cameron separated the two, Matt's nose was bleeding.

"What are you doing?" I stormed, holding a tissue to Matt's nose. "You're acting like idiots."

"Laur—" Matt pleaded, while Seth watched me with narrowed eyes as I cared for Matt.

Seth shook free of Cameron and walked over. "I only came out here because Piper was helping with the compost pile and heard from the kitchen staff that you guys got a ride out to the D&O."

Matt shoved Eli away and strode up, eyebrows together. "Oh, so you just had to wait for her, did you? Thought you'd catch her alone?"

Seth sent him a withering look but didn't make a move. "I waited because Gollum got wind of it from Emily, who heard Piper and Alex talking. He's waiting at the end of the road to catch you. You're all going to be kicked out of camp." The way he looked at Matt, he didn't look at all sorry about the idea of that becoming a reality.

"Hate those Munchies' Manor girls. They are such fun suckers," Hannah griped beside Matt, then looked at me. "No offense."

"Hey," I began, but Seth cut me off.

"Look, I know a back way in. Gollum will never know."

Kayla smiled at me. "I totally see why you dated him."

I gave her a half-hearted grin, wondering if she'd be next in line to fall for Seth. The boy had no lack of admirers.

"Remember the pinky swear," Brittany hissed at her.

"Oops," Kayla giggled. "I was kidding!"

"How do we know you aren't leading us right to him?" Hannah accused. "Be honest."

"Honestly?" Seth looked around the skeptical group, zoomed in on me, then dropped his eyes. "Because I don't want Lauren to go."

And with that he turned and disappeared into the woods. I stood in shock as something inside me thawed. The boy who casually waved me off at the end of each summer had finally owned up to needing me. Was Seth changing too? Opening up?

"The pinky," Brittany breathed in my ear before following Kayla and the rest into the woods. Matt, Hannah and I brought up the rear.

"How would he even know this way?" Hannah yanked the hem of her fringed top from a scrub tree.

"His grandparents own this place. He could find his way blindfolded," I said, trudging behind them.

If only he knew me that well. How could he think I'd drink or betray my friends? He might be ready to reveal more of himself, but that didn't mean I'd like what I saw.

Chapter Eighteen

We owed Seth big-time for sneaking us back into camp.

The word around the bonfire the next night was that Gollum had been furious when he'd waited two hours in the dark trying to bust us. He gave us all a stern warning at dinnertime, but since he hadn't caught us he could hardly punish anyone. Even Matt grudgingly admitted that what Seth had done for us was cool. Seth's favor was almost enough to make me forgive him for thinking I'd been drinking and that I'd stolen Trinity's diary.

Almost.

The whole experience had brought me closer to the Divas' Den girls, which felt like a betrayal to my old friends, but I was so tired of being judged for things I didn't do that it felt good to be part of a group again. I'd even scored a purple warm-up jacket that said Divas' Den on the back. Kayla had given it to me, and although Hannah had grumbled about it, she hadn't ripped it out of my hands.

Now, on Sunday afternoon, Kayla and I sat in front of ancient computer screens in the small lounge attached to the office. The communications lab was open only to senior campers and counselors, and even then we could only use it during our hour of "plugged in" time each week. I'd opted for the computer time instead of my cell phone this week so I could work on my latest wedding chore.

Siobhan and Alex were there too, but they paid no attention to us. I was pretty sure Siobhan was emailing some of her work home so she could stay on track with the rigorous study program her parents demanded of her. I used to come here with her sometimes. Now it looked like Alex was filling my shoes, although she seemed to be cyber-shopping more than she was helping with calc.

"What exactly are you looking for?" Kayla asked, looking over my shoulder at a webpage selling engraved silver boxes.

"Gifts for my sister's bridal party." I was supposed to have spent this summer working on the essay portion of the Aerospace Scholars application, not micromanaging bridal gifts. Of course, it probably would have helped if I'd told my mom and sister that instead of mutely accepting the duties they'd delegated my way. Siobhan would have never ignored her studies for the sake of slave labor.

"Want me to ask my mom for ideas?" Kayla offered. "She reviews tons of products for the magazine where she works."

"Really?" I was so tired of looking at knickknacks and keepsakes that I would even have accepted Gollum's suggestions at this point. But Kayla's fashion-editor mom might actually have some good hints. "That'd be great."

"We were messaging each other a minute ago." Kayla clicked open a dialogue box and started typing. "Let me just see if she's still there."

While I waited, I keyed in the address for the NASA Aerospace Scholars Program, to re-check the application date. I still had until September, but since Dad hadn't bothered to get my letter of reference from the congressman, it didn't look good. Maybe when I got home I could call the politician's office and ask for a meeting on my own. I'd met him at some family corporate events before. It seemed like a long shot...and daunting. They must get hundreds of requests like that.

"She sent us a link," Kayla announced, double-clicking on the text. "She said this jewelry designer is new and—oh! Look at this stuff."

I peered over at her screen to see the thin gold-wire pieces shaped around tiny gemstones. The jewelry was fine and delicate, but the shapes were kind of organic and unusual. Plus, most of the necklaces came with multiple charms, so you could layer an initial over a horoscope sign or a soccer ball with a fairy-tale castle.

"Awesome," I breathed, already seeing the possibilities.

"Look!" Kayla pointed. "There's even a wedding dress. You could engrave the date on the back of the dress pendant for everyone, then personalize the rest of the charms to the other attendants."

"That's so cool. Maybe I can find out the zodiac signs or birthstones for everyone and do their first initials." I was already typing a note to my mom to help me find out that information from all the bridesmaids.

A ping on Kayla's computer announced another message.

"My mom says she's friends with the designer." Kayla scrolled down the note. "If we send her the shipping address and the information, she'll make sure the jewelry gets there on time."

"She will?" I was so used to being the one who got things done that it felt weird and really great to have someone else take over a job. And I'd never even met Kayla's mom. "That's so generous."

I toyed with the zipper on my new Divas' Den jacket, thinking I would have had a lot to offer the Kindness Cup this week. Too bad they didn't have such a thing in my new cabin.

Kayla shrugged. "She works all the time and I don't get to see her much. But when she can help out with stuff like this...yeah, I guess she is pretty cool about it."

When my mom messaged me with the information I was looking for, I forwarded it to Kayla to give to her mother. I didn't even wince when my mom added a note about my leaving camp a few days early to attend final dress fittings and a bridal luncheon. I'd known all along that was a possibility and, given the way things had gone for me at Juniper Point this year, I didn't think I'd be missed all that much anyhow. At least I'd be able to stay through the Talent Show.

"My dad works all the time, too," I admitted to Kayla, keeping the news that I'd be leaving camp early to myself. "He never used to be that way, but he took a new job this year and he's gone constantly."

I still hadn't opened the excuse-letter thing he'd sent me. Then again, I hadn't seen it since the day Kellianne gave it to me. It had to be somewhere in my old cabin. That is, if my former friends hadn't tossed it in the trash.

My eyes went to Siobhan and Alex as they stood to leave. Siobhan flicked her eyes at me, then strode past us. But Alex slowed her step and gave a quick wave hello.

"Nice jacket, Lauren," she said.

For a moment, I thought she was being sarcastic about my new Divas' Den gear. But when Siobhan turned around to glare at her, I realized she must have been sincere.

Alex hurried to catch up to Siobhan, but she covered her mouth to whisper, "Purple looks good on you," as she darted past.

"Thanks," I called, regretting that Alex wouldn't stay and hang out with us. With a pang, I remembered purple was her favorite color.

"Ready?" Kayla asked, hitting the send button on the note for her mom and shutting off her computer. "Our time is almost up."

"Yes." I was relieved to have the bridal party gifts taken care of, but torn about not being able to hang out with Alex. I gathered my things and shut down my computer. "Do you ever wonder how we all got so divided here?"

Kayla frowned.

"You mean, the Munchies and the Divas?"

"Yes." We waved to Leslie Kim, the dance instructor who was still working on one of the computers, as we went left. "Remember when we first started coming to camp? We all caught butterflies and made macaroni necklaces together. There wasn't this huge gulf separating us like we were from different planets."

"We grew up, I guess." Kayla's face looked wistful for a moment, the expression so fleeting I thought I imagined it. "We made new friends and lost some too," she added in a voice full of longing. I wondered if she thought of Nick, her oldest camp friend before she'd become a Diva. He'd been in the Wander Inn and I was pretty sure her friends had convinced her not to hang around him.

We stepped outside and waited for a barrage of junior campers to pass us as they streaked toward the Field of Dreams. The younger campers must have one of their big playoff games. They carried glittery signs to cheer on their teams and a few were already chanting, "We want a pitcher, not a belly-itcher."

"I'm just so tired of the whole clique thing." I followed Kayla toward the dance studio where we were supposed to meet up with the other Divas' Den girls to practice our routine for the talent show. "It's even worse here than at my school."

"Really?" Kayla hitched her floral bag higher on her shoulder. "This is nothing compared to my school. I don't even rank on the popularity scale there since we're not as rich as everyone else."

"You're kidding." I felt embarrassed as soon as I said it. "Um. Not about the rich part. I mean, I can't believe you wouldn't be popular anywhere you went."

"You're not like most people, Lauren. *You* don't judge a book by its cover." Kayla might have said more, but Hannah and Rachel met us on the path and started asking for opinions on the dance routine we were planning.

I didn't answer, thinking about what Kayla had said. Sure, I wished I were the kind of person who didn't judge until I knew someone, but that wasn't necessarily true. I'd gone headlong into the most popular crowd at Jefferson Davis High this past year, seeking out the cool kids to give myself a safety net in a new school. I was totally guilty of judging books by covers.

But it wasn't too late to change.

"I've got an idea for the dance." I announced before I'd thought it through. We were all inside the studio now. Brittany and Rachel were already rehearsing some dance moves, trying to put together a routine.

"Congratulations," Hannah said dryly.

"Let's hear it," said Brittany, her ponytail bobbing in time to her step as she came toward me. "We're stumped."

"You know how Gollum is pushing healthy food on us and trying to brand the camp as environmentally friendly?"

"*Sustainable* is the new black this season," Kayla added. "Even the fly paper in the dining room is made out of bamboo."

"Eww." Brittany made a big show of pretending to retch. "Like, who gets close enough to the fly paper to notice?"

Rachel rolled her eyes while she practiced her power jumps to one side of the dance floor. "There's a huge sign in the dining room that lists everything that's made of bamboo now. Duh. So what's your idea, Lauren?"

I hoped they wouldn't see right through me, because I totally had an ulterior motive. But my heart was in the right place and my motives were good. Or so I thought.

"Well, think how many points we'd score with head judge Gollum if we did a dance routine that was an ode to Mother Earth or a save the rainforest theme."

Hannah was already shaking her head. "No way am I dressing up as a tree frog to score a few points from Mr. Woodrow." She did a butt-shaking move and tossed her hair. "I'd rather win the popular vote."

Brittany tapped a finger against her lips as if she was deep in thought. Finally, she nodded.

"Nature can be sexy." She pirouetted around. "The wind can flow through our hair and we can get high-cut blue skirts to represent the ocean." She did a belly-dance move that looked like one long wave.

Rachel stopped jumping and came closer. "We could do some yoga stretches toward the rising sun in the background." She did a back arch that would undoubtedly make a few boys swallow their tongues.

Even Hannah looked impressed. "You really think we could come up with hot outfits for this?"

"My mom will find us whatever we want," Kayla volunteered.

"My dad will pay for it," Brittany offered.

I checked my watch. "The computer lab is already closed—"

The rest of the girls laughed.

"Cameron sells prepaid 4G cell phones," Kayla informed me. "Brittany is his favorite customer."

Given her legendary bank account, that made total sense.

"We can use Michael Jackson's 'Earth Song,'" I chimed in, the energy in the room tangible now.

Hannah squealed and went back to booty-shaking. "Love MJ. Now you're talking."

We spent the next hour working on routines and I realized that I was totally happy.

This was what I'd missed about Camp Juniper Point. It wasn't just about kisses and boys. It was also about friends and fun. And if a little piece of my heart wished I had someone to sit next to tonight at the bonfire, I quickly smothered the thought. I was figuring out who I was and what I wanted, which was the first step in understanding who—if anyone—I should be with.

For today, I was content to enjoy the moment. And hope the Divas didn't kick me out of their cabin when they realized I'd given them a dance routine that perfectly complemented the performance art piece the Munchies' Manor cabin already had planned.

*   *   *

Two days later, we gathered after breakfast for the senior scavenger hunt. It was one of the few events where we skipped regular activities to do something special, kind of like the overnight canoe trip. We would be paired up and armed with lists of stuff to find in the woods or around the campgrounds.

The Divas had sprinted from their seats after breakfast as soon as Gollum announced that the pairings were posted outside.

"I'm Matt's partner!" Hannah squealed as she arrived at the list. Her shrill announcement rang out over our group while the rest of the senior campers caught up to us.

Hannah practically knocked down Brittany in her haste to find Matt. No wonder she was happy. They'd be alone together all day. I tried to ignore the knot in my stomach. Unlike the rest of the Divas, Hannah had refused to take the "boy-free" summer pledge.

"Don't worry, Lauren." A familiar voice in my ear surprised me.

I turned to find Emily dressed in a camouflage shirt three sizes too big for her that could only belong to Bam-Bam. She'd dressed it up with white denim cutoffs and rhinestone pins on the sleeves that gathered the material away from her shoulders to make it look sleeveless.

As soon as Emily said, "don't worry," I worried.

"Why?" I looked past her to where Alex and Piper were shoving Rachel out of the way to check out the list for themselves.

Gray storm clouds were moving in overhead, but that wasn't the only reason I sensed trouble.

"Because the counselors helped choose the partners and I put in a good word for you, even though you deserted us." She winked at me before she went over to Siobhan and Jackie.

"*Ohmigod.*" Kayla latched onto my arm. "I'm with Vijay and you're with Seth."

That was Emily's favor to me? I stared at her, wondering what she'd been thinking. Alex marched up to us, no doubt aware of the news. I braced myself for her reaction, knowing how much she liked Vijay.

"Looks like you got my guy and I got yours." Alex snapped her gum and gave Kayla an even look. "Or at least, he *was* your boyfriend." She pointed to Cameron. "How about we make a deal that I won't take your man and you won't take mine?"

Kayla rolled her eyes. "I'm taking a break from guys, so you can have Cam if you want him. But I promise Vijay is totally safe with me."

"For real?" Alex raised an eyebrow and looked skeptical.

While Alex quizzed Kayla about her commitment to not dating anyone, I couldn't help but notice Breyanna and Seth exchanging some terse words.

I grabbed a list of the items we were supposed to find and waited for Seth.

All around me, kids were pairing off and heading in different directions. Hannah had Matt's sleeve and was practically dragging him down toward the beach. He looked back at me, and I shrugged, helpless to save him from her clutches.

Besides, I was still a little mad at both him *and* Seth for the way they'd acted the other night. They fought about me *after* I'd broken up with both of them. I might as well be one of Hershey's chew toys.

Was I important to either of them, or just a small part of the bigger reasons they didn't like each other? The guys in the Wander Inn didn't get along with the Warriors any better than the Munchies girls got along with the Divas. I was problematic for everyone because I didn't fit in anywhere.

I'd messed up all the boundaries that everyone else had been perfectly happy with.

"Are you ready?" Seth asked, appearing out of nowhere.

I nodded, wishing I'd brought a rain jacket in case those clouds let loose. "I've got the list."

Seth took the extra copy from me and studied it, his sandy hair falling over one eye.

"*Asimina triloba,*" he read aloud with a laugh. "That's a common pawpaw." He flipped the paper around to show me the "points" column. "That plant is worth a lot and I don't think many people will even know what it is, let alone where to find it. Are you up for a hike on the other side of the river?"

Was he asking so that we could win the game? Or was there a chance he was trying to be alone with me? I didn't think any other campers would be making that long trip, especially since it was off the approved grid. My indecision must have shown, because he stuffed his list in his back pocket and turned his full attention on me.

"You know that, if we stay by camp, our every move is going to headline the gossip over dinner, right?" He surprised me with that one, but he had a good point. "I don't think that'd be any more fun for you than it will be for me."

"Agreed." I didn't need to draw any more attention to myself. With only one more week left for me at Juniper Point, I was keeping things low-key. "But we could just split the list in half to divide and conquer. If we're not together, no one can accuse us of..." My cheeks warmed as I thought about the way we'd ended up kissing. More than once. "...anything."

"It's a team game," he protested. "I don't want to get disqualified when we can win easily with pawpaw. The winning team is excused from chores for the rest of camp."

I *did* hate waking up early to set tables in the dining hall...

"Fine. I just hope it doesn't start raining." I looked up at the clouds. Maybe they were moving away from us.

I wondered if I should lay down some ground rules to make sure things stayed platonic. But since he seemed to be moving forward with Breyanna, why should I worry? So as I followed him into the woods, I kept my eyes on the trail ahead instead of Seth's broad shoulders. Honest.

Yet every step I took felt even more dangerous than when I'd snuck out of camp to go to the D&O. I couldn't shake the feeling that I'd signed on for a lot more trouble.

Chapter Nineteen

"How much farther?" I groaned as we slogged up another muddy hill.

A light rain had been falling for the last half-hour. Even though I was wearing a hoodie, my hair was plastered to my head. Seth had been quiet and so had I, the awkward silence feeling as chilly as the weather.

We'd passed the hermit's hut a few minutes earlier without so much as a comment. Hard to believe that I'd occasionally daydreamed we'd go there this summer.

"Depends." Seth stopped a few yards ahead and waited for me. The rain didn't look bad on him. In fact, his wet T-shirt clung to all the major muscle groups. "What does the compass say?"

"As if that will help." I pulled it out of my sweatshirt pocket, irritated that I had noticed anything attractive on a guy I was still mad at.

It was one thing for the Munchies to think the worst of me with Trinity's diary. But Seth? We'd known each other so long. He should have believed me.

"It does help," he said gently, tugging the device out of my hands. My skin tingled at our brief contact, like he'd transmitted electricity through my skin. "Staying on course will get us there faster."

A few weeks ago, having this alone time with Seth would have been a huge thrill. Now, I couldn't stop thinking about how quickly things had fallen apart for us. Had he been right to break up with me at the end of every summer, knowing one of us might find someone else? Or had his insistence on breaking up every year been the wedge that helped drive us apart?

I pointed at my soaked sandals, practical in dry weather but a slippery disaster in a summer storm. "I can't go faster. These aren't the right shoes."

"Just like the other night when you were coming home from the bar?" His straight eyebrows lowered over his eyes as the rain fell between us.

"Exactly." I folded my arms, daring him to suggest I'd stumbled that night for any other reason. "I fell because of the shoes, Seth, not because I had been drinking. Do you think I'm a liar now?"

He held my gaze for a long moment before looking down at the compass.

"We went too far west." He peered around the woods as fog started to roll in. "When did we start drifting off course?"

Annoyed that he'd avoided my question, I yanked the compass away and chucked it into the mist. "I'll tell you when we started drifting."

"What are you doing?" he demanded. "I needed that."

"Well, I needed you. But we got off-course when you stopped caring about me. How did that happen?"

Thunder rolled in the background, the deep bass startling a brown rabbit. It flew into the brush, its white tail bobbing.

"I've never stopped caring." Seth gazed after the animal. "I'd better get you back before things get nasty."

My blood simmered at the double meaning behind his words. Once again, Seth was avoiding a serious talk about our relationship. So much for thinking he was opening up. I could ask him about the life cycle of a fruit fly and he'd speak for an hour, but one question about where we stood and he ran for the hills—or straight to another girl. Suddenly I saw Breyanna for what she was. Not competition. She was a distraction. To avoid dealing with missing me, he spent time with her. It was another way for him to escape his problems.

"Lauren, we need to keep moving if we want to get back before dark," he urged, then headed downhill.

I stomped after him, swiping rain off my cheeks as the wind picked up.

"I'll tell you where we got off-track," I fumed, shivering despite the anger that fired me up inside. "How dare you tell my friends you helped us get back into camp because you didn't want me to leave. What a joke. You've spent half the summer either hanging out with Miss Headband, avoiding me, or accusing me of stuff I didn't do."

"Are they really your friends, Lauren?" Although his voice was steady, his tone sounded grim. "They're encouraging you to sneak out at night and betray your old friends."

"Now wait a minute—"

"Are you going to deny that you let them into your cabin and gave them Trinity's stuff?" He paused to squint through the rain as if trying to get his bearings.

"I didn't give them anything! They stole it."

"Yet now they're your friends." Seth brushed back his dripping curls and looked at me, his golden eyes moving down my face from nose to mouth to chin. "Come on, Lauren. Does any of that make sense?"

I strained to hear Seth's voice in the howling wind. Rain lashed my face, ran down my neck and pooled at my clavicle.

"I'll admit Hannah's a bitch." I raised my voice over the intensifying gusts. "But the rest of the girls are really nice. Besides, the Munchies *wanted* me to leave. They didn't want to hear my side."

Something inside me deflated like an untied balloon. I'd never imagined all my old relationships would fall apart so fast.

"Right now we've got a bigger problem." The anger drained out of his expression. "We're lost."

"Excuse me?" I pivoted on one heel to survey our surroundings, argument forgotten. "You know this area backward and forward. How can we be lost?"

"I can't see." He swiped a hand through the mist. "Between the rain and this fog, I have no idea where we're going anymore."

"Then let's backtrack." I turned around again to check where we'd come from and saw lightning fork on a distant mountain. I shivered. "They've probably called off the scavenger hunt anyway."

"We could if we knew which way we came from." His amber eyes were filled with concern.

He had me seriously worried. If Seth didn't know where we were, how would I ever know? I picked a direction and pointed. "That way."

"But how long can we walk 'that way' without a compass or being able to see anything?"

I looked down and noticed my knees disappeared in the mist.

"Oh. My. God." With a sinking feeling, I began to understand why he looked so concerned. "I'm sorry I threw the compass. I had no idea—"

He waved away my panicked apology. "I could probably find our way back by following lichen growth." His face creased in concentration, then lifted as another lightning bolt streaked across the sky. "But that would take too long. We need to get out of this weather now."

He looped an arm around my shoulders and pulled me close. Cold and scared, I didn't protest. The fog transformed the woods into a shrouded, eerie place.

"How will we get back?" We couldn't walk all that way in this weather. For that matter, it felt weird to even put my foot down when I couldn't see the ground in front of me. I could twist an ankle or step off a cliff.

With the pelting rain in our ears, would we even hear the river when we got near it? I tucked my head against his shoulder, comforted by his warmth.

"We won't make it until the fog lifts." He held a tree branch up so we could duck under it. "We'll be lucky if we can find our way back to the hermit's hut."

I missed a step, and it didn't have anything to do with the weather.

Seth squeezed my shoulders, holding me steady.

"The hermit's hut?" It shouldn't matter that kids went there to make out and...much more. We were lost and needed shelter. It was a practical solution. So why did it feel like we were doing something wrong?

"Safety first." He sounded as concerned as I felt. Rumors were going to fly if we were stuck out there for long. "Let's hope the weather clears soon and we'll make it back before dark."

Something sharp pinged against my head as a small building came into view ahead of us.

"Hail!" Seth shouted, grabbing my hand and racing us to the shadowy outline of the hut. Lightning crackled and thunder boomed as we pulled open the door and ducked inside. I turned to survey the nightmarish scene before shutting it. Fifty-foot trees bent like saplings in the moaning wind. Smaller branches flew by like a scene from the Wizard of Oz. I half-expected to see Hannah ride by on a bicycle wearing a witch hat.

I shut the door and leaned against it. If there was a chance we'd make it back to camp before nightfall, it was a slim one.

* * *

Night came early in this kind of weather.

By the time the mist started to lift and the hailstorm ended, it was too dark to try making it back to camp.

Luckily, Seth hadn't waited to make preparations. He'd unearthed abandoned cabin loot like candles, blankets and those chemical fireplace logs that burned with just one touch of a match.

Knowing I hated thunderstorms, Seth distracted me. He found all the hiding spots where various visitors had stashed their supplies and piled them in the center of the planked floor. He made up a game to guess who'd left which items. It was so fun I barely flinched when thunder shook the hut or hail drummed so hard on the tin roof that I thought it'd break through. So far we'd speculated that the Army-issue utility knife was Bam-Bam's and the gold glitter comb belonged to Emily. We laughed imagining Rob's reaction if he'd discovered the two. It'd been fun watching the super-confident hunk crash and burn attempting to seduce Emily. Neither of us mentioned our own relationship woes. We were finally having a good time together.

A Yankees baseball hat could belong to most anyone. I pulled on the hat, attempting to hide my humidity-expanded hair. If only someone had left behind a hair straightener... The pink satin sleeping bag monogrammed with a capital M was no challenge, given Madison's reputation. No doubt I'd have one as well after spending the night here with Seth.

"I know you didn't steal the diary," Seth said out of the blue as we huddled on the sleeping bag before the crackling fire.

"Finally." My breath rushed out. "What made you realize that now?"

Seth's amber eyes darted to mine. "Deep down, I always knew. I was frustrated about the way things were between us. That you couldn't make up your mind between Matt and me. "

Seth took my hand and ran one of his fingertips down my palm. My throat tightened. I tried to ignore the nervous electricity that pulsed through me at his touch.

Even though I was determined to keep things platonic between Seth and me, I could imagine what it would be like to sit in front of this fire with the right guy. Making out. Seeing what else happened...

"Are you cold?" he asked me suddenly, rubbing my arm with warm fingers.

I couldn't stop the small thrill that shot through me. "I'm fine," I insisted, though my voice sounded tight.

"I know you're worried about what will happen when we go back tomorrow." He rested his hand on the side of my face, his thumb skimming my cheek.

I frowned and pulled back.

"Tomorrow?" I'd been holding out hope we'd still go back to camp soon. "But kids come out here all the time in the dark. Can't we at least try?"

"Kids who plan to come up here bring flashlights." Seth shook his head. "The river will be dangerously high anyway. It's not safe tonight, even if we could see."

Was I crazy to trust the judgment of a seventeen-year-old boy so much? All I knew was that Seth had hiked and climbed all over these mountains; if he said it wasn't safe, I wasn't going to risk it. Gollum could toss me out if he wanted. But I really hoped he didn't. I wanted to perform in the talent show and spring my last surprise on my cabin mates—new and old.

"Even if Gollum believes that, you know the other kids won't. They'll think we hooked up." An image of Matt's livid face, Hannah whispering in his ear, came to mind. "We'll get all the blame and none of the fun."

"I'm having fun." He pressed his forehead to mine and flattened his palm against my back.

In a friendly, reassuring way? Or a way that meant he was hitting on me? I had no radar with him anymore. Seth had surprised me at every turn this year.

My heartbeat picked up. The warmth of the fire sent a pleasurable heat through me. Or was it Seth's touch?

Boy-free summer. I repeated it like a mantra.

"Can I ask you a question?" I'd been dying to ask him this for years, but the old me had been too afraid.

"Shoot." He wrapped his arms around his knees and locked a hand around his other wrist.

I gathered my courage. "Why did you want to break up every year after camp?"

In the quiet that followed, I traced the white stitching on the embroidery that outlined Madison's initial.

When Seth finally answered, his voice was low.

"It's easier to end things on good terms than risk something going wrong during the school year."

"Why assume the worst?" I'd never given him reason to doubt me.

"I saw what my dad went through after my mom left us." He reached for a stick to shove the logs around in the dusty fireplace as I marveled that he'd finally admitted what I'd suspected. When Seth's mom abandoned him, she'd left a huge hole. No wonder he had trust issues. Still, we could have worked through that if he'd given me a chance. Opened up to me like this before.

"I always figured I'd wait to get serious with anyone until I was...really sure," he continued.

"And you were never sure of me?"

His crooked grin made a surprise appearance, but his tone was dry. "I was hoping this would be the year we'd be ready to take that step."

Something inside me collapsed. My chest felt so tight that for a minute I couldn't breathe. We'd been so close to developing something amazing.

"Instead, I showed up with someone else."

Outside, the wind rubbed tree limbs against the cabin, making a squeaking scrape.

"It wasn't just that." He put the stick down and looked at me. Really looked me. "You showed up *as* someone else. Someone I didn't recognize with a new look, new clothes, new interests."

I opened my mouth to protest but stayed silent when I followed his gaze to my trendy sandals.

"I didn't know who you were anymore," Seth went on. "Since when did you prefer dancing to stargazing, tanning to pursuing your Aerospace Scholar dreams? That wasn't the Lauren I knew. The Lauren I loved."

I flinched. Who knew a verb tense could cut as deep as a knife? Seth no longer loved me because I'd changed.

How ironic that I'd come back to camp to get back to the things I'd loved, especially Seth. But Matt had stopped that chance and, suddenly, I was glad he had. What was so wrong with liking dance *and* astronomy? Cheering and the science club? The popular and the outsider cliques? The problem was, I hadn't realized I could do both, *be* both. If I'd gone back to Seth, I would never have learned that.

I looked over at my drying wedge sandals by the fireplace. They were awesome, even if they had slowed us down. And yeah, I was the girl who worried about weather-induced hair frizz.

So maybe I had changed. And Seth had a point about letting my dreams lapse. But why couldn't he see through the make-up and clothes to the person who still thrilled at the site of a meteor shower and drew constellations on her notebook covers?

I laid back, tired of justifying myself. "That girl's gone, Seth. I'm different now."

Seth stretched beside me. His amber eyes searched mine in the dim light, a wistful smile lifting the corners of his mouth.

"It's not a bad thing," he agreed, his fingers toying with my curls. "I just miss the old you sometimes."

I closed my eyes and enjoyed his touch, knowing it wasn't going any further. After all, he cared about someone else, someone I'd never be again.

"Sometimes..." I edged a little closer to ease the empty ache inside. "...so do I."

Chapter Twenty

I wrung my dishrag over a bucket of soapy water and draped it across the handle. Back aching, I stretched and surveyed the sparkling mess hall tables. Seth's mop clattered in its holder nearby. Our eyes met in weary satisfaction. After two hours, our breakfast cleanup—punishment for straying off the scavenger hunt trail—was over.

"Finally!" Seth whooped, then skidded across the slick floor, losing his footing as he reached me. I caught him at the last minute, my arms gripping his to keep us both upright.

Laughter erupted outside the screened windows. Hannah pointed at the two of us as we broke apart. *"Boy-free summer*, my ass," I heard her say. "Wait till Matt hears about this." As they moved past the building, Kayla and Brittany looked back, their faces a matched set of betrayed expressions.

Seth pulled out a chair for me and sat on a table, his calves swinging. I buried my face in my hands.

"Hey. It's not that bad." His fingers brushed back a clump of uncombed curls. The moment we'd stumbled into camp, Gollum had blasted his whistle and set us to work with only a brief bathroom break.

"Yes it is." My muffled voice rose through my fingers. "Did you see how the Munchies left breakfast the minute we arrived? They despise me more than ever." I sighed. "If that was even possible."

Seth pried my fingers away, his earnest eyes meeting mine. "Maybe they were finished?"

"Jackie still had French toast on her plate. No way were they done."

Seth shook his head. "It was whole-grain bread. Not a lot of kids ate it. Trust me. I dumped enough plates to know."

"It *was* pretty gross-looking," I admitted, a smile starting. I inhaled his distinct outdoorsy scent.

Seth's sandal snagged my shoe. "At least I won't miss the food here next year," he said in a quiet voice.

"What will you miss?" The question popped out without thinking.

His eyes skirted mine as he scratched the back of his head. "This." He cleared his throat. "You."

"But you can come back next year as a junior counselor, right?" We'd discussed that possibility last summer.

"Yeah. But I'm not so sure now. I mean, I'd love to work with the kids outdoors, teach them about nature, but..."

He broke off, his eyes following mine as Matt stalked past the mess hall. Jeez. Hannah hadn't taken long to spread her poison. And knowing Matt's possessive side, he'd decided to check things out for himself. I gripped the chair, keeping myself from following him as he rounded the bend toward the baseball field.

"You want to go after him."

I looked up. "Huh? No."

Seth's eyebrows rose. He held my gaze until I looked down.

"Okay. Yes. But we're better off apart."

A large hand descended on my jittering knee. "Sure about that?"

A startled gasp sounded from the screen door. Breyanna stood behind the crisscrossed wire, a jar of swimming creatures held in her hand. Her headband slid to her forehead as she twirled away.

Seth shot to his feet. "Breyanna. Wait."

She turned and held up the glass bottle. "They changed into metamorphs yesterday and they're ready for the release we planned. I told the kids to be ready for us." She looked at me, mouth drooping in disappointment. "But I'll just go myself."

The hurt on her face echoed my own pain. They'd raised tadpoles together? Seth and I used to do that, giving them names and having a ceremony when they were big enough to survive in the river. I thought it was our special thing. But like Seth said, things had changed. And that included us.

Breyanna nudged her headband back in place.

"Go," I whispered to Seth. I'd broken up with him, after all. I had to accept the consequences.

"Are you sure? We still need to talk." But he was already on his feet, and that said a whole lot more than his words.

He wasn't waiting for me any longer.

"If we're meant to be, we'll be. Right?"

Seth shook his head, eyes wide. "I think that's the stupidest thing I ever said."

He jogged after Breyanna, nudged her shoulder, and grabbed the jar. The sun shimmered through the green water, illuminating the little lives ready for their moment of freedom. I'd worked hard to have mine; now that I was all alone, I realized it wasn't so great after all.

*   *   *

I trudged down the dirt path to the baseball field, to Matt. Although nearly everyone in camp seemed to hate me now, his dismissal hurt the most. Maybe it was because I understood him the best. I'd spent so long believing that Matt was "the hot guy" I was lucky to have that I hadn't seen how much we had in common. And I knew, without question, that he would feel the sting of me spending the night in the woods with Seth. I owed him an explanation, even if we weren't together anymore.

At the park, my fingers curled around the links in the chain-link fence above the backstop, but there was no sign of him. I remembered the day we'd arrived and Matt's awe when he saw the field. I'd scoffed at his fascination with all things athletic. But now I saw the beauty in the pristine white bases, the perfectly shaped red pitcher's mound and diagonally mowed grass. Who was I to judge if someone else's dreams were worthy? Meaningful? I'd been hard on him...hard on us both.

If only he were here. Suddenly, arms wrapped around me from behind. I held back a sneeze, senses overwhelmed by a flowery scent. It was Emily, not Matt.

"Hey home girl! You looked so lonely I thought you could use a hug." Emily's pink gums flashed.

"Thanks, Em." My lips refused to shape themselves into a smile, even at the sight of her red cut-off "That's what she said" T-shirt. "You might be the only person still speaking to me."

"But not the only person talking *about* you, right?" Her elbow dug in my side as her high-pitched laugh rang in the sweltering, mid-morning air.

"Right." A burning started behind my eyes. I blinked and pretended to study the envelope clutched in her hand.

"I have a present for you." She thrust the envelope at me. "Alex found it behind your bunk when we were cleaning up the cabin."

Through watering eyes, I recalled my dad's apology letter. As the camp's social outcast, it felt good to have a piece of home in my hands. He'd asked me to open it during our phone call. Why had I waited so long to look for it?

"Yo! Em! You coming?" Bam-Bam boomed from the main building. He jangled a pair of keys, the bright sun glinting off the metal.

"Oops. Gotta go. We're heading into town to get supplies for tomorrow's talent contest. You'll be there, right?"

I cringed at the reminder, imagining everyone's scornful looks. Then a thought struck me. Emily could help me change that.

"Would you do something for me at the talent show?"

She leaned in conspiratorially. "What?"

When I finished whispering, she nodded, eyes wide.

"Done deal!" She jogged backwards a few feet, then stopped. "You know I've always got your back."

Alone again, I studied the envelope, wondering what the note said. I ripped through the seal and readied myself for disappointment. When it came to Dad, it hadn't paid lately to get my hopes up.

But a receipt with a familiar stamp appeared. NASA. The paper shook so hard in my hands, it took me a couple of seconds to read it then process what it meant. No wonder it'd felt so light. He'd sent in my letters of reference. They must have received my application for the Aerospace Scholars Program! My heart pounded. How had that happened? I remembered leaving the uploaded application on his computer the morning I left for camp, but since I didn't think he had gotten the letters of reference, I hadn't thought he cared.

But my father had thought of everything, even a quick note of encouragement and a reminder to submit my essay online for early acceptance.

My throat constricted. Dad might have put aside his dreams, but he hadn't forgotten mine.

Now I needed to write the admission essay and my application would be complete. It had been my childhood dream. But after a summer of focusing on boy and friend drama, I hadn't given any thought to what I'd write about.

The papers hovered over a nearby garbage can.

"Don't even think about it." Siobhan's reasonable voice sounded behind me.

I squinted at her irreverent look—a knee-length Elmo T-shirt, red-banded gym socks, and a penguin hat—at odds with her serious expression.

"Excuse me?"

"The application you're throwing out."

"What?" I pulled the envelope farther from the bin.

"Duh. It was all you talked about last year. Remember? We even strategized about the essay you'd write. When Alex found the envelope, I remembered the phone conversation you had with your dad and put two and two together."

"You eavesdropped?"

"Get real, Lauren. The porch windows are covered with screens, not soundproof glass. And you were wrong when you told your father life was too complicated to have what you want. It's only as complicated as you make it."

I pointed to her school work. "You're one to talk."

Siobhan shrugged and hoisted her backpack, bowing slightly under the weight. "My parents may make me do this, but I'd do it anyway. I want to be a doctor. Do you think that after all the opportunities they've given me I'd—" she gestured to the trash, "throw it away?"

"At least you've worked for it. All I've done is mess everything up."

"Opportunities come to all kinds of people. It's what you do with them that's important. Think about it."

She gave me a small smile as she headed toward the lounge, the only quiet place during the activities-filled day. Gollum must have relaxed the rules for her, given that camp was nearly over.

"Are you coming?" she called.

My heart squeezed tight at the invitation from my old friend. Whether I deserved her friendship or not, she'd held out a hand when I needed one.

I was an idiot if I wasted this chance, with her friendship and with the Aerospace Scholars. I'd lost a lot this summer, but I'd be damned if I'd lose this opportunity too.

"Got a pen?" I shouted, sprinting past Siobhan.

* * *

Massive fans whirled overhead, moving hot air around the oversized common space. Siobhan curled up in a frayed chair, her dark brows knit as she pored over a science book. I sat across from her on a sagging couch that creaked whenever I moved. I'd filled out the application last spring without a problem. It was the essay question that stumped me.

"What makes you a good fit for this program?"
Last year, the words would have rolled off my pen. I'd known exactly who I was and what I wanted—to be an astronomer. And Seth had reminded me not to forget those old dreams, so I started with that.

Wonderment is a word often associated with children. There is so much they wish to explore, thrilling at each discovery in their new world. While Earth held many such surprises for me growing up, my young eyes were also drawn to the heavens, imagining what I might someday find there.

Some say the night sky is like an old photograph. Light takes so long to reach us that many of the stars I admire have burned out. Yet their memory is as bright and vivid as ever, a dream that should never be forgotten.

These stars have guided many travelers home. I'm no exception. When I've lost my way, their lights, like old friends, guide me back. It's a breathtaking vista and a quiet reminder that, no matter how complicated life becomes, the sky will always be my simple, universal truth.

So far so good. But what came next?

I put down my pencil, slowly becoming aware of a soft tune playing in my head. Or was it? I'd been concentrating so hard I'd missed the faint piano notes coming through the wall the lounge shared with the arts center. Something about it sounded familiar. I strained to hear more, then froze. It was the same melody Matt had hummed in my ear during the camp dance.

The couch squealed in protest as I stood, drawn to the music. Other than that one time I'd heard Matt hum the song, I hadn't ever heard it before.

Siobhan glanced up and frowned. "Are you bailing?"

"No. I just need to think through the end of the essay," I fibbed, unable to concentrate until I found out who was playing that music next door. My eyes wandered to the wall, the notes trickling through it like a spring rain shower.

Siobhan shook her head, penguin ear-flaps lifting. "Just as long as you come back."

"I will." I stacked my papers on the scarred coffee table.

She gave me an assessing stare as I passed by her chair and studied her homework.

"I assume you know you need to use the sis form of that isomer," I pointed out, my brain firing on all cylinders today.

She stopped nibbling her eraser. "I do now. Thanks."

"Hey. Can I ask a favor?" I really needed an ally in the Munchies cabin to pull off my plan tomorrow, and I knew Trinity would never give me the time of day.

Siobhan's pencil stilled. "I'm listening."

I whispered my plan about the Talent Show. She remained silent for moment, her eyebrows disappearing into faux penguin fur.

I grinned when she finally nodded; it was on now.

*   *   *

Lyrical chords rose and fell as I eased inside the arts center, the mystery song drawing me forward. My eyes adjusted from the bright outdoors to the interior gloom. Normally activities would be running this period, but it was free time. With the clock winding down at camp, everyone was outside. Except Matt.

His straight dark hair, longer than he'd ever worn it, obscured his face as he bent over the keys. His hands were a blur of motion across the black and white strip, halting once in a while to yank a pencil out of his mouth and scribble on a sheet of music paper.

Holy. Crap.

I'd heard Matt mess around on a piano once, but I'd never known he could really play. Write songs. Compose music.

I'd thought he was a sight to see on the football field. But watching him create music took my breath away.

I must have made a sound because the song cut off with a discordant note. On shaking legs, I wove through the maze of art stations. He stared at me, his eyes following my body from my head to my feet, not lingering anywhere—a wary, defensive gaze.

I tugged up my tank top strap, then stuffed my hands into the pockets of my shorts. Matt looked awesome in a faded-black racer-back tank that showed off his biceps, veins popping. Who knew piano playing could look so hot?

"What are you doing here?" He glared at me, though his green eyes looked thoughtful. Their peculiar shade had always fascinated me, the color set off by a fleck of gold in his right iris.

"I could ask you the same thing." I moved closer and rested my hand on the worn piano lid. "Why didn't you tell me you could play?"

"Why didn't you tell me you were spending the night with Seth?" His nostrils flared, the twitch under his left eye appearing.

Air hissed between my teeth and I looked away. Would Matt ever trust me? "We didn't," I made air quotes, "'*spend the night.*' We got caught in the storm and had to wait it out."

Matt spoke to the peaked ceiling. "How convenient."

My nails drummed on the hardwood. "Actually it was cold, dark, and a little scary, but thanks for your concern."

His eyes flashed to mine. "I was worried. Rob and Bam-Bam had to keep me from going after you."

For the first time I noticed a nasty shoulder bruise and what looked like finger marks on his upper arm. I reached out to touch the spots.

"Are these from—"

"Yes." His jaw tightened as my fingers swept over the discolored skin.

Touched, I blurted, "I'm so sorry. Believe me. I wanted to get back but Seth said it was too dangerous."

Matt's laugh was bitter and hard. "And you believed him."

"Since he knows these woods and is my friend, yeah. I trusted him."

"We both know he's more than a friend." His low voice echoed in the empty space. "Hannah saw you hugging him in the dining hall this morning."

Of course. Hannah. Would that girl ever quit? Then again, with Matt close to being hers, why would she? Since it wasn't her last year of eligibility for camp, or Matt's, they could plan to meet up again next summer. My heart clenched. Maybe they already had.

"The floor was wet and he slipped." I sat on the piano bench, encouraged that he didn't leap off the seat when I did.

His bottle green eyes searched mine, a light in them growing as tense seconds ticked away. Finally, he exhaled, his shoulders lowering.

"You're telling the truth."

"Duh. I told you I didn't want to go out with anyone right now, and I meant it."

"So have you figured things out yet?"

I shook my head. "No. But I'm writing my essay to become an Aerospace Scholar at NASA's Johnson Space Center."

Matt's smile made my stomach flip- flop. He grabbed my hands. "That's awesome. Why didn't you tell me you wanted to do that?"

"It'll mean I might not have time to cheer next year." I knew cheerleading wasn't everything, but I liked it and I would miss it.

"That's perfect, because I'm going to be hanging out in the music room instead of playing football."

"We're both geeks—" we said at the same time. "Jinx, you owe me a soda," we chorused again and laughed.

"That makes us geek chic." I pushed up my square frames.

"I prefer nerd cool." Matt punctuated his statement with a cascade of chords.

"Definitely cooler." I smiled and gestured to the piano. "Why didn't you tell me you played?"

"I've gotten used to keeping it under wraps." His words were punctuated by two ominous chords. "It never fit with my father's image of a dedicated jock." He deepened his voice in a decent imitation of his dad. *"Keep your focus on the game, son."*

"That wouldn't have mattered to me."

"You cared a lot about cheerleading and your popular friends. What was I supposed to think?"

I opened my mouth and closed it. Had I made him believe I wouldn't accept this different side of him? That I would think like his father? I'd been so busy trying to fit in with my family's expectations that I had failed to realize that others, even confident kids like Matt, did the same.

Matt's hands danced across the keys, a jaunty melody springing from them like magic. "And I'm not taking over the car dealership when Dad retires, either." He trailed his fingers along the length of the board to punctuate his declaration of independence. Butler men had sold cars in Texas since Henry Ford was alive, and probably sold horses before that. My mind reeled.

"What will you do instead?"

"My mom said I can study music after I graduate."

"Wow, Matt, that's amazing." I hugged him quickly, then pulled back.

Matt shook his head, looking as shell-shocked as me. "Crazy, right? I used to know where I'd end up, but everything is different now. I'm not afraid to do what I want—be who I am anymore." He rubbed his hand across his forehead. "I sound like a fortune cookie."

I squeezed his hand. "No. You're making perfect sense." I nodded at his music sheet. "Is that what you're writing about?"

Red bloomed under his tan cheeks. "No," He cleared his throat. "It's a love song."

"Oh." I stood and wiped my damp palms on my shorts, not sure if I wanted to know who he'd written it for. Given my behavior, I doubted it was me.

"Maybe I'll play it for you someday," he said, his voice pitched low.

"I'd like that." I backed away. "But I've got to finish my application essay today or I won't get in."

His eyes shone with confidence. "You'll get in, Lauren. There's no one better."

I shut the door behind me and stopped to catch my breath. Never in a million years would I have imagined Matt Butler choosing music over football. It was too unreal to process.

The lounge was deserted when I returned. I wished Siobhan had stuck around, but I was glad for the privacy. My head felt like a tornado had blown through it, my thoughts twisting all around. Matt and Seth had changed this summer. Then a thought struck me. I had, too. A different Lauren would return to Texas, just like a new Lauren had left it. The only difference was that now I accepted those changes. Like Matt said, I shouldn't be afraid to be myself.

I picked up my pen and got back to the essay.

At first glance, the universe appears to be a constant. But I've learned that things are rarely as they appear. New stars form as I write, while others fade away, their light dimming to allow room in the sky for the next generation. Such change is not to be feared, but celebrated.

The unknown is a gift, a promise, a journey worth more than its destination. As an Aerospace Scholar, I will bring my passion for this dynamic, ever-growing entity, the primordial origin of life. My thirst to uncover the many secrets the heavens hold will make me a dedicated student and a fascinated observer of the wonder that lies above.

I'd convince Emily to let me type and email it tonight. Then I'd make copies. Two individuals had taught me a lot this summer, and I wanted both to see what I'd learned.

As I passed Siobhan's empty chair, I noticed a note propped against its back.

L- If I could write you a letter of reference it'd go like this: I'm pleased to recommend Lauren Carlson. She's the smartest girl I know and the one I'd vote as most likely to change the universe. She will always be one of my closest friends, and you'd be lucky to have her. We were. See you at the talent show, Lauren! Can't wait—the girls will freak. Love ya, Siobhan.

I swiped at my damp cheeks, incredulous that by some miracle I'd kept at least one friend. Would tomorrow's risky plan help me win back the rest, or would I lose them forever?

*   *   *

After spell-checking for the tenth time, I hit send a few minutes before the computer lab shut down for the day. I took a deep breath and crossed my arms. Wow. I'd completed the NASA application and taken my first step toward the life I wanted. After all I'd been through, I never would have guessed that the guy who'd help me realize my dreams would be my father.

When I returned to Divas' Den, my belongings were heaped on the porch, with an "I'm sorry" note in Kayla's handwriting. My shoulders slumped as I processed their unspoken message: I was no longer welcome. Spending the night with Seth hadn't gone over well after promising to keep the summer "boy-free." Kayla might have believed me, but what chance would she have stood against Hannah's harsh judgment?

I packed my clothes in my suitcase and left it there on the porch with the rest of my stuff. Grabbing some leftover trail mix from my bag, I set out to hike along the Nantahala River, something I'd always liked doing when I came to camp. I wanted at least a few camp memories that weren't about boys and cliques. Much later, when the campers gathered at their final bonfire, I snuck back and grabbed my sleeping bag.

Lying on the dock, I listened to an orchestra of crickets and the lapping water below. There was nothing like sleeping outdoors on a clear night. Luckily, Victoria's deep sleep habits meant I wouldn't be missed.

Brilliant stars twinkled down from an onyx sky. I drew my flannel-lined sleeping bag around me as the first breath of crisp night air caressed my shoulders. Summer was ending.

I watched the steadfast universe I'd always loved—Polaris, the North Star, and the Big and Little Dippers. But the familiar formations left me restless, and I scanned for signs that the heavens changed like us, something I no longer feared. I could evolve eternally and shine just as bright.

A flash of light streaked across the midnight sky. As it fell like a sparkler, I made a wish. I'd finally figured who I was and what my place in the world should be.

The question was, who to share it with? And would he want to share it with me?

Chapter Twenty-One

The day of the talent show passed in a blur. After hours of prep work running errands for counselors and helping paint scenery, I stepped out of the shower. Outside the window, kids chattered on their way back from dinner. They shoved, giggled, and screeched, their excitement for our end-of-the-year event palpable.

I blew out my hair, straightening every inch until it reflected the waning light. I withdrew my dance outfit from my suitcase, my breath catching as I tore off the plastic. Kayla's fashion-connected mom had come through and gotten us gorgeous costumes in record time.

Mine was a toucan. I pulled on the emerald-green tights and slipped the matching leotard over them. A cropped jacket made of yellow, green, and white faux feathers, and a green mask complete with a bright orange beak, completed the ensemble.

After donning the last two pieces, I gasped at my exotic reflection. The green darkened my eyes, giving them a mysterious look. The feathers floated around me, lending me grace before I started moving. I felt transformed, an endangered animal about to execute a dangerous plan—one I was less and less sure of as the hour drew nearer.

A towel-clad Kayla bumped into me as I stuffed my feet into matching green jazz shoes and headed for the door.

"Sorry," we both blurted, then looked away.

"That looks great." Kayla swung her shower tote in her hand. "I'm sure Seth will love it."

I didn't bother responding to that one since she would believe what she wanted anyhow. At least she hadn't ignored me. I was fortunate that the choreography for our number meant they couldn't exclude me from the routine. After our planning session, we'd held more formal practices in which my part, like the others, became an integral part of the dance.

Before I could think of anything to say, Kayla had already turned on the shower spray.

I slipped off the mask, put it in my bag, and lugged my suitcase down the shower house steps. Where to go? Then inspiration struck. Within minutes, I reached Emily's cabin. *My* former cabin. The other Munchies would already be at the arts building.

"Polly want a cracker?" Emily croaked when she opened her door. She wore a glittering pink bustier and a green mermaid's tail that nearly reached her red platform heels. Hopefully this was her talent show outfit. But with Emily, who knew?

"I need a place to store this until tomorrow," I gestured to my luggage. "Can I keep it here?"

Emily stopped giggling and looked at me, her smile fading. "Lauren. Are you okay?"

A lump formed in my throat. I nodded, unable to speak.

Emily put a thin arm around my shoulder, led me to her bunk and sat me down. "No, you're not. I can see it. Honey. I know a lot has happened to you—at least, according to Trinity's diary—but these are supposed to be the best years of your life."

A bleak laugh escaped me. Emily squeezed me tighter.

"Hey. Do you think I was always this confident? That everyone liked me the way they do now?" I swallowed back a gasp as she continued. "For years I tried to be everyone's friend, fit in, be what they wanted. Look—" She grabbed a spangled purse and pulled out a picture of a stylish young woman wearing an argyle sweater and dress slacks, standing with a preppy family. "That's me."

I looked from the photo back to Emily's outlandish outfit, trying to comprehend that this was the same person.

"The only difference?" she continued, tapping the picture, "I was miserable there."

I examined the snapshot, noting the huge ring on her finger and a man as handsome as Rob standing beside her. Was this an engagement party? My eyes flew to her bare left hand.

Emily followed my gaze and wiggled her acrylic tips. "Yep. Single—well, kind of." She plucked at the dog tags that hung from her throat.

"Bam-Bam said I could keep these, so I guess that means we're together."

"Why not Rob?" I blurted. He had always seemed like the ideal man. And he'd made it clear he liked Emily.

Emily laughed. "Oh. I've dated a hundred Robs before. Almost married one to please my parents." She lowered her voice and leaned in. "My family's loaded, and they expect me to marry someone who's either rich, gorgeous or preferably both."

She tossed the photo aside. "But in the words of the late, great rocker Kurt Cobain, 'Wanting to be someone else is a waste of the person you are.' I didn't want to waste a minute of my life being with guys like that, so I came—"

"—here," I breathed, taking a guess.

Emily's broad smile appeared. "How did you know?" She walked over to her mirror, a tube of lipstick in hand.

"I did the same thing."

Emily met my eyes in the mirror, her bottom lip painted a bright fuchsia. "Weird. No wonder you're my home girl. We're exactly the same, except," a furrow appeared between her brows, "you didn't get your Prince Charming."

I hung my head. "Nope. Definitely not. But I turned in my application to the Houston Aerospace Scholar program." My chest loosened, recalling the satisfaction I'd felt in making the deadline.

Emily pulled me up and caught me in a tight hug.

"That's awesome. Who needs men anyway? I didn't come to camp looking to find someone, and I ended up with Bam-Bam."

"And I came to camp looking for someone and ended up with no one," I said with more than a touch of irony.

She released me and shook her head. "You did find someone." She jabbed her finger at my chest. "Yourself."

I nodded. For a girl who dressed like a dancer in an old music video, gave up her supposedly perfect life, and dated an eccentric war veteran, she made a lot of sense.

Whether or not my plans to win back my friends and the guy I loved worked, I would always have myself and, hopefully, the Aerospace Program. Anything less, according to Kurt Cobain and Emily, was a waste of my life.

*   *   *

The recreation room had been transformed into what looked like an underwater wonderland. Blue and green streamers undulated from the rafters while blue and white cardboard waves covered the walls. Cutouts of fish swung from the ceiling, and a papier-mâché replica of coral, complete with clay sea creatures, dominated the center of the room.

Bam-Bam tested the sound and light system while Emily lined up chairs. I lent her a hand, unfolding the last chair while the youngest campers trooped in, their leader ushering them to the front. The intermediate campers followed and filled up the center seats, while senior campers took the back rows.

I handed out programs, hurt when none of the Munchies, except for Siobhan, took one. As always, the Divas saved their grand entrance for last. Hannah breezed by me in a skintight leopard costume and sat beside a smiling Matt. I grabbed Kayla's arm, careful not to damage her silk brown-and-white-spotted moth wings.

"Will you promise me something?" I asked.

She wrenched free and crossed her arms. "Like the way you promised to stay away from boys?"

"I haven't broken that promise. But listen, this is about something else."

Kayla shrugged, then looked away.

"Whatever happens during our act, will you just go with it?"

Her eyes flew to mine and narrowed. "What's going to happen?"

Brittany, clad in a fitted black fruit bat costume, yanked Kayla away before I could answer.

"Promise?" I called to her retreating back, hurrying to take my seat as the house lights dimmed.

Her shoulders lifted and dropped as she left without a backward glance.

Sighing, I settled into my chair in the back. Alone. After three hip-hop dance numbers, a cheer routine, a jaw-dropping contortionist act, and bicycle tricks that made everyone gasp, Matt stood.

Silence descended as he mounted the steps. Hannah swayed behind him, flicking out her costume tail before sitting on the piano bench beside him. His deep-green eyes caught mine as he turned to the audience and spoke into the microphone. "This is for someone special."

His baritone filled the room, powerful and hypnotizing. I gasped, never imagining he had so much talent. Gazing more into the audience than at the pages Hannah turned, he sang,

When the cold
Freezes you body and soul
And it seems like
There's nowhere to go
I could offer you
The warmth you need
And wrap you in my love

When the sun falls
And the stars emerge
And it feels like all your
Dreams are submerged
I would listen
Till your blues are purged
And wrap you in my love

I know you're guessing
If the one is me
If I'm the guy
Who fits all your dreams
Take a chance
And trust how
Good we'll be
I'll wrap you in my love

I'd move mountains
I'd scour the ocean floor

I'd go to hell and back
To prove I love you more
No one has ever made me
Feel more sure
That you are my love

The stars are shifting
In the twilight sky
But nothing could ever
Change you and I
The future's certain
Since you've opened my eyes
So won't you be my love?

Come back and be my love.

Our eyes locked as his final note lingered in the silent room. I felt my heartbeat everywhere, even in my toes. Captivated, I was on my feet. I even took a step forward, then stopped when Hannah threw her arms around him. The crowd rose and cheered. The rafters shook with stamping feet and shouts for an encore.

"I'll give you an encore," Hannah yelled and kissed an uncomfortable-looking Matt. The crowd went wild. Cameron grabbed Kayla's hand while Eli threw his arms around Brittany. On the Munchies side of the room, Vijay put his head on Alex's shoulder while Seth tugged at Breyanna's headband. I turned away before I saw more. Halfway to the exit, Emily stepped in front of me.

"You're on next. Remember the plan."

I brushed away my tears and pulled down my mask.

Matt and Hannah and Seth and Breyanna had had their moments. Now it was my turn.

"Thank you Matt. That was–ah–surprising," Bam-Bam, our MC, announced as the Warriors cabin erupted into another bout of raucous cheering. Matt grinned and waved to a younger girl who screamed, "Marry me, Matt!" He jogged down the aisle to rejoin his friends, incredibly handsome in a light blue polo shirt that darkened his eyes and clung to his muscular build.

Bam-Bam tapped the microphone, but the excited crowd kept cheering until Emily shouted, "Free ice cream!"

After nearly eight weeks without refined sugar, that got everyone's attention. Even Alex and Vijay came up for air.

Emily toyed with what looked like a seaweed boa and smiled. "Kidding." The room groaned. "But I've got something even better for you. We've saved the best for last. Let's give it up for 'Earth Song.'"

The Divas scooted out of their seats, but froze when the Munchies took the stage. They were dressed in brown leggings and pulled-up hoodies, branches attached to their heads and wrists.

The group lined up, their limbs pointing in different directions.

Piper stepped to the front. Even from the back of the room, the shaking of her knees was visible. "There are over three hundred different species of tropical rainforest trees, a few of which are depicted behind me." Her words tumbled over each other like a rushing waterfall. "While the rainforest provides over 40% of the earth's oxygen, it now covers only 7% of our planet due to human encroachment."

Hannah leaned across to a monkey-suited Rachel and hissed, "Earth Song's the title of *our* dance routine."

Rachel shrugged, her dark-rimmed eyes creasing in confusion.

One of the Warriors yawned loudly when Piper stopped for a quivering breath. "When's the talent part start?" His stage-whisper made Eli and Devon burst out laughing.

"Shut it," Matt commanded, stopping Hannah mid-giggle. "This is interesting."

The group quieted, and Piper's knees stopped knocking. I shot a grateful look at Matt, amazed at how far he'd come from the boy who'd high-fived Crash for breaking the hovercraft.

I glanced over at Seth, who'd leaped to his feet at the insult. He and Matt exchanged a strange look before Seth sat. For a moment, it'd looked like respect.

Piper cleared her throat. "Scientists estimate that more than half the world's plants and animals live in tropical rainforests." She nodded at Bam-Bam, who inserted a disc as she rejoined the tree line. As the opening music to "Earth Song" began, the group swayed, their branches swooping and bending in unison.

Hannah stomped over to Emily. "That's our song."

Emily arched a brow. "Then you'd better shake a leg, or should I say your tail, and get up there."

"This is a joke. Turn that music off," Hannah snarled, her leopard whiskers twitching.

"Sorry." Emily shrugged. "If you want to be in the show, this is your only chance. We're out of time."

Hannah groaned and signaled to the rest of the group to follow her on stage. Kayla gestured for me to follow.

Since the opening music was so long, we took our positions as the lyrics began. The Munchies group looked at us in shock. Jackie started to head for Hannah, but Siobhan put out an arm and stopped her.

"They're dressed as rainforest animals," she whispered, dipping to the beat with the rest of the puzzled-looking trees. "Just go with it. It's not what we rehearsed, but it still works."

As we'd practiced, the animal-clad Divas dove for the floor, rolled, leaped to their feet and reached to the sky, arms spread. Then, somewhere near the middle of the song, Brittany slipped. Before she crashed, Jackie caught her and improvised a dip. The move must have inspired Kayla, because she flitted to Siobhan, fluttering her wings as she encircled the tree. As the song headed into its final chorus, we stopped following the routine and improvised a dance with the trees. Hannah snorted but joined the rest of us.

When Bam-Bam played a chainsaw sound at the end of the song, the Munchies toppled over. In solidarity, I threw myself down beside Alex and played dead. Through slit eyes, I watched the Divas do the same.

Immediately, the audience broke into wild applause. We held our lifeless positions for a second more, then stood and bowed. The cheering went on so long that Gollum had to blow his whistle three times before the crowd took its seats.

"As camp director, it has always been my greatest pleasure to watch my campers grow and mature each summer," he began, his chest swelling like a puffer fish.

"Go Gollum," Alex said out of the side of her mouth.

"My Precious," Kayla whispered back. The girls smiled at each other while Brittany and Piper smothered their giggles.

"Seeing these two very different groups of young women join together for such a noble cause, well—it—ah..." He coughed, pulled a white handkerchief out of his pocket, and blew his nose.

"Didn't know there were geese in the rainforest," Siobhan mumbled behind her hand.

"Maybe we should have asked him to join our act," Rachel put in, her voice low.

Now all of us held hands over our mouths, shoulders shaking as we held back our laughter. I couldn't believe that these archenemies were finally getting along. Was my far-fetched plan actually working?

Gollum tucked the cloth away and took a deep breath. "This act proved to me that camp is truly a special place. There is a magic here. It catches from person to person, soul to soul."

I followed his gaze, taking in the tentative accord forming on stage, the way Emily leaned back against Bam-Bam, the fleeting smile Seth gave Matt. He was right. Camp was magic. And I'd been right to come back and try to share it with the person I now realized I loved with all my heart. If only I hadn't been such an idiot for letting him slip through my fingers. Then again, without spending time on my own, I wouldn't have had the perspective to figure us both out.

Mr. Woodrow held up a gold-colored metal trophy with the words "Talent Show Champions" inscribed on its base. He handed it to Rachel who, to my surprise, passed it to Jackie.

"We've got the Volleyball trophy. I think your cabin should keep this."

Jackie let out a whoop and raised the trophy overhead. "To the Diva Munchies!"

"Diva Munchies!" the crowd roared, the noise moving outdoors as the campers exited the building.

Alex turned to the group. "Let's celebrate."

Kayla nodded, her felt antennas wiggling. "Definitely. How about the beach?"

"Let's change and meet up in fifteen," Siobhan smiled at everyone, even me. "Later." She and the rest of the Munchies followed her out.

"They're actually nice," Brittany mused, wrapping her bat wings around herself, then releasing them.

"Why didn't we get to know them before?" Rachel leaped off the stage. "We could have used them on our volleyball team."

"Could you see Jackie in one of our jackets?" Hannah snickered.

Silence descended. Kayla put her hands on her hips. "Yes, actually I can."

Hannah stepped back as if slapped.

Brittany tramped down the steps.

"You're not seriously going to hang out with them?" Hannah called.

Kayla grabbed my hand and pulled me down the stairs. "We're going to have *fun*. And for once, everyone's invited. Even you, Hannah. TTFN."

I looked over my shoulder at a stunned Hannah. She stood in the now-darkened room, her eyes darting around the empty space.

"I'll meet up with you, okay?" I let go of Kayla's hand.

"You better." She gave me a quick hug.

Back inside, I ran to the stage. Hannah sat on its edge, head down, legs swinging.

"You know it won't be the same without you."

"Look. You win. I get it." Hannah's voice was heavy with tears. "Just leave. I don't need my face rubbed in it."

How could she say that when she'd already won Matt?

I stepped forward. "If you mope in here any longer, I might rub your face in the sand."

Hannah laughed faintly. "I always knew it'd come down to mortal combat between us."

"Can't we settle this over marshmallows instead?"

She removed the elastic that held her plastic nose and whiskers in place and looked up. "Why are you being nice to me?"

I sighed in exasperation. "In case you haven't noticed, I'm a little short of friends and I could use one."

Hannah sniffed. "Even after everything?"

"Nothing's happened that can't be fixed or forgotten." It was one of my mother's favorite expressions. "Although I don't know if the other girls in my cabin will be so quick to forgive you for the mean stuff you've pulled."

I tried not to think about where she might go if left to her own devices. Was Matt waiting for her even now? Swallowing back the jealousy I had no business feeling, I tried one more approach.

"Hey. This is my last night of boy-free summer." I held out my pinkie. "Are you in or out?"

Hannah's eyes gleamed as she wrapped her finger around mine and smiled.

"So in."

*   *   *

After a quick change at the showers, I jogged down to the beach wearing a navy bikini and matching cover-up. My flip-flops skimmed over the thick layer of pinecones on the trail, unable to keep pace with my racing heart.

The first part of my plan had succeeded better than I'd imagined. At last, I had my friends back; even better, they all liked each other. I ignored the twinge of worry that the second part of my plan might not end as well, and felt even less sure I'd make it into the uber-competitive Aerospace Program. But I'd think about that tomorrow. Tonight belonged to the girls who were dancing under the beach's spotlights.

"Lauren!" the group chorused when I broke through the trees. One of them had started a small fire, a major infraction usually not punished by counselors on the final nights of camp. Besides, we'd made Gollum so happy, he'd probably give us his precious whistle if we asked. Victoria was monitoring things from her beach blanket a few yards away, her nose buried in a book.

I pulled off my wrap and splashed into the river, goose bumps rising on my legs. "Last one in is a rotten—"

Water closed over my head as someone tackled me from behind. I sat up and blinked until I could make out a laughing Jackie.

"Gotcha!"

I reached out and yanked her ankle, pulling her legs out from under her.

"You—" she sputtered, shaking her head at me, water flying.

Rachel jogged into the shallows, Alex on her back. "Chicken fight," she hollered. "Unless you're chicken."

Jackie scratched the back of her head and cocked an eyebrow at me.

"They're so dead," I whispered, jumping on Jackie's back. We gave chase. Within minutes the river was filled with mixed pairs of Divas and Munchies who grappled, screamed, and laughed until we toppled over. It was a war without sides, the only objective to have fun.

Later, we huddled together around the fire roasting marshmallows.

Alex raised her marshmallow-tipped branch. "To Lauren!"

The rest of the girls followed suit, shouting things like, "Miss you, Lauren!", "Can't wait till next year!", and "Goodbyes suck."

Tears filled my eyes. "Thanks, guys." I waved my stick. "I can't tell you what this means to me. What you all mean to me."

We thrust our marshmallows into the fire, shoulder to shoulder. I swallowed my half- burnt, half-raw sugar puff and flopped back on my towel, contentment curling inside me.

I stared up at the stars, thinking back to my lonely night yesterday and how hopeless everything had seemed. Alex lay down on my right, Kayla on my left. I reached out and held both their hands. Now that I'd accepted myself, my friends accepted me.

For tonight, that was enough.

*   *   *

Before boarding the shuttle the next morning, I slipped an envelope under the cabin door of both Warriors' Warden and the Wander Inn. Although both contained a note and a copy of my essay, only one held a wedding invitation.

It was for someone I very much hoped— despite the odds—would be my plus one.

Chapter Twenty-Two

A week at home passed in a whirlwind of last-minute bridal preparations. I attended a bridal luncheon, dress fittings, spa treatments, hair consultations and—finally—the rehearsal dinner.

I sat at a table with a few out-of-town guests, catching up on the news from Ithaca with my aunt and uncle. The party wouldn't go late with the wedding tomorrow, but for now Kellianne and Andrew made the rounds, visiting with relatives who'd converged on Highland Park for the big event.

"The bridal party gifts were gorgeous, Lauren!" my mother confided as she went past with Aunt Flo, probably trying to prevent her from doing a Tarot reading in the middle of the rented hall. "Great job!"

Mom seemed happy tonight and—amazingly—so did Dad. With all the bridal events, I hadn't seen him much since I'd returned from camp, but I had thanked him for all the work he did to get me into the Aerospace Scholars program. When he'd insisted that I'd done all the work by putting myself in a position to succeed, it had been almost like having the old Dad back.

"I can't take all the credit," I told Mom about the gifts. "I had some help from a friend."

I owed Kayla and her mom some thank-you notes, something I was an expert at writing after my wedding duties. But these would come from the heart. I'd learned not to rule out potential friends just because they were in one cabin or another. This year, I'd Facebook with the Divas and the Munchies on the camp page and keep our newfound unity going.

I might be single, but at least I'd left camp with girlfriends.

"That's nice, sweetheart," Mom told me. "Now please check your mascara and powder your nose. You're a little bit shiny."

She gestured toward my forehead and gave me a look that told me this was an important assignment I needed to address *pronto*. Not bothering to argue, I grabbed the navy-blue satin bag that matched my rehearsal dinner dress and hustled toward the bathroom.

The hall was attached to a local museum funded by my grandparents' oil company; the bathroom was across an atrium where the night sky was visible through a high glass ceiling. The hint of stars twinkling beyond the glass reminded me of the application I'd finalized with the essay I'd sent last week. As much as I wanted to join the Aerospace Program, I took some comfort from the fact that, if nothing else, writing that essay had helped me understand myself better. Had given me the courage to go after what I wanted, even it if didn't fit with other people's expectations of me.

"Hey, Lauren." My sister greeted me from her seat at the bank of mirrors in the bathroom lounge, her pale pink dress and matching jacket making her skin glow. "Did you get sent back to the drawing board on your makeup job too?"

"What gave me away?" I asked as I dropped into a seat beside her. "My shiny nose? Collapsing hairdo? Smudged eyeliner?"

Apparently I'd forgotten some of the beauty tips my mother had tried to drill into me during the school year. But then, I'd let that kind of thing go at camp for the most part.

Kellianne surprised me by smiling. "None of the above. I just know that Mom's nervous tonight, and she's reverted to perfectionist mode."

"Really?" I paused in the middle of dotting powder on my cheeks. "You think Mom's a perfectionist?"

"Why do you think the wedding planning nearly killed me?" Kellianne tucked a lipstick—matte, I noticed—into her tiny sequined handbag. "Mom has high expectations."

With an effort, I did not remind Kellianne that, on the contrary, planning the wedding had nearly killed *me*. It was so rare that we got along that I hated to disrupt the harmony. Another lesson I'd learned from camp. Savor friendships.

"It's funny she ended up with Dad then, right?" I smiled to think of my father's slouchy suits and perpetually crooked ties, hoping that the tension that had been growing between my parents had eased this summer.

"Honestly?" Kellianne stared down at the huge rock on her left finger that would be joined by even more bling tomorrow. "I think being with Dad has kept her grounded. At least, it did until we moved back here."

Right. Now they were both married to their jobs, although Mom was doubling up with her mother-to-the-bride responsibilities.

I wanted to ask her more about Mom and Dad, but she rose to her feet and clicked her tiny purse shut.

"I just hope Andrew understands that *I'm* not going to be a slave to some ideal wife image." She tucked a loose strand of my hair back into a rhinestone barrette and patted me on the shoulder.

"Why would he think that?" I asked carefully, surprised to see a side of my sister that I hadn't been aware existed.

I had to admit that I'd pictured her as the ideal traditional wife. Or at least, the traditional genteel southern lady. She seemed born for the role.

"He's already talking about having a family and I—" She broke off. "It's nothing. It'll be fine."

My jaw was still on the floor when she marched out of the bathroom lounge. I hurried to finish up and rejoin the rehearsal party, wondering if Kellianne was going through some of the same things I had this summer. Except for her, the consequences for a wrong choice were much bigger.

I was still hurting over the way my love life had fallen apart this summer, but at least I could fix it or move on. Kellianne would be marrying her guy tomorrow, so any fixing needed to be done now.

I searched for her across the atrium, but she was already at Andrew's side. Near her, my parents stood together by a small rolling bar. My father held up a glass and clinked a spoon against the stem. The tinkling sound quieted the crowd and turned all eyes toward him.

"May I have your attention, please?" He looked handsome in a charcoal-gray suit and crisp white shirt, way different from the tweed blazers he used to wear every day for teaching.

Beside him, my mother looked expectant. Excited.

What was up?

"My lovely daughter has given us permission to steal her spotlight for a moment, because she's as thrilled about our announcement as we are," Dad continued, surrounded by family and friends. Grandma and Grandpa Hartman stood behind my parents.

"As of September first, Hartman Oil will be launching an eco-friendly energy division." There was a polite smattering of applause. "Even better, I'd like to announce that Christine will be heading the new division."

Dad led the room in a noisy cheer for Mom while I observed the way they smiled at each other. Like partners. Apparently a lot had changed while I'd been away this summer. Maybe that was why no one had quizzed me about Matt when I came home. They'd all been too preoccupied with this news.

"Thank you. And since he's too modest to tell you himself," my mother took over without losing a beat. But then again, she was good at appearances. "Paul will be the head research scientist in our new venture. He'll be leading the way to find green initiatives that will supplement our traditional business at Hartman."

After the announcement, a few close friends gathered around my parents to offer congratulations. I was thrilled for them and curious what it meant for us as a family. Would I see Dad more often? Less?

I knew he didn't always have choices about his job, but I hoped that at least he'd be happier in this new work environment. I reached Mom and Dad the same time Kellianne did. We hugged, all of us, in a way we hadn't done in ages.

After we talked about the new branch of the company, that had apparently been Dad's brainchild all along, Dad squeezed Kellianne's hand.

"And don't forget we're looking for good people in the new division," he told her. "You'd be perfect."

Maybe because I was looking for it, I noticed the flash of interest in my sister's eyes.

"Paul, don't be silly," my mother chided him. "Kellianne and Andrew are anxious to start a family."

Was I the only one who saw my sister's shoulders slump? My sister, who normally had the most perfect posture ever?

But Mom and Dad had moved on to say their goodnights to relatives and rake in good wishes on their new career moves. With the rehearsal dinner breaking up, I took the initiative to steal the bride-to-be.

"Come on," I told her, dragging her toward the back of the atrium where she'd parked.

"But Andrew..." she protested half-heartedly, waving feebly at her fiancé.

"You're all his tomorrow," I insisted. "He can spare you for your last night as a free woman."

We stepped out into the dark and hurried for her convertible Beemer. The top was up even though the night was warm and pleasant. No doubt she'd wanted to keep her hair in place on the ride over.

Sliding into the car, I shoved off my shoes while she shut her door.

"What gives?" I asked, not waiting for her to start the engine.

She didn't even bother putting the key in the ignition. Instead, her head fell to the steering wheel.

"I don't know," Kellianne muttered.

"If you're not ready for a family—"

"It's not that," she denied. "Okay, maybe a little it's that. I want a family. I just—I'd like to see what it would be like to use my degree for a little while first."

"And Andrew doesn't want you to?" I was prepared to give Andrew Buford III a piece of my mind.

Even if Kellianne could be a royal pain, she was family. Besides, there was obviously a whole lot more to her than I'd given her credit for.

"It's not so much Andrew. It's Mom. His mom. Grandma..." She straightened in her seat and I saw through the perfect exterior she normally showed to the world. "They all want me to join their clubs and charities and have babies. I just wish sometimes I was more like you, Lauren."

I nearly fell out of my seat.

"Me?"

She shrugged. "You're not afraid to go against the norm."

I shook my head, amazed that she'd noticed something about me beyond good penmanship. "I wish you'd told me sooner. It took me all year to figure that out."

She rolled her eyes, but she was smiling while she did.

"So I told you what's on my mind." Turning in her seat, she faced me across the console. "What about you? You said you broke up with Matt, but you didn't really say why. Is it that Seth guy?"

"No." It was past time for me to take responsibility for what I wanted and who I wanted to be with. "I was just confused about why Matt and I were together."

"Meaning?"

"I thought Matt only wanted to be with me because I was a cheerleader and we were in the same crowd."

"There are worse reasons to date than having things in common."

"I know, but I think I pushed Matt away because I was trying to become someone else. Actually, that's not totally accurate." I took a deep breath and admitted the deeper truth. "I kept thinking everyone was trying to categorize me, to slap a label on me as a geek or a popular girl, when all the time I was doing the same thing to Matt, to Seth, and to my friends."

I'd gone into camp with a script in my head where Hannah was the mean girl and Seth was my ideal guy. Two months ago, I think I'd secretly assumed that Matt would eventually tire of me and hook up with someone else. I'd also assumed that Emily would fall for Rob, that Brittany was the biggest airhead on the planet, and that Alex and I would share all our secrets. It never occurred to me to see beyond my expectations to the real people beneath my preconceived notions.

"Your real friends don't run away just because you mess up. And neither will the right guy." Kellianne started the Beemer now that the foot traffic had cleared out of the parking lot. "But that doesn't answer the bigger question."

I leaned back in my seat, surprised to have shared my deepest insights with the sister who'd demanded I write her shower thank-yous. But seeing all the work that had gone into the rehearsal dinner, the bridal luncheon, and the spa day in just this week alone, I realized that she must have taken on a fair share of wedding duties herself in order to pull off the big event.

Maybe she'd been as stressed as I was this summer.

"Which is?"

"Who is going to be sitting with you at the wedding reception tomorrow?"

We'd never finalized the seating chart. Why hadn't she asked me this before now?

Yet, in all honesty, what could I say?

"The truth is..." I hadn't heard back from my invitee. I would most likely be alone for the wedding. But I didn't want the bride to worry more when she had a lot on her mind. "I'm not sure."

Chapter Twenty-Three

I tried to tell myself that it was okay that I attended Kellianne's wedding solo.

After all, I was in charge of things like arranging my sister's mile-long train when she was at the altar so that the custom-sewn inset of vintage Alençon lace showed to its best advantage. Then there were the last-minute hair repairs for the bride before the photos, the endless posing for those pictures, and patiently fielding comments from relatives about how "grown-up" I looked in my bridesmaid gown.

But no matter how practical it might have been to attend the wedding alone, I was hurt inside. Maybe the hollow feeling in my gut as the bridesmaids' limo reached the reception hall was what I deserved after the way I'd played both Matt and Seth this summer. Not that I'd meant to.

I'd had good intentions about being there for Matt. About staying away from Seth until Matt and I were no longer together. Unfortunately, I hadn't been able to separate my feelings for them any better than I'd been able to separate the old and the new me. They were both a part of the real me—the Lauren that was a nerd *and* a cheerleader, a wannabe astronomer with a Diva's eye for fashion.

Too bad I'd hurt people I cared about to finally be okay with who I was inside.

Now, smoothing any wrinkles from my lavender chiffon Vera Wang custom dress, I blinked hard to banish any trace of tears. This was Kellianne's big day, and I wasn't going to let regrets about my camp boyfriends steal a moment of the bride's happiness. She looked happy enough, but I still worried about her after our talk last night. I hoped she came to her senses and started voicing her needs instead of following everyone else's expectations for her.

Guests poured into our country club for the reception as valets scurried to keep up with new arrivals. I'd be lying if I said I wasn't secretly scanning the vehicles in a futile hope for a late arrival. Forcing myself inside the banquet hall, I mingled with a few cousins while we all waited for the bride and groom's big appearance.

"Congratulations, Lauren!" A meaty hand clapped me on the shoulder, and I turned to see an older gentleman who looked vaguely familiar in a dark blue suit with an American flag pinned to the lapel.

A distant uncle? A friend of my father's?

"Thank you," I said automatically, wondering if he'd somehow mistaken me for the bride. Since I was a brunette wearing lavender instead of a blonde in white, that didn't seem too likely.

"Aren't you going to ask me what for?" he teased, a big grin on his face, his polished white teeth standing out against very tanned skin.

Like a politician's, I thought.

That's when it hit me how I knew this guy. From TV and the paper. He was our local congressman, a friend of my grandfather's.

"*Ohmigod.*" I let the comment slip out, unguarded. "You're Representative Fawkes. Thank you so much for the letter of recommendation for the Aerospace program. I just sent you a thank-you note—"

"You're welcome." He took a glass of champagne off a passing waiter's tray and gave the man orders to start sending over the folks with the hors d'oeuvres. Then Representative Fawkes leaned closer to me. "But I'm not congratulating you on *applying,* young lady."

My head reeled. My knees felt weak. Could he be saying what I thought he was saying?

"Excuse me?"

"I talked to the folks over at the Aerospace Scholars program just this morning." He took a sip of his champagne and I wondered if he was enjoying the suspense because it was definitely killing me. Then, with all the drama of a man who knew a thing or two about sound bites, he whispered, "You're in."

I couldn't hold in the scream even though I bit my lip. It came out as more of a screech. I launched myself in his arms and hugged him, almost spilling his drink.

"Thank you!" I couldn't wait to tell my dad. "Thank you so much."

"It wasn't *my* hard work that got you in," he reminded me. "We need strong women to lead us into the future." He patted me on the shoulder, still grinning, while he intercepted a waitress with a tray full of bacon-wrapped shrimp. "Make good use of this opportunity."

"I will," I promised, wishing I could share this news with Siobhan after the way she'd encouraged me to apply.

For that matter, Seth deserved some credit for reminding me to follow my dreams. Matt, too, would be so proud of me...

The ache in my chest returned with new bittersweetness. I wouldn't be seeing any of them next summer, since the Aerospace Program would be my priority. I wouldn't be going back to camp. I wondered if this hurt inside would go away by then.

Funny how some dreams came true at the same time old ones faded away.

"May I have your attention please?" The DJ's voice came over the sound system just as the lights dimmed in the country club. "Ladies and gentlemen, I have some very special introductions to make."

Knowing my sister must have arrived, I hurried to the back of the room to get ready for the DJ's introduction of the bridal party. Kellianne and Andrew got to make their big entrance as husband and wife, and then they'd dance. Then, finally, we could all relax and eat.

Hopefully that would help ease the butterflies that had come out of nowhere. I shouldn't have been nervous, but it had been such a roller coaster for the past few weeks. I saw my mom and dad gathered with the bridal party as the first bridesmaid and groomsman were called to the dance floor, but I didn't say anything about my big news. This was Kellianne's time.

"Where's Kellianne?" I asked my mom, peering around the entrance to the restaurant.

"With Andrew," she said vaguely, a big smile pinned to her face, as if that could erase the hint of worry in her eyes. "Around the corner, I think."

My stomach cramped. They couldn't seriously be having a disagreement two hours into their married life. Guilt swamped me for not hashing things out with Kellianne last night when she'd expressed some worries.

While the next bridesmaids were announced, I hurried toward the alcove my mom had indicated, a little lounge near the bathrooms. I hadn't rounded the corner yet when I heard Andrew's thick southern accent speaking softly.

"Honey, you know I just want you to be happy. You should take that job if you want it."

And my sister's voice answering him. "But what about your mom? You know she can't wait for a grandbaby."

"We'll just keep reminding her she's too young to be a grandma, okay?" He chuckled over that and something else he said—too low to overhear—made Kellianne laugh.

My heart melted as Andrew Buford III's stock soared in my book.

"Maid of honor, Ms. Lauren Carlson," the DJ's voice suddenly boomed through the sound system as I was being announced "and best man Mr.—"

Crap.

I sprinted to the best man's side and looped my hand through his arm for our entrance, but not before I gave my mother a thumbs-up so she would know everything was okay with Kellianne. Seeing my sister's happily-ever-after come together so well made it a little easier to feel okay about not getting one for me. At least I had the Aerospace program.

I took my place off to one side of the dance floor with the other wedding attendants. We were supposed to wait there while Andrew and Kellianne took their first quick turn around the dance floor. Apparently it was a tradition in the Buford family to do this lone dance before dinner—an unorthodox practice that my mother had tried politely arguing about, but this was one arena where Andrew's family got some say.

"And for the bride and groom's first dance," the DJ announced as a spotlight hovered on Andrew and Kellianne. "We have a special guest to serenade them with an original song."

Special guest?

I hadn't heard a word about this, and wondered if the Bufords had tried springing more last-minute surprises. But my mother's face showed no hint of aggravation. In fact, she smiled at me. As did the bride.

Why where they looking at *me*?

Then the DJ continued, "Please welcome Matt Butler to sing to the new Mr. and Mrs. Buford!"

I didn't fully comprehend that introduction until I heard the gorgeous strains of a melody I knew well even though I'd only heard it a few times before. It felt like I was in a dream as I eased away from the best man to see the source of the music.

In the shadows of the stage, off to one side, Matt sat at the piano, dressed flawlessly in a black tuxedo, his broad shoulders leaning forward over the keys.

"When the cold/freezes you body and soul..."

His green eyes met mine in the slow, spinning squares of light filtered over the dance floor. While the rest of the room watched Andrew and Kellianne, Matt and I only had eyes for each other.

He came for me.

I knew he would never be sitting here, singing in public for probably the first time in his life outside of camp, just because Kellianne wanted him to. No. If Matt was here, at this wedding that I'd asked him to attend with me, it was because he wanted to be here for me.

As my date. And—I hoped—my boyfriend.

"When the sun falls/and the stars emerge," he sang, lifting his voice with lyrics that had never been about Hannah. I understood now that *Come Back and Be My Love* was about me.

Us.

The tears that had threatened earlier were falling now, and I didn't even care. It was dark anyhow, and the only one who saw was Matt. Frankly, he deserved to see how much I cared. After he'd waited all summer for me to figure out what I wanted. After he'd eventually forgiven and even understood about me and Seth.

After he'd reached deep inside to write the most beautiful song I'd ever heard... Yeah, Matt Butler had earned the right to know how much his love touched me. How much I loved him back.

The notes swirled around me like the rose-colored lights, the music reaching out like a hug across the space between us.

"The future's certain/since you've opened my eyes/So won't you be my love?/Come back and be my love." The final chords of the song died away, and Matt straightened back from the keys, his eyes still on me.

The room erupted in thunderous applause for the couple in the spotlight while I sought the man behind the music.

"Matt." I put shaking hands on the piano as he rose from the bench. "That was amazing."

The spotlight flashed over to him for a minute and the applause rose again. He took a bow, that dazzling smile of his winning over anyone in the crowd who wasn't already in love with him. No matter that Matt had found his inner geek, he was still seriously hot. Nerd cool and geek chic. It was a sexy combination.

I was glad I saw a lot more than that in him, though.

"Sorry I'm late." He turned toward me after taking the bow, his hand reaching out for mine. A half-grin kicked up one side of his face. "I thought I'd make an entrance."

"You definitely accomplished that." I took his hand while everyone else started taking their seats for the meal.

"Hey." He frowned and put his arm around me. "You're shaking like a leaf. Everything okay?"

"I thought you weren't coming," I confessed, tilting my head onto his shoulder. He felt so solid. So real.

"I wouldn't miss it, Lauren. You worked so hard on this wedding all summer, even when you were supposed to be having fun with your friends." He squeezed me and guided me toward a door that led outdoors where a few patio tables were set up for anyone wanting to catch some fresh air despite the heat. "Come on, we can take a minute to talk while they get seated."

Looking back over my shoulder, I saw he was right. People who'd missed Kellianne and Andrew in the receiving line were swarming them now. Mom and Dad were talking to old friends. Dinner would be a while.

Following him outside, we could see Turtle Creek in the valley below the country club. Torches were already lit even though it wasn't dark outside yet. A white canvas tent was set up with fans for outdoor dancing later.

"When I didn't hear from you after camp, I thought maybe Hannah had finally convinced you..."

"No." He shook his head. "Lauren, I'm crazy about you. I wouldn't have been hanging out with Hannah at all except that she was always there any time I turned around this summer."

He shrugged. "She's going through some tough stuff at home and I related, but when she started to think it meant more than friendship..."

"You don't have to explain it to me." I didn't want to be the kind of couple that needed to question each other's every conversation with someone of the opposite sex. "You trusted me plenty of times. I trust you, too."

He smiled. "That feels really good. But I have a confession to make before you trust me too much."

My heart fell. "What?"

"I talked to Seth on the bus to the airport after camp."

"You're kidding." I couldn't picture the two of them doing more than snarling at each other.

"No. And I'll admit I asked him—you know—what his intentions were toward you."

I rolled my eyes. "So you only trust me now that you believe Seth and I are really through?"

"Hell, no. Lauren, that guy will always be a little in love with you, and I'm going to have to live with that. But hearing him talk about you reminded me that I'd be a jerk to let stupid jealousy keep us apart."

My eyes burned all over again. Because even though it was Matt that I loved, I had Seth to thank for pushing us together. Seth, who would always have a place in my heart too. But now I understood that it was as my friend.

"Seth and I were friends for a long time, and I hope someday we'll be friends again." Twilight was falling now, the sky turning purple in the west as a few fireflies lit the bushes nearby.

Photouris pyralis, I happened to know, thanks to a friend.

"I get that." Matt nodded. "That's cool with me."

"So how did you end up singing at the wedding?" I asked, wanting to get back to us. Matt was my future after all, and I couldn't wait to start it.

"I called your sister a few days ago to pitch my case." He turned me toward him so that we stood eye to eye. "I had to submit a demo tape first."

"Of course." I laughed. "I can't believe she kept it a secret."

"It was her idea to make it a surprise." He put his hands on my hips and drew me closer.

My heartbeat sped at his nearness. He smelled so good.

"I can't believe that I worked so hard to make friends this year—both in school and at camp—and it turned out the person who had my back the most in the end is probably my sister."

"She even got me a fitting for a tux at the last minute so I could look almost good enough to hang out with you." He smoothed his palm to my back where a hundred little buttons held my dress in place. "You look incredible."

"So do you," I whispered hoarsely, already imagining the night that I let him lead me into the privacy of the trees down by Turtle Creek, where couples went to be alone under the stars...

Speaking of stars.

"Guess what?" I blurted just before he kissed me.

"Mmm?" he asked, his mouth already brushing mine gently.

He had distracted me so thoroughly it took me a minute to remember what I was going to say.

"I got accepted into the Aerospace Scholars program." I still couldn't believe it. The news felt all the more special now that I had someone to share it with.

"That's fantastic." He hugged me hard. "I'm so proud of you."

Laughter filtered out through the bank of windows from the party inside, reminding me we should probably get back indoors before someone missed us.

"Thank you." I was pretty proud of me too. "I'm really excited." I could hear the DJ's voice inside, calling people to their tables to be seated now. "But we'd better go in."

"On one condition." He held me there, a teasing light in his eyes. "If you're going to be an astronomer, you have to promise you'll take me stargazing one of these nights."

"Stargazing?" It sounded a little old fashioned. Possibly a little geeky. And just right for us.

I looked skyward just in time to see the first stars come out. Cicadas chirped in the tall grass as the night songs started early.

"Only if you sing to me some more." I wanted to know the musician much better than I'd gotten to know the football player.

"Deal," he whispered, just as his mouth came down to mine.

And, wedding or no wedding, I decided this kiss deserved all the time in the world.

Acknowledgements

Joanne and Karen would like to thank their editor, Patricia Riley, for caring as passionately about this book and the characters as they have. Special thanks to Kate Kaynak for giving *Camp Boyfriend* the exciting honor of being the first book in the Spencer Hill Contemporary line. We are grateful to Danielle Ellison for putting her special stamp on the story, our publicist Cindy Thomas who made sure people found out about the book, the multi-talented Jenn Rush for the fantastic cover art, the West brothers for their fun and funny YouTube show, "This Week in YA" that featured *Camp Boyfriend*, along with the many other Spencer Hill Press staffers who helped fine-tune our story including Britta, Christina, John, Lauren, Rich, Shira, and Taryn. Finally, we would like to send the very warmest thank you to our agent, Barbara Collins Rosenberg for encouraging us in our quest to write a story about summer camp.

From Joanne:
To Dean—thank you for believing in my dreams and encouraging me to pursue them. Huge thanks to my critique partner, Catherine Mann, who is ready to brainstorm no matter what time her phone rings. Much love to my parents for sending me to summer camp, hugs to my cousins, Karen Pickup, Susan Newkirk and Michele Murray for sharing those memorable summers with me, and a special shout-out to my three sons, Maxim, Camden and Taylor Rock, who know that "I'm

on deadline" means they'll be making their own dinners for a week. Finally, this book would not be possible without the talent, enthusiasm and creativity of my sister-in-law, Karen, who inspired me to write a YA novel with her deep respect for the genre. It turned out to be *very easy* to merge two voices that have talked as long and often as we have over the years! Thank you to the Rock family for bringing us together, for throwing the best parties, and for giving me the best in-laws any girl could ever ask for.

From Karen:
To Greg—the 'Rock' in my world. Thank you for your unfailing support, encouragement, faith and love. There is no greater gift than knowing that I get to spend the rest of my life with you. A big mom hug to my tell-it-like-it-is daughter Danielle who brought out the best in me and my writing with her patient, honest, and tough critiques. I love you both so much. Thank you as well to my wonderful in-laws, my father, and sister, Jeanne for being such a caring family to me. Much appreciation as well to my wonderful SCBWI writers group Marjorie Light, Kate Messner, Jaramy Connors, Amy Guglielmo, Lucy Cooney, and Jacqueline Tourville whose talent and positivity have been a great source of inspiration, and to my Friday Night Book Club members Jennifer Giumbruno, Elizabeth Gibbs, Michelle Oullette, and Elaine Ostry who keep me laughing and reading great literature every month. Thanks as well to my co-teacher and friend extraordinaire Penny Manor, and my fellow English teachers Andrew

Ducharme, Nancy Strack, Michelle Walpole, Sue Wilson, Erica Buskey and our incredible librarian Russell Puschak and his amazing assistant Carol Passno-I absolutely do not know how I would get through a day without you. Finally, I am most grateful to my wonderful sister-in-law and dearest friend, Joanne Rock. It's hard to believe that we came away from a Burlington shopping trip one year with the greatest prize of all- our writing partnership. To steal a line from one of my favorite books, *Freak the Mighty*, "I never had a (writer's) brain, until (Joanne) came along and let me borrow hers for a while". If it wasn't for Joanne, I never would have had the courage to share my writing with others. Because of her faith in me, I believe in myself and, most of all, the wonderful stories we have to share.

DISCLAIMER:

While the NASA Aerospace Scholars' Program is fictional, there is a real program that promotes the study of Aerospace Science, Technology, Engineering, and Mathematics for high school students called the Texas Aerospace Scholars. For more information about this fantastic program, please visit: http://has.aerospacescholars.org/

Jenna Oliver doesn't have time to get involved with one boy, let alone two.

All Jenna wants is to escape her evaporating small town and her alcoholic mother. She's determined she'll go to college and find a life that is wholly hers—one that isn't tainted by her family's past. But when the McAlister twins move to town and Jenna gets involved with both of them, she learns the life she planned may not be the one she gets.

SPENCER HILL CONTEMPORARY • spencerhillcontemporary.com

About the Authors

J.K. Rock is the pseudonym for writing partners—and sisters-in-law—Joanne and Karen Rock. After selling some adult romances on their own, they thought it would be fun to write YA together and *Camp Boyfriend* was dreamed up while floating around the pool at a family party. F visit jkrock. net

A full-time eighth grade teacher, Karen Rock recently sold her first romance to Harlequin Heartwarming. Prior to her work with Harlequin, Karen published numerous YA short stories in and a YA screenplay designed for high school drama clubs. An active member of SCBWI and RWA, Karen has helped several students to publish their own work. She has a wide following as a "Cynsation" blogger on Cynthia Leitich Smith's website. She lives in the Adirondack Mountain region with her husband, her much-appreciated beta-reader daughter, and two King Cavalier spaniels that have yet to learn the concept of "fetch" even though they've taught her the trick! *Camp Boyfriend* marks her debut as a YA novelist. Learn more about Karen at www.karenrock.com

An unapologetic romantic, Joanne Rock started writing while working toward a Masters degree in Literature at the University of Louisville, craving a creative outlet to break up her studying. Today, she is the author of over sixty books for a variety of Harlequin series. She has been nominated for the RITA, the romance genre's highest honor, three times. She's also been a Romantic Times Career Achievement Nominee and multiple Reviewers' Choice finalist. Her work has been reprinted in twenty-six countries and translated into twenty languages. Her three teenage sons encouraged her to try writing YA, a venture that's been non-stop fun. For more information on Joanne's books, visit www.joannerock.com